Presented by
AO JYUMONJI

Illustration by
EIRI SHIRAI

level.18 The World Hates Me

Grimgar of Fantasy and Ash

The Ironblood Kingdom was in the Kurogane Mountain Range. In reality, it was made up of hundreds, maybe even thousands, of vertical and horizontal mine tunnels.

The Walter Gate was halfway up the western slopes of the Kurogane Mountain Range. The way to the gate went through a canyon, up a valley, and between the gaps in broken hunks of rock.

Grimgar of Fantasy and Ash

GRIMGAR OF FANTASY AND ASH, LEVEL. 18

Copyright © 2021 Ao Jyumonji
Illustrations by Eiri Shirai

First published in Japan in 2021 by
OVERLAP Inc., Ltd., Tokyo.
English translation rights arranged with
OVERLAP Inc., Ltd., Tokyo.

No portion of this book may be reproduced or transmitted in any form without written permission from the copyright holders. This is a work of fiction. Names, characters, places, and incidents are the products of the author's imagination or are used fictitiously. Any resemblance to actual events, locales, or persons, living or dead, is entirely coincidental. Any information or opinions expressed by the creators of this book belong to those individual creators and do not necessarily reflect the views of Seven Seas Entertainment or its employees.

Seven Seas and the Seven Seas logo are trademarks of Seven Seas Entertainment. All rights reserved.

Follow Seven Seas Entertainment online at sevenseasentertainment.com.
Experience J-Novel Club books online at j-novel.club.

TRANSLATION: Sean McCann
J-NOVEL CLUB EDITOR: Adam Fogle
COVER DESIGN: Kris Aubin
INTERIOR DESIGN: Clay Gardner
INTERIOR LAYOUT: Karis Page
PROOFREADER: Jack Hamm
LIGHT NOVEL EDITOR: T. Anne
PREPRESS TECHNICIAN: Melanie Ujimori, Jules Valera
PRODUCTION MANAGER: Lissa Pattillo
EDITOR-IN-CHIEF: Julie Davis
ASSOCIATE PUBLISHER: Adam Arnold
PUBLISHER: Jason DeAngelis

ISBN: 978-1-63858-264-9
Printed in Canada
First Printing: January 2023
10 9 8 7 6 5 4 3 2 1

level. 18 — The World Hates Me

Presented by
AO JYUMONJI

Illustrated by
EIRI SHIRAI

Table of Contents

1	Short-Lived Homesickness	11
2	Bonds Don't Break, Even When You Cut Ties	19
3	Memory	31
4	Why Do We Repeat Ourselves?	47
5	Paper-Thin Stubbornness	63
6	It's All in How You Say a Thing	73
7	Not So I Can Remain Myself	83
8	For Now	111
9	Wild Nature	133
10	LOVE	155
11	Inscrutable Causality	169
12	Like No Other	197
13	A Legend	219
14	All in One	237
15	HATE THE WORLD	279
	Afterword	324
#1	937 Days Later	325
#2	Fire, Stay with Me	329
#3	Into Shelter	333

Grimgar of Fantasy and Ash

1 | Short-Lived Homesickness

Nick, a soldier with the Frontier Army, had been on guard duty at the watchtower of Alterna's north gate since ten o'clock the night before. He was on what you'd call the night shift, lasting until the first bell tolled at six o'clock in the morning the next day.

The north gate's watchtower had no roof. At twenty-seven years of age, Nick was of middling height and weight, but the moderately high walls of the watchtower only came up to his chest. He looked out over them, his eyes cautiously monitoring the area outside the barrier that protected Alterna. He was almost completely exposed to the wind. It was a chill wind that left him feeling awfully cold. On top of that, with dawn approaching, a thick fog had been hanging over the area.

"I've got no luck at all," Nick muttered, rubbing his face with gloved hands. He was standing next to the watch fire for warmth, but his nose had been running pretty badly for a while now.

"Why's it gotta be so damn cold? And the fog makes it impossible to see too..."

"Quit your bellyaching," his coworker Chad, a man the same age as him, said with a laugh. "It'll be dawn soon enough, and we'll be relieved right after that. You can hang in there a little longer, can't you?"

Nick cast a resentful sideways glance at the buddy he never seemed to be able to get rid of. "Hey, Chad."

"Yeah?" Chad took a long swig from his leather water bottle. "What is it, Nick?"

"I've been wondering about something."

"Yeah?" Chad responded with a generous shrug. "About what? Out with it, man."

"About that water bottle," Nick said, snatching it as soon as the words had left his mouth.

"Ah! Hey, you jerk!" Chad hurriedly tried to snatch it back.

"Oh, shut up. Who're you calling a jerk, you jerk?" Nick countered, blocking Chad's hands with one arm as he took a whiff of the contents of his bottle. It was faint, but he smelled something. "I knew it. Booze."

"No, it's not—" Chad said in a panic before slipping into a more coaxing tone. "D-don't be silly, Nick, buddy, you've got it all wrong. It's not booze. Not at all. Of course it isn't. I mean, if it was, I'd get drunk, right? Right? If I was drinking the whole night while I was on guard duty, I'd end up totally sloshed. Do I look drunk to you? I don't, do I?"

"I'll know for sure once I take a swig myself."

"Oh, I dunno about that. Maybe you shouldn't? I mean, I put my lips on that bottle and all. Not that it would bother me if you wanna go ahead with it. But you're the sort who makes a big deal about stuff like that, aren't you?"

Nick didn't let that stop him from taking a sip.

"A-yep… This is some watered-down hooch. There isn't much, but it's in there. Definitely. This's got booze in it. Without a doubt."

"Fine," Chad said, putting a hand on Nick's shoulder. "Yeah, yeah, yeah, you got me. That's what it is."

"Oh? Trying to go on the offensive now?"

"Just listen to me. I admit it, Nick. Like you said, I mixed a little booze into my water. Only a little, though. So little, you can barely tell it's there. The perfect amount, really. If it doesn't affect my work, what's the problem, am I right?"

"Do you really think Commander Jin Mogis would let that slide?"

"I'm not talking to the commander, I'm talking to you. So, let me turn the question around. It's cold, right? And we're on night duty. At night. That's why it's called night duty. It's tough, isn't it? Of course it is. Yeah, I'm gonna mix a little booze into my water. It's the least I can do. It'd be crazier not to. You get me? Nick, buddy, you're the one who's a little crazy here. What I'm doing is totally sane."

"What the hell? I've got a crazy guy telling me I'm crazy now? What even is this? Chad, pal, what do you think common sense and regulations are for?"

"I'm telling you, it's fine." Chad took the bottle back from Nick and took a swig before winking at him. "Totally fine, buddy. You don't need to worry. Come on. Think about it. Our Frontier Army and those uppity volunteer soldiers just finished slaughtering the enemy at Mount Grief, right? If you'd actually use some of that common sense, you'd realize there aren't any enemies around here. No way. Times like this, we can afford to loosen up regulations a little. Yeah? We're just human. Let's take it nice and easy, okay?"

"But, man, there're goblins right over in Damuro, aren't there?"

"They aren't gonna come attack us. What do you think the commander forged an alliance with them for? To tame those barbaric little shit-monkeys, right?"

"And you trust them? They've got no scruples. They'd eat you without a second thought; eat their own kind too while they're at it."

"Yeah, yeah." Chad started massaging Nick's shoulders. "That's the thing. What an idea, forging an alliance with creatures like that. It's crazy, isn't it? Absolutely insane, that's what our commander is. I hear he's secretly been feeding us goblin meat too."

"Huh...? The hell?"

"It's just a rumor, but..." Chad lowered his voice. "A guy on duty in the mess hall looked inside one of the barrels in the larder, and there was a goblin, all sliced up and pickled in brine..."

Nick covered his mouth, feeling a sudden bout of nausea. "Are you serious...?"

"Like I said, man, it's just a rumor," Chad said with a laugh, handing Nick the bottle.

SHORT-LIVED HOMESICKNESS

Nick accepted it, taking just a sip of the water that tasted faintly of alcohol. "But...knowing the commander, he might well do it. I mean, sure, we've got guys out gathering up the livestock that were being kept in the outlying villages, and looking for other stuff we can eat. Question is whether that's enough..."

"They say the commander's got a stock of supplies hidden away. And there's talk about how we're getting regular shipments from the mainland resupplying us."

"The mainland, huh?" Nick returned the bottle to his fellow guard, crossing his arms as he looked off into the distance. A light sigh escaped his lips. "Wish I could go back," he said. "But even if I did, I've already cut ties with my folks, and I've got no other way to make a living. Nothing I can do about it..."

"That's north, Nick. Mainland's the other way," Chad said with a laugh, shaking the bottle to check how much was left.

Nick sniffled. "I know that. I'm just being attentive in my duties. Getting clobbered by our superior officer for messing up'd be one thing, but damned if I'm gonna get myself executed by the commander."

"Yeah, you've got a point..." Chad looked outside the wall. "He might suddenly start purging the ranks to enforce discipline. I wouldn't put it past him... Oh. The mist's—"

"Yeah." Nick looked out over the area around Alterna as the fog dissipated. "It's clearing—"

Then, as he was looking almost straight down, Nick stopped short.

He grabbed Chad's arm.

15

SHORT-LIVED HOMESICKNESS

"Hey."

"Hmm?"

"There's someone there. In front of the gate," Nick said, squinting. Chad stood on his tip-toes and leaned out over the chest-high wall.

"Oh, yeah...?"

The ground was still hazy. Someone was standing in front of the north gate, and he could see well enough to tell they were human but couldn't make out their face. It was a man, though. Bearded. The guy looked filthy. Nick scowled.

"A dog...?"

The man wasn't alone. He had a critter with him, four-legged and doglike. But was it really a dog? It looked awfully well built.

The bearded man looked up. Probably at Nick. He waved his hand.

"Chad!" Nick shouted, and Chad grabbed the crossbow that was lying against the chest-high wall.

"What do we do, Nick? Should I shoot him?!"

Chad looked ready to pull the trigger any second. His shoulders heaved. His nostrils flared. Seeing his colleague all fired up, Nick's head rapidly cooled.

"Hold up. The guy looks human."

Chad took a deep breath. "Sure does."

"Who goes there?!" Nick shouted at the bearded man. "What are you doing?!"

"Waiting for the gate to open," the man answered in an awfully calm voice. "I'm Itsukushima. I used to be in Alterna's hunters' guild. I don't know what the situation is here, but I'd like you to take me to someone in a position of authority."

2. Bonds Don't Break, Even When You Cut Ties

"Haru-kun! Hey, Haru-kun! This is huge, Haru-kun!"

Shaken awake by Yume, Haruhiro hurried to the basement of Tenboro Tower with Ranta, Kuzaku, Merry, and Setora. Neal the scout, in his deep-green cloak, called after them to stop, but the group ignored him and headed downstairs. Neal didn't force the issue, instead following them to the basement.

The man had been relieved of his possessions, stripped of even his cloak and boots, and shut behind a set of iron bars in the dank, cold stone dungeon. He was unshaven and lacking in cleanliness, looking more like a beast than the unkempt man he was.

"Master!" Yume cried, clutching at the bars with a level of intensity that made it look like she might sink her teeth into them. "It's you! Yume's been so worried! Thank goodness you're okay!"

"Y-yeah..." The scruffy man looked more weirded out by this display than relieved. "Sorry about that. I hate to worry you...

Oh, right. I was too. Worried about you, that is. You know, just thought I'd say that..."

"Erm..."

As Haruhiro was looking at the man sideways, trying to figure out the situation, Ranta gestured at the man with his chin.

"He's Itsukushima, of the hunters' guild. He'd be the equivalent of a mentor in the thieves' guild, or a lord in the dread knights' guild. The hunters' guild called theirs fathers or mothers, depending on gender. So, that makes this guy Yume's father."

"He looks like a savage." Setora never minced words.

"Well, thanks." Itsukushima didn't seem to mind. "It's true, I prefer living in the remote mountains to being among people."

"So, the thing about Master is he's kinda like Yume's dad. Right, Master?"

"Yeah, um... Your dad?" Itsukushima clearly didn't know what to say. "Y-your dad, huh? I'm Yume's dad..."

"And if you're Yume's dad, then that makes Yume your daughter, right?"

"Y-yeah, I guess by that logic you would be..."

"You're a fitting pair," Setora commented, and it was hard to be sure if she was being sarcastic or just blunt about how she felt.

Haruhiro leaned over to whisper in Ranta's ear. "Don't you need to introduce yourself?"

"Huh...?!" Ranta jumped into the air, overreacting. "Introduce myself?! Huh?! Wh-wh-wh-why?!"

"Well, I mean, this *is* Yume's dad and all."

"Not her *real* dad! A-a-a-a-a-and even if I did meet her real dad, I still wouldn't need to! Wh-wh-wh-wh-wh-why would I have to do that, you moron?!"

Merry scowled and shook her head. "The echo in here just makes him louder and more annoying..."

"Wah! Wahhh! Wahhhhh! Take that and suffer some more, dumbass!" Ranta shouted.

Haruhiro sighed. "You're as bad as ever..."

"Hold up..." Kuzaku's brow furrowed. "What's Yume's master, or father, or whatever he is, doing in jail?"

That was the problem, yes.

It turned out that around when Alterna fell, Yume, Itsukushima, and Ranta had been working together for a time. Yume and Ranta went on to rejoin the Volunteer Soldier Corps, but Itsukushima headed north.

"Master was sayin' he'd go up to the Killing Game Mountains with Poochie."

Yume's explanation honestly didn't make a lot of sense. Her master stepped in to help.

"Poochie's one of the guild's wolf dogs. And it's the Kurogane Mountains, not the Killing Game Mountains, okay?"

"Ohhh, that's the place with the, uh..." Kuzaku said, scratching his head, "the something-or-other kingdom. Where those dwarven people live."

"The Ironblood Kingdom. And just calling them 'dwarves' is enough," Setora said, looking at him coldly.

Kuzaku seemed suddenly deflated. "'Kay... I'll try to say that from now on."

"Gah ha ha ha ha ha!" Ranta let out a vulgar laugh. "That's right! You'd better watch yourself! In all sorts of ways!"

"You're the last one I want to hear that from, Ranta-kun..."

According to Yume's master, he had friends living in the Ironblood Kingdom. If the enemy had a next target in mind after Arnotu in the Shadow Forest and Alterna, it was probably the Ironblood Kingdom. That was why he'd gone up to the Kurogane Mountain Range to warn his friends there.

It went about as he'd expected. More than a month ago now, a massive army of orcs and undead had invaded the Kurogane Mountains. With centuries of history on its side, the Ironblood Kingdom was a massive underground fortress. The dwarves who lived there had dug it out of the bedrock. It was basically an interconnected series of mines, both large and small.

The enemy had tried to storm the entrance on the surface, the Great Ironfist Gate. That was the main way into the Ironblood Kingdom, located near a massive river called the River of Tears.

Of course, according to Itsukushima, the dwarves weren't totally without any plan for how to handle the situation.

"The dwarves never got on with the elves of the Shadow Forest, but the iron king made the bold decision to take in refugees from Arnotu. And I gave them what little intel I had too."

"The dwarves knew what the enemy was up to, then, huh?" Ranta said, nodding like an insufferable know-it-all. "Which means they had time to prepare for the attack."

"How did they fare?" Setora asked.

BONDS DON'T BREAK, EVEN WHEN YOU CUT TIES

Itsukushima responded without any real emotion. "I left the Kurogane Mountains twelve, thirteen days ago. They hadn't fallen then, at least. The enemy seemed to be struggling to seal their victory."

"Hweh." Yume's eyes widened. "That's amazin'! The dwarfies're real tough, huh! Mwungh-hungh..."

"Arnotu went down in no time, though," Ranta said, keeping up the know-it-all act. He probably felt the need to look cool in front of Yume's master, seeing as he was like her dad and all. "And, Yume, how long are you gonna go on making weird noises? You sound like an idiot—"

Suddenly, the iron bars rattled, causing Ranta to let out a squeal of surprise and start trembling.

It was Itsukushima. He hadn't so much pressed on the bars as smacked them with the palms of his hands. "An idiot? Did you just call Yume an idiot?"

"Ah...! No, I didn't say she's an idiot, I just said she sounds like one..."

"Take it back. Or I'll chop you up and feed you to the bears."

"S-s-sorry. I-I-I take it back! I-I-I-It was just a turn of phrase, or something..."

"Bears? Scary!" Kuzaku looked less than amused. As for Yume herself, she was blinking in confusion. She didn't seem to get what had happened.

"So, here's the thing..." Itsukushima said, clearing his throat loudly as he tried to get back on track. "I didn't know about it until this most recent time I went to the Ironblood Kingdom,

23

but the dwarves have a secret weapon. Thanks to that, not only has the enemy been unable to get through the Great Ironfist Gate, but they can't even encircle it."

Haruhiro touched his cheek. *A secret weapon.* Just hearing the words was a bit embarrassing, but at the same time they set his heart all aflutter. Ranta was beside himself with glee, his eyes needlessly sparkling.

"Whoa, whoa, whoa, whoaaaa! Are you seriously serious?! Secret weapons are for real?! Hot damn, I want one! A secret weapon! Gimme one too!"

"Uh, no, they're not gonna give them away..." Kuzaku told him, sounding exasperated, but he couldn't completely mask his own interest. "I would like to see for myself, though. What're they like? Secret weapons, I mean..."

Setora let out a thoroughly exasperated sigh. "You people..."

It seemed Itsukushima had long been treated like some kind of representative of the human Kingdom of Arabakia in the Ironblood Kingdom. It had just ended up that way because he'd tell the iron king about Alterna when asked, and no other humans from Alterna were around.

Itsukushima and his dwarf friends had participated in the battle to defend the Kurogane Mountain Range, but only until the second day of the fighting, when things intensified, and both sides started taking a substantial number of casualties. In that two-day period, the Ironblood Kingdom lost twenty-seven people, while the enemy piled up hundreds of corpses.

From then on, there were only sporadic clashes, and the

Ironblood Kingdom was ready to strike back if the enemy showed any openings.

From the enemy's perspective, an attack from the rear would be devastating, so they couldn't afford to carelessly retreat. Itsukushima took an opportunity during an audience with the iron king to suggest that they simply let the enemy withdraw without pursuing. He was told that wasn't an option.

"The iron king's impressive. I don't know how to describe it. Like an amalgamation of everything good about the dwarves..."

According to Itsukushima, the iron king wasn't bellicose by any means and was in fact very thoughtful, but dwarves as a race tended to be hot-blooded. It was easy to rile them up, and they were incredibly tenacious too. As was sometimes said, "A dwarf's fire burns for a hundred years."

When they fought, they went all out. Such was the way of the dwarves. And in this case, the other side had started it. There was no reason to let someone who'd picked a fight with them slink away unharmed. The dwarves had a saying: "Always hang a robber." If someone tried to force their way into your home, just capturing them and roughing them up wasn't enough punishment. If you didn't string them up, it reflected poorly on you. That was what it meant.

Ranta snorted smugly.

"Once things get started, it's kill or be killed, nothing else, huh? Can't say I'm against that. Actually, I like it. I bet I could share some good drinks with the dwarves."

"Do you *know* how much booze a dwarf can consume?"

Itsukushima said with a nasally laugh. "They could drink even our hardiest barflies under the table. That's their Achilles' heel, though."

Yume nodded enthusiastically. "They're a bunch of whiners. Always have been, right?"

"Uh, yeah..." Itsukushima looked like he was going to both smile and cry. "I don't think that's the word you were looking for. Winos, maybe? Sorry to be picky..."

Yume was troubling him, but he wouldn't have had it any other way. He even looked happy about it. That said, Haruhiro couldn't let this drag on forever, so he tried to help.

"The dwarves can't hold their liquor? Is that it?"

Itsukushima shook his head.

"No, not at all. They drink booze like water and are totally fine. It's normal for them to drink for good cheer in the middle of a battle."

As a massive underground nation, the Ironblood Kingdom maintained food stores large enough to feed their people for several years. But alcohol was another matter. For the dwarves, booze was a necessity. Obviously, they brewed and distilled it themselves, and had significant amounts in storage. However, they drank a lot more in wartime than when they were at peace, so their stocks had been gradually falling. Normally, they'd be able to import more from the Free City of Vele, but with an enemy force out in the Kurogane Mountain Range, they couldn't count on that.

If they ran out of booze, they ran out of booze. Was it really something to make such a big fuss over?

Yes. Yes, it was. For dwarves, running out of alcohol was a huge problem.

According to Itsukushima, when rumors had spread that they might not be able to partake freely anymore, the whole Ironblood Kingdom had immediately started to get brutal. All dwarves drank a lot, but even among them there were some who were especially heavy drinkers, and they became the targets of a sort of condemnation. *If you're going to drink so much, then I am too!* The situation turned into a sort of pathetic competition to see who could drink the most. Their consumption grew explosively. They'd get hopelessly inebriated, fists would fly, and kicks would follow. There were bloody fights all over.

The way things were going, people were going to get killed. Worse yet, the booze might run out. It was their own fault for drinking so much of it, but ultimately the primary cause was the enemy army. They had to pay for this.

The infighting over alcohol among the dwarves of the Ironblood Kingdom had intensified, setting their hostility and battle fervor ablaze.

"The truth is, the iron king is struggling hard to keep all those drunken dwarves from exploding."

And as that was going on, they'd received information that a human faction had managed to retake Alterna.

The news had made it to the enemy forces first somehow. The Ironblood Kingdom had only come to learn of it through their intelligence gathering activities.

"So the iron king gave me a letter to bring back to Alterna.

I never would've imagined it was retaken by reinforcements from the mainland, though."

Haruhiro glanced over at Neal the scout, who was watching from a short distance away with a smirk on his face.

"Yeah, reinforcements..."

"Hey!" Yume yelled at Neal. "Yume wants you to let Master out of this jail! Master's real nice, you know! And Yume loves him!"

"I'm not the one you need to talk to," Neal said with a shrug and a smile. "Why not ask Commander Mogis directly?"

"He'd probably force us into doing something again..." Merry muttered. Setora was quick to agree.

"It's possible. No, it's more or less guaranteed." Haruhiro rubbed his stomach. It suddenly felt heavy, like a solid lump had formed in it.

"Yeah... You've got a point."

"Nnnnnurrrrrrrrrrrrghhhhhh...!" Yume filled her mouth with all the air she could, letting a snarling sound escape through her nose. She was absolutely livid.

"Anyway, I gave Jin Mogis the letter," Itsukushima said, trying to calm Yume down. "I don't get along well with people who are that full of themselves. Maybe I should've flattered him, even if it was a lie, but I couldn't. Look, he probably only jailed me to try to be intimidating. He's not gonna kill me. I'm technically an envoy from the iron king, you know?"

"Masteeer..." Yume stuck her fingers between the bars.

Itsukushima seemed unsure what to do for a moment, but he ended up gently stroking her fingers.

"I'm all right, Yume. You just worry about your own comrades."

"Heh..." Neal smirked. "You've got me tearing up here."

How about I make you cry for real? Haruhiro thought, but he didn't say it out loud. If he was going to do it, he was better off not announcing his plans first. No need to give his opponent any time to prepare himself.

Grimgar of Fantasy and Ash

3. Memory

STILL, what exactly should I do?

It felt awkward hanging around in the room Jin Mogis had given them in Tenboro Tower. No, more like downright unpleasant. So Haruhiro and the team decided to go outside. The weather today was dismal, with a cold rain falling on and off since morning. Sometimes it even turned into freezing rain.

Kuzaku shivered. "Sure is cold..."

"Perfect for helping you cool your head." Setora was fine with the weather.

"Looks like we've got another problem on our plates now, huh?" Ranta said from behind his mask, raising two fingers. "First, there's taking Shihoru back. And now we've gotta save that old guy, Itsukushima, too."

Merry was looking around constantly. It was a given that Neal the scout was tailing them. If they kept their voices down, he wouldn't overhear. Still, she couldn't help but worry.

Kuzaku groaned, cocking his head to the side with a frown. "Y'think Shihoru-san's really in the Forbidden Tower? I mean, it's forbidden and all."

"Yeah, that's strange, isn't it?" Yume was still upset that Itsukushima had been jailed. Her expression was harsh. But only by Yume standards. "They call it the tower that doesn't open, right? Well, if it doesn't open, what's she doin' in there? How'd she even *get* in, huh?"

"Well, yeah. That's the thing," the masked man said, nodding. "We call it the tower that doesn't open, but it's not like it can't. If it really couldn't, there'd be no way to get in from the outside."

"You sure solved that one quickly, huh?" Haruhiro said, causing the masked man to cough awkwardly.

"Wh-wh-what?! It's not that hard, man. We've known each other for how long? Give me a break. Yeah, I get it. This is a whole thing with you. You've got the thing with your memory, so this kind of thing might not make sense to you, but it's a normal thing, being able to understand her."

"This is a thing. That's a thing. So many things are 'things' with you..." Kuzaku said, sounding exasperated.

"Grahhh...!" The masked man sprang toward Kuzaku with the terrifying speed of a bird of prey zeroing in on its target. Then he stomped on Kuzaku's foot.

"Owww?!"

"Yahoo!"

"Wh-what was that for?!"

"You should've been able to dodge that, you loser! If we've

gotta rely on a dunce like you to tank for us when your only good point is your size, then honestly, I'm worried about us. Get good, you blockhead!"

"I'm not slow; you're just too fast! But hearing that'll make you happy, won't it? Man, you're such garbage! You're absolute trash! And listen, I'm not just big, I'm sturdy too!"

"Can't you come up with anything more?" Setora asked in a dry voice. Kuzaku crossed his arms and thought about it.

"Huh? Anything more? Hrmm, what else is good about me...?"

"I'm sure there's something," Haruhiro said, but, awkwardly, nothing was coming to mind. "There has to be, right? All sorts of stuff. Gotta be. I mean, there can't be nothing..."

"Oh, yeah?" Kuzaku asked. "Really? Like what?"

Yume clapped a hand on Kuzaku's chest. "You're real good at followin' Haru-kun's orders, yeah? Oh, and probably, this's just what Yume thinks, you're good-natured too."

"I'm good-natured? Uh, sure, I guess. What Haruhiro says is absolute, though."

"Are you a moron?!" The masked man interposed himself between Yume and Kuzaku before pointing at Haruhiro. "Seeing this worthless loser's word as absolute? That's so stupid, I don't even know where to start with you, you imbecile! You dumb, dumb bum!"

"I may be dumb, but I'm not a bum!"

"Shouldn't you be making the opposite objection?" Setora said in a sneering tone. Kuzaku looked at her blankly.

"Oh, yeah. Guess you're right. Ah ha ha."

"Oh, and there's more," Yume continued, snapping her fingers. "He's got a real refreshin' smile. You see it, and you feel ripe as grain!"

"How's he make you feel right as rain?!" Ranta shouted instantly, impressing Haruhiro.

"You picked up on that one fast..."

"Yeah," Kuzaku agreed.

"Ripe as... What was it? Grain? Whatever she said just now. You instantly knew she meant 'right as rain...'"

Yume pressed a finger to her lips and cocked her head to the side. "Fwuh?"

"I-It's not that hard, man!" The masked man stamped his feet indignantly. "You just haven't trained enough! Train, man, train! Train like mad! What are you training at...? Hell if I know!"

Haruhiro caught himself having a little fun teasing Ranta, and he wasn't sure how to feel about it. This wasn't the time to play around. But the trouble was, no matter how hard he thought about it, no matter how much he racked his brain, would he ever find a solution to their problems? He couldn't stay on edge twenty-four seven. And he was fortunate to be with comrades he could let his guard down with. He had to blow off steam like this when the opportunity arose, buckle down when he had to, and wait for a way out of the situation to present itself.

Haruhiro found himself glancing at Merry. Not like he was looking to her for agreement. It was just, she was being awfully quiet, unlike the others, so he was a little concerned. No, not a little—a lot.

Merry was staring into space all alone.

She was clearly not seeing Haruhiro and the others. Her eyes were turned upward a little, and off to the side. Her lips were drawn taut. Was she gritting her teeth? Her jaw looked tense.

He hesitated to ask, *You okay?* Maybe it was a bit much to think this based on the evidence, but something seemed off about her.

"The Forbidden Tower, huh?"

Was it Merry who'd said that? It seemed like it. But the voice was awfully low for her.

Haruhiro gulped. His mouth felt dry. There was something weird with his throat too. "Merry...what'd you say, just now?"

Merry turned and looked at Haruhiro.

It was strange, frankly. Nothing felt right about it. The way Merry was looking at Haruhiro. It was like she wasn't seeing him at all, and that hurt. Merry had suddenly become a total stranger. That's how it seemed to him. Or perhaps Merry didn't know who Haruhiro was? If it wasn't something like that, she wouldn't be looking at him the way she was.

"Is there a way inside the Forbidden Tower?"

Was Merry asking Haruhiro that?

"Huh? Uh..."

But Haruhiro had no answer. Merry should have known that. Or did she not know now? Did she even care?

"The Forbidden Tower, huh?" Merry repeated, then suddenly started walking.

Ranta shifted his mask aside to shoot Haruhiro a dubious glance. *What's with her? Is something up?* he seemed to be asking, but that was what Haruhiro wanted to know.

Kuzaku glanced at Merry's back. Then he looked at Haruhiro. "Something up...?"

I'm telling you, I don't know, Haruhiro nearly snapped at him. It wouldn't have been terribly mature, though, so he reconsidered and held it in. He was more uneasy than angry. What was happening with Merry?

"Merry-chan, is somethin' the matter?" Yume ran after Merry. Haruhiro followed suit. Yume quickly caught up to the priest and started walking next to her. "Merry-chan...?"

When Yume called her name, Merry simply glanced over. That was all. She was just checking what was beside her, not showing any interest in Yume's existence.

Yume and Kuzaku both looked befuddled. Ranta and Setora were blatantly suspicious. All of them, however, were silent. Everyone, Haruhiro included, was nonplussed.

Merry headed straight for the north gate. It stood open, guarded by soldiers of the Frontier Army. Obviously, they stopped her.

"I'm paying respects to the dead," Merry told the soldiers without hesitation. "My comrades lie buried on the hill just over there. Once I visit their graves, I'll come right back."

The soldiers were confused, but they ultimately let Haruhiro and the others pass. When he saw how easily they let the team go, Haruhiro almost felt disappointed.

A thought crossed his mind. Maybe he was overrating Jin Mogis.

It seemed Mogis hadn't taken Shihoru captive after all. She was likely in the Forbidden Tower. Had she lost her memories and was now being manipulated by the master of the tower?

He could assume that it was Mogis's men who'd abducted Shihoru. But after that, she'd been handed over to the master of the tower, and she was no longer in Mogis's custody. That meant Haruhiro and the team had no reason to obey Mogis.

It wasn't a good idea to actually take Mogis on since he possessed a powerful relic. They ought to just ignore him and desert the Frontier Army. They'd bust Yume's master, Itsukushima, out of jail first, then flee with him. The situation was complicated, with the goals of many different factions in play, but Haruhiro and the rest didn't care. They could act independently for their own benefit. That was simplest, and it didn't seem like a bad idea.

Merry began climbing the hill. She'd said something to the guards about visiting graves, but she seemed to have no intention of doing so.

It wasn't raining, but a thick, unbroken carpet of clouds covered the sky. Something flashed in the distance. Lightning. A few moments later, a low rumble like the rolling of a heavy iron ball followed.

The well-trodden path that led from Alterna to the hill was damp and soft. Merry paid it no mind as she climbed to the top, gazing up at the imposing Forbidden Tower.

Haruhiro looked up at the tower too. Upon careful inspection, something about it seemed unnatural. Was it stonework? It was constructed out of blocks, that much was certain. But *were* they stone? Their size, shape, and texture were too uniform for that. Maybe these blocks weren't quarried from rock. Were they something like concrete, then? Or perhaps, despite their lack of luster, they might be some kind of metal.

The Forbidden Tower stood taller than Tenboro Tower in Alterna. Unlike the former seat of the margrave, it wasn't ostentatious, so it didn't give off the impression of being an impressive building, but it was sturdy.

Tenboro Tower seemed like something you could build if you assembled a large amount of manpower, knowledge, and tools. But what about the Forbidden Tower? It didn't feel like something people had constructed. It would have been more believable if someone said that it had always just been there.

"This is a relic," Merry said. Haruhiro was surprised, of course.

A relic. That's it, thought Haruhiro. *The Forbidden Tower's a massive relic. But...why? Why did Merry say that?*

Haruhiro should have asked her. There was definitely something wrong with Merry. Even so, no matter how you looked at her, Merry was still Merry. Nobody else. She'd been with them through thick and thin, both before and after they'd lost their memories. A precious comrade, worthy of their trust. If he had doubts, he could ask Merry about them. It shouldn't have been hard, so why? Why were not just Haruhiro but Yume, Kuzaku, and Ranta all so silent?

Thunder rumbled once more in the distance.

Ice-cold rain struck Haruhiro's cheek.

"Who are you?" Setora asked, breaking the silence.

It was probably the right question, one that cut to the heart of the matter. Which is why Haruhiro couldn't have asked it. He was sure it shouldn't have been asked.

Why not, though? Merry was unquestionably Merry, yet for some reason she seemed not to be. In the unlikely event that Merry wasn't Merry, then who was she? Wasn't that exactly what Haruhiro wanted to know?

Was Haruhiro scared? He might have been.

Obviously, he sensed something was wrong.

Yume and Ranta had been off doing their own thing, but Haruhiro, Shihoru, Kuzaku, Merry, and Setora had all passed through another world together. And while he didn't know what had happened there, they had eventually come back to Grimgar. Something was done to them in the Forbidden Tower to steal their memories, leaving Haruhiro, Shihoru, Kuzaku, and Setora with no recollection of anything beyond their own names.

Merry was the sole exception. She was fuzzy on what had happened in the other world, seeming to barely remember it, but her other memories were intact. What did that mean? Merry herself claimed not to know. Whether it was the work of a relic or something else, it was baffling that she had lost only some of her memories. Was it just chance that it was only partial for her? It didn't seem completely impossible.

MEMORY

But that wasn't the only issue. There was more than just her memories to consider.

Merry had used magic.

Magic Missile.

Hiyomu had been surprised.

"You're a priest, but you just used magic," she'd stammered.

This had been not long after they'd returned to Grimgar without their memories. At the time, it hadn't meant anything to Haruhiro, but now he understood. Merry became a volunteer soldier as a priest. She'd been one ever since. There was no way she should have been able to use a mage's spells.

Besides, it felt like Merry had been acting weird back then. She'd seemed to suffer after firing off that Magic Missile.

Merry suddenly gulped, her eyes widening. Haruhiro understood. He sensed it keenly. It wasn't a subtle change. Even when they're just standing around, people have distinctive habits. Things like resting their weight on one leg, or holding one of their shoulders higher. She had changed completely. What had changed, and to what degree? That was hard to explain. But it undoubtedly had. It was significant enough that he could be certain of it.

"Merry...?" Haruhiro's voice was shrill, cracking.

Merry looked at Haruhiro. Then blinked. She was staring at him like she didn't understand the situation she was in. Haruhiro could predict what would come next. She'd try to act like everything was normal.

And she did. Merry quickly looked around, probably figuring out where she was.

"Uh... What?"

It sounded like a, *Sorry, I was a little out of it for a moment there,* kind of response. If Haruhiro were to ask her, *What's wrong?* that was surely what she would have said in response.

Huh. Uh, okay. Well, it happens. It does...sometimes. It does. It does.

I can't say for sure it doesn't—or I shouldn't be able to.

Haruhiro was forcefully trying to convince himself. There was something like a well in front of him. When he looked into it, he couldn't see the water. Instead, he sensed something he couldn't identify down there. Was it really a well at all? Rather than checking, Haruhiro wanted to put a lid over it. If he blocked it off, it wouldn't look like anything more than a covered well. It might still be something else, but its true nature would remain a mystery. He didn't have to know.

"Don't you 'what' me." Setora's voice was level. She was more or less calm. Still, she was showing far too little emotion. Maybe she was shaken up in her own way and was trying to hide it.

"You were a totally different person a moment ago. Why do you think we're here? It was you, Merry. You brought us out here. More precisely, you started walking to this tower on your own. We came after you."

"Uh, S-Setora-san, hold on, you could have said that differently. Maybe to sound a little less accusatory...?" Kuzaku said, trying to mediate with Setora.

"Accusatory?" Setora narrowed her eyes a little. "That is not my intention in the slightest. I just want to make things clear.

MEMORY

Was Merry always like this, or has something changed from before? I can't tell because I don't remember, and I was never a volunteer soldier to begin with. I can't have known any of you all that long. How about you, Yume?"

"Fwhuh?!" Yume let out a weird noise.

Setora looked closely at her. "You haven't lost your memory, and you didn't leave the party like Ranta."

"Y-yeah... That's true and all, but..."

"In your eyes, has Merry changed?"

"She's... Erm... Well... Hrmm..." Yume looked down and clutched her head. "She's changed... Maybe? Has she? Uhhh. Yeah..."

It was unbearable to watch. But if he averted his eyes from the struggling Yume, where exactly was he supposed to point them? What should he be looking at?

Ranta removed his mask and looked up at the Forbidden Tower. The freezing raindrops lashed him, one after another, leaving his face soaked in no time.

"Yume," Ranta said in a low voice, uncharacteristic of him. "You've told me all sorts of stuff that happened while I was gone. But there are things you haven't told me, aren't there?"

Yume glared at Ranta. Her eyes were accusatory. "Well, Ranta... That's your fault for leavin', now isn't it? You're the bad one here, okay? Maybe bad's the wrong word, but still, if you were with us then, Merry-chan wouldn't've—"

"The hell...?" Ranta wiped his face before looking at Yume again. "What...happened to Merry?"

"M-Merry-chan..."

Yume clutched her left shoulder with her right hand. Her other hand was already clutching her side too.

"M-Merry-chan, she d-d-d—"

Yume kept stammering. What was she trying to say? The word was stuck in her throat, refusing to come out.

Died.

Died?

"Ahhh...!"

He remembered now.

What he'd seen then. The sounds. The smell. It all welled up inside Haruhiro.

"Ahhhhhhhhhhhhhhhhhhhhhhhhhhhhh...!"

There was a large gorilla-like creature covered in a hard dark-brown carapace standing over Merry. He tried to do something about it. He didn't have the strength.

But he had to save Merry. Had to hurry. Quickly.

Merry could only open her eyes halfway. She was trembling. Quivering. She coughed. Blood came out.

"Magic," Haruhiro called out to her. "Merry, use magic. You have to heal. Hurry. Merry."

Right. Merry was the priest. The only one here who could heal wounds. The only one. Merry had to know that too. That was why she was trying to raise her hand, her right hand. She had to make the sign of the hexagram. But her arm wouldn't rise.

It's okay. Don't worry. I'll help you.

He took Merry's hand, trying to assist. Merry groaned. She shook her head.

It hurt. It hurt too much for her to bear.

"Merry? Merry?!" he cried. "Wha... Wh-what should I...?"

Something. Merry was trying to say something. Haruhiro brought his ear to Merry's lips.

"Merry? What? Merry, what are you saying?!"

I can't hear you, Merry. Your voice is weak. Too weak.

"Ha."

"Yeah. What?"

"...Haru."

"Huh?"

"I..."

"Yeah?"

"Haru...you're the one...I..."

"The one you what? What is it, Merry...?"

"...!"

Merry was trying to say something. To communicate something. But maybe she couldn't say it? Could she not force herself to speak any longer?

He moved his face away a little. Looked at Merry. When their eyes met, she smiled.

I don't get it. Why? Aren't you in pain? Aren't you suffering? You're scaring me.

Why are you smiling, Merry?

There was no response. And there never would be one. In that moment, he realized it. Clearly.

Her pupils were dilated, unfocused. Merry wasn't seeing anything. She probably couldn't hear either. Couldn't think. Couldn't feel.

I'm the one you what? Tell me, Merry.

Oh, he remembered now.

Merry had died once before.

4 | Why Do We Repeat Ourselves?

"Hey, Haruhiro!"

The next thing he knew, Ranta was grabbing him by the shoulders and shaking him.

"Haruhiro! Haruhiro! Why're you acting like there's something wrong with you now too, man?!"

There's nothing wrong with me. Haruhiro shook his head. *Nothing's gone wrong with me. That's not it.*

You're wrong.

If anything, there was something wrong with me until just this moment.

Why had he forgotten? That was a mystery to him. There was no way he should've been able to forget something like this. In fact, Haruhiro remembered everything. He'd never lost his memories at all. They'd been right there inside Haruhiro's head all along. If they hadn't, he couldn't have just remembered them.

"Haruhirooo!"

"Oh, shut up!" Haruhiro shoved Ranta away.

You're giving me a headache. You're too stubborn, man. What the hell? Damn it.

Calm down, Haruhiro told himself. *Cool your head.*

As if I could calm down, he thought.

It wasn't just Ranta. Kuzaku, Setora, Yume, and even Merry were all looking at Haruhiro dubiously.

"Hold on..."

Don't look at me like that. I've been messed up all this time, but I'm finally back to normal. Or at least, I feel like I can finally get back to normal, but you guys are gonna make me go crazy all over again.

"Could you give me a moment...? I need to sort through some things. Just for a bit..."

Haruhiro started walking. He didn't have anywhere to go. He just didn't want to be here. This was too close to the Forbidden Tower.

It had all started in this tower.

He'd heard someone's voice.

"Awaken."

He remembered that clearly. It was a dark place. Under the Forbidden Tower. Ranta was there, and Yume, and Shihoru. Renji. Ron. Adachi. Sassa. Chibi-chan. And Kikkawa. Then there was Moguzo. Manato too.

His feet led him there without him even thinking about it. Haruhiro came to a stop in front of the off-white stone that marked his comrade's grave.

"Moguzo..."

Haruhiro reached out toward the gravestone. He wasn't hoping that if he touched it something might happen. Nothing did. It was just an off-white rock. Nothing but a cold, wet stone.

Haruhiro remembered. Renji and his team had helped them carry Moguzo to the crematorium on the outskirts of the city. Moguzo, always bigger and kinder than anyone else, had turned to bone and ash. They had buried him themselves under this very stone.

Manato's grave had been within sight of Moguzo's. Right. It was over there.

Haruhiro walked across the sloping grass. The others followed. He noticed that. But Haruhiro didn't turn around. What was Merry doing? Was she following him like the rest? He wondered about that. If he cared so much, he should have just checked. It was so simple, and yet he couldn't do it.

"Oh, yeah..." Haruhiro crouched down in front of Manato's grave. "That's right, isn't it, Manato...?"

When they'd left the Forbidden Tower, the wall had risen up behind them, sealing off the entrance. There had been a lever of some sort inside. That lever. That was what opened and closed the door.

The moon.

After leaving the tower, he'd seen the moon.

A red moon is just weird.

He remembered thinking that.

He didn't remember anything that happened before he awoke in the basement of the Forbidden Tower. But he felt like, if he just

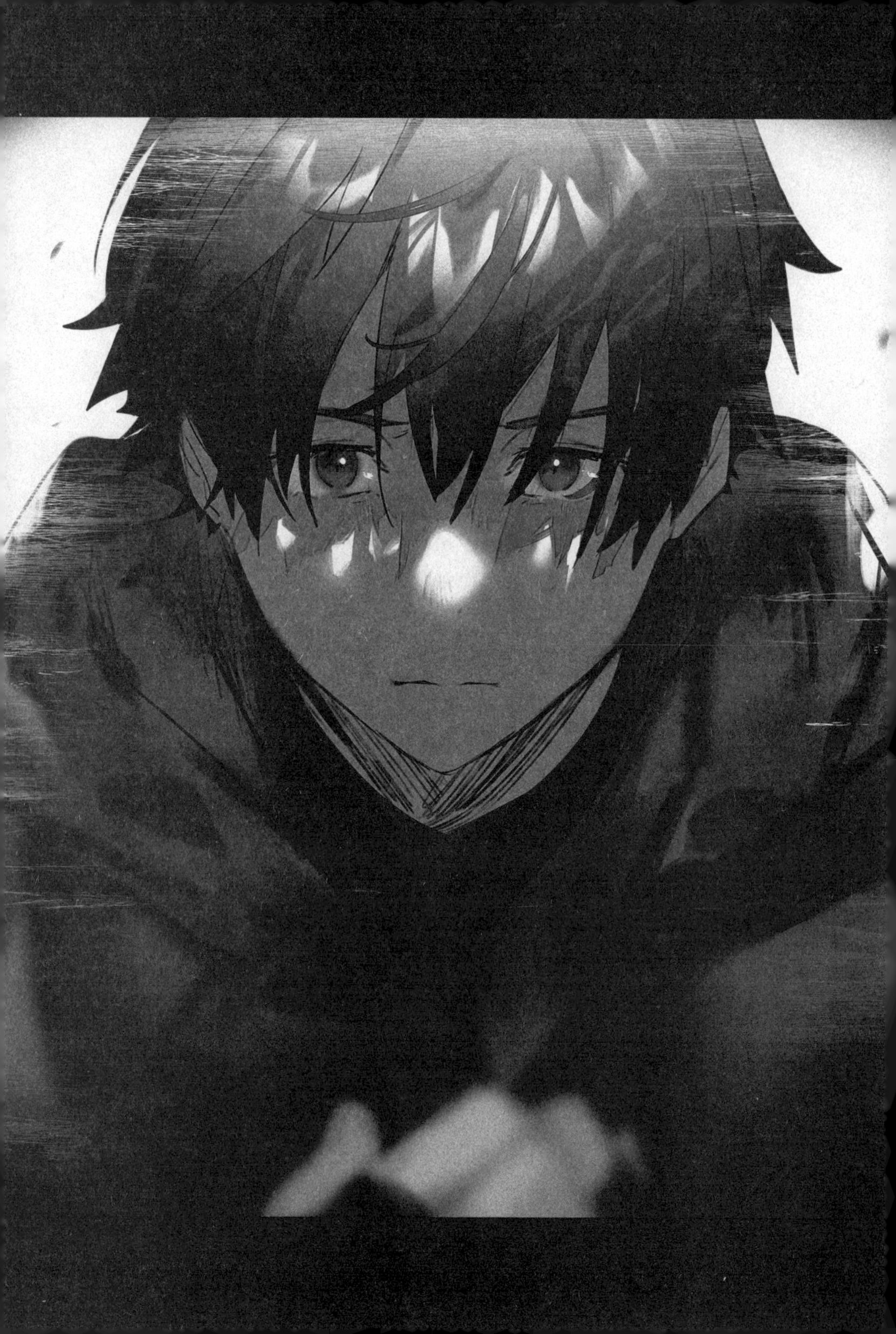

WHY DO WE REPEAT OURSELVES?

had some kind of lead, he could. It didn't have to be anything big, just something to start from, and it might be surprisingly easy to recall the rest from there.

The parents he must have had, for instance. His family. Or maybe a friend.

If he could meet someone he used to know again, it might suddenly jog his memories. It didn't even have to be a person. Maybe a tool he'd used regularly.

Regardless, there was one thing he was absolutely sure of.

He hadn't always been here.

"Awaken."

Before he heard that voice and awakened, Haruhiro had been somewhere else.

Not Grimgar.

The moon probably wasn't red there. What color was it? That I don't know. But it wasn't red. A red moon is just weird.

Haruhiro had gone from Grimgar to other worlds. Through the Wonder Hole to the Dusk Realm. Then through the gremlins' flats to Darunggar. From there he'd gone through the passage on the fire dragon's mountain and returned to Grimgar once more at Thousand Valley, where he'd met Setora and parted company with Ranta. Then there was Parano. They'd entered the Leslie Camp, and as a result were forced to spend a long time in that mind-bending other world.

Grimgar.

The Dusk Realm.

Darunggar.

Parano.

There had to be other worlds in addition to these. Many worlds. Countless, perhaps.

Haruhiro had come to Grimgar from one of them.

"I need to sort through all this... I'm confused, Manato..."

When he closed his eyes he could see Manato's face.

Haruhiro's memories were still a mess, all jumbled out of order. It had been a long time since Manato died—since Haruhiro got him killed.

I let him die.

It was the same with Merry. Haruhiro had basically let her die. He was the leader, so it was his responsibility.

Ranta had left the party in Thousand Valley. Haruhiro and the others had been traveling east through the southwestern portion of the Kuaron Mountains to avoid wyverns. They were attacked by a colony of guorellas in the mountains, and came across a village as they fled. The villagers weren't human. They were gumows, a mix between orcs and either humans or elves.

No, there was one human.

Jessie. He had blond hair and blue eyes, and he said he was a former hunter.

Right. A hunter. When he learned Yume was a hunter, Jessie revealed he had been one too.

Itsukushima. Yume's father. The guy currently imprisoned in the basement of Tenboro Tower. Haruhiro remembered Jessie saying his name. He'd asked Yume, "Are you Itsukushima's apprentice?"

Jessie was a hunter.

But he could use magic too.

That wasn't a contradiction. It wouldn't be strange if an ex-hunter became a mage.

Jessie Land.

That was the place where Merry died. She was completely bereft of life. And yet, Jessie said there was a way.

"She can come back to life, like me, who already died once."

"But there is a price to pay."

"She'll be coming back in my place."

"You people aren't stupid, so you understand, right?"

"This isn't normal."

"It's common sense that people can't come back to life, and that's a fact."

Haruhiro dropped to his knees. If he didn't put his hands on his thighs for support, he was going to fall over.

Jessie was a mystery, and not a man to be trusted. But it hadn't seemed like he was trying to deceive them.

Manato and Moguzo had taught them something. People die. Lives can be lost. Every life ends in death.

That was why, as Jessie had explained it, Merry's revival was a special occurrence, and it came with unique conditions. It was no miracle. Like with a magician's tricks, no matter how mysterious it seemed, there was a proper explanation behind it. But Jessie said he couldn't spoil the trick. Merry would come back to life in his place. He couldn't tell them any more than that.

Haruhiro and the party had the right to choose.

No, Haruhiro did.

Haruhiro had made the call himself, without consulting anyone.

He couldn't bear it. Merry becoming no more than a memory, like Manato or Moguzo. The pain he'd feel as he looked back on the time they'd spent together. He didn't want that. This was no joke. Of course he didn't want it. If he'd had the option, Haruhiro would have made the same choice for Manato or Moguzo. If he could get away with not having to accept the death of someone close to him, accept losing them forever, nothing could be better.

No matter how repulsive the act, it was better than having to bury Merry. He'd learned that well enough the first time. And yet, he'd been unable to avoid going through it twice. He didn't want to feel that way a third time. He'd had enough.

But what was that? What did Jessie do?

The wound in Merry's shoulder had been pretty deep. Jessie had slit his own left wrist and pressed it against Merry's injury. He'd stayed like that for a long time. Eventually, all that was left of Jessie was a husk of skin, no bones—as if Jessie had poured everything that had been inside him into Merry.

When Merry woke, some foul-smelling liquid, not blood but something else, gushed from her mouth, nose, and ears.

If the same amount came out as went in, then the volume was unchanged.

Whatever had been filling Jessie moved inside Merry. If nothing had been displaced by it, there would be no balance. No matter how you looked at it, that wouldn't have made sense.

Basically, whatever was supposed to happen happened, and Merry came back to life.

Was that how Haruhiro had interpreted it at the time? Or rather, was it the only way he could have interpreted it? Had he stopped thinking because any explanation was going to feel forced? He might have.

"That was the start of it..."

Haruhiro looked up. He'd never been so aware of the weight of his own head as he was now. He turned his gaze to the right, where his comrades were.

Ranta shifted his mask aside, frowning at Haruhiro. Kuzaku looked worried, or maybe just bewildered. Yume was putting a supporting hand on Merry's back as Merry hung her head.

Setora had her arms crossed and her chin up, her silent gaze fixed on Haruhiro.

"*The dead don't come back.*"

That was what Setora had said to him that day. Even if Merry started breathing again, it wouldn't be the sort of revival he was hoping for.

Merry.

I thought it would be all right.

Did I try to believe because I wanted to think it would be?

"*The woman who comes back may be a different person from the one who died.*"

Setora had been persuasive. She was a necromancer from the Hidden Village, after all. The necromancers had given birth to the golem in their attempts to bring back the dead. They had tried to overcome death through repeated trial and error, but were never able to reach that goal. Using the parts of dead bodies as material, they'd created terrifyingly loyal servants. That was the best they could do.

"I hope she's not some unknown monster, at least."

She's not.

When she came back, Merry was still Merry. Not some monster.

Absolutely not.

"She's not... Right...?"

But that was the start of it.

Merry was unquestionably Merry. But there were some things that were strange.

Jessie Land had been attacked by a pack of vooloos, wolflike creatures the size of bears. The team had made it through that somehow. The problem was what happened next.

There was a rumbling, like an earthquake, and a hill came at them. Obviously, that wasn't what actually happened. It wasn't really a hill. It was a mass of giant black caterpillar-like creatures.

Was that a natural phenomenon? Was that just the kind of creatures they were? Whatever the case, Haruhiro had never seen or heard of anything like them.

But Merry knew what the mass was.

He felt like she had called it "sekaishu."

Then there was the magic too. Right. Merry had used magic. An Arve Magic spell called Blaze Cliff. But she said it wouldn't be enough to eliminate the sekaishu.

It was probably Setora who asked the question. "What is sekaishu?"

"I don't know," Merry had answered. It was a word she'd said herself, yet she claimed not to know.

Merry shouldn't have been able to use Arve Magic, but she had. Blaze Cliff. Strangely, the former hunter Jessie had shown them the same spell. Strangely?

Was it really a coincidence?

Leaving Jessie Land, they'd headed for the sea. It was on the way there that he'd had a chance to talk with Merry alone.

"There must be something wrong with me. I'm making everyone worry. I know that."

Merry understood something was wrong inside her. That she must have changed. If she was messed up, she said, she wanted him to tell her. She also said she wanted him to stop her.

"I'm here. And yet, I don't know. It's not always, but there are times I just don't know. The wind is strong, and I feel like I'm going to be blown away. Where am I? Someone tell me. I—"

When they came back from Parano, the master of the Forbidden Tower probably gave Haruhiro and the others a drug of some sort to make them lose their memories. Haruhiro had forgotten all this until just now.

For some reason, it was different for Merry. She said she didn't really know what happened in Parano. Everything else, she remembered. Merry was different from the rest of them.

Haruhiro put a hand on the ground for leverage and stood up.

The rain was closer to sleet now. It was pretty cold. Feeling a chill, Haruhiro shuddered.

Let's go home. Not that I know where home is. For now, anywhere that gets us out of the wind and rain will do.

"Merry."

He called her name, but she didn't raise her eyes. She was pressing herself against Yume, looking frightened. Who was she afraid of? What intimidated her? Was she looking to Yume for protection? *Yume will defend me.* Maybe that was what she thought.

Would Merry really think that? If she was the Merry that Haruhiro knew? Besides, why wasn't she answering him? Haruhiro had called her name. Would it kill her to say something in response? Or did she have some reason she couldn't?

"Are you Jessie?"

When Haruhiro asked that, she shuddered, still hanging her head. She made no attempt to look up.

Her shoulders rose and fell as she took a breath. The motion repeated, again and again.

"Merry-chan...?" Yume asked, leaning in to look closer at her face. Still, the woman did not respond.

Her breathing grew faster, shallower, with each breath. Yume tried to rub her back, but she brushed Yume's hand aside. Then she went further and pushed Yume's entire body away from her.

"Wha—" Ranta instinctively put himself between Yume and the woman.

"N-no...! No...!"

The woman shook her head, making a mess of her hair.

WHY DO WE REPEAT OURSELVES?

"Ahhhh!"

Her voice was almost a scream. No, it *was* a scream.

"Ngahhhh!"

Was she hurting somewhere? Was she in pain? The woman was squirming.

"No...! No, no, no, no, no, no...! I'm...!"

If she was suffering, it was because of Haruhiro. The woman was Merry. She looked just like her, after all—and nobody else. And yet, what had Haruhiro called her?

He'd called her Jessie.

Was he trying to say that she was that mysterious man? She couldn't be.

"Merry! I'm sorry, Merry!"

That day, when the two of them talked. That night, when she revealed her insecurities to him. Haruhiro had held Merry tight. Merry hadn't rejected him. What was it she'd said?

"I've always wanted you to do this."

He remembered. That was what Merry had said to him.

That had been Merry. And this woman here now, writhing in front of them, was also Merry. Merry hadn't been looking for Yume to defend her. Merry realized something was wrong with her, but she couldn't do anything about it herself, so she'd clung to Yume without meaning to. Basically, the same as that night. Merry trusted Haruhiro and Yume as comrades. That was why Merry had relied on them. And what had he gone and said to her?

Haruhiro tried to rush to Merry's side. That was when it happened.

Merry's gaze was wrenched up toward the heavens. It was such a sudden jerking motion that you could almost hear it. Instantly, her eyes rolled into the back of her head. Her mouth fell open and a groan escaped it. This wasn't something happening of her own will. No, it looked more like some external force was doing it to her. Not that someone had grabbed Merry's head and pulled it back. There was nothing like that happening.

"Merry...?"

"No."

That was Merry's voice. At least that part was the same.

But she was different.

"He's not here." Her chin still raised, only Merry's eyes moved to look down at Haruhiro. "To be more precise, he's lost the ability to perceive himself. As such, he can no longer come out."

Jessie? Was the "he" she was talking about Jessie? Haruhiro had brought it up. He'd suggested that while she looked like Merry, she might really be Jessie. Merry had denied it. No, that wasn't quite right.

She wasn't Merry.

She no longer had any intention of hiding that she wasn't. Everything, the way she spoke, the way she stood, the way she moved, it was all different from Merry. Anyone who knew her even a little could tell the difference. That was how big the gap was.

"I think this goes without saying, but..." the woman said, "it's wrong of you to blame her for this. She is not the one who made the decision."

Her. She.

"Try saying it in a way we can understand..." Ranta had Yume back away, also taking a half step back himself. "What're you even talking about?"

She glanced at Ranta. Inclining her head slightly, as if nodding, she directed a distinctive gaze toward him. It wasn't a gesture Merry would ever have used.

"I am saying she is not responsible for this in the slightest. It was not she herself who roused her from the fate of those who die. Nor was it I who chose her."

"The fate of...those who die?" Ranta bit his lip. "You're telling me she bit the big one? Merry...died? But she's alive... Or am I wrong? You're not Merry, are you? So, what's going on is, there's... something else inside Merry—you, the one who's talking to us right now... Is that it...?"

"You should show her compassion."

This thing that was clearly not Merry spoke of her in the third person, using Merry's face and voice.

"You should not oppress her, hurt her, or force her into isolation. Because none of this is her fault. As things stand, she still has her memories, her will, the things that make up her personal identity. However, you would do well not to assume those will continue to exist indefinitely regardless of the conditions she is placed in. From what I have observed, the sense of self possessed by creatures of your kind, despite some individual variance, is not particularly stable. In fact, it is incredibly fragile and prone to collapsing."

"Like I asked!" Ranta shouted at her. "What the hell are *you*, the one who's rambling on at us?! Before you go on talking like you're better than us, give us your damn name!"

"I have no name."

"Don't try to dodge the question!"

"No." Not-Merry shook her head gently. "I have no name. Only a thing I am called."

"Then tell us what *that* is!"

"I am that which frees the dying from—" Not-Merry began to say, then seemed to stumble a little, as if feeling faint. She held her head and lowered her eyes. "It seems she wants to come out... She is not yet ready to accept it..."

Before she even finished speaking, Not-Merry began to change. Haruhiro could tell. She let out an audible gulp. Her eyes opened and she stared into space.

"Merry...?"

When Haruhiro called her name, she looked at him, then immediately away. She hunched over, clutching the base of her neck with both hands and taking shallow breaths.

"Merry-chan..." Yume tried to approach her.

"Stay away!" she screamed.

It's Merry. Haruhiro was sure of it.

"Stay away from me... Please..."

Merry's back.

Merry had died once, and now she had someone inside who wasn't her. Perhaps multiple someones. Merry was inside Merry too. But the one rejecting Haruhiro and the others wasn't one of those Not-Merrys, it was Merry herself.

5. Paper-Thin Stubbornness

Haruhiro and the group had decided to return to Alterna. When he'd said, "Let's head back for now," Merry had nodded. She followed behind them, keeping her distance. *That's good, at least,* was something Haruhiro couldn't bring himself to think. *There's nothing good about this. Not one thing.*

They entered Alterna through the north gate. The soldiers were pretty suspicious, but they let the party through.

Neal was waiting for them in front of Tenboro Tower.

"What were you people doing outside?"

Haruhiro told him they were visiting graves.

"Visiting graves, in weather like this?" Neal said, incredulous.

"*Because* the weather's like this."

Haruhiro knew he was putting on a tough front. He was almost frantic. Obviously, he shouldn't have been letting himself lose his cool. But even though he knew that, it was hard to stay in control, given the circumstances.

"Commander's calling for you," Neal said.

"For whom?" Haruhiro asked in a nonchalant tone.

"You."

"Just me?"

"Yeah."

"Do you like being his errand boy?"

"Huh?" Neal's face flushed red with anger. Haruhiro clapped him on the shoulder.

"Where do I need to go?"

"The great hall," Neal answered, shaking off Haruhiro's hand. "You'd better not be looking down on me..."

Haruhiro went into Tenboro Tower without bothering to respond. *That wasn't very mature of me,* he thought. Not that acting mature was going to fix any of his problems. What *would* fix them? Honestly, he couldn't even imagine.

Haruhiro sent Ranta and the rest back to their room before heading to the great hall on the second floor. Jin Mogis sat pompously on a chair atop a platform. In addition to Mogis, there were five black cloaks in the great hall. One of them was General Thomas Margo, who had been a regular black cloak before his promotion. He wasn't especially fat, but he had pudgy cheeks, and his hairline formed an M-shape that looked like he shaved it that way. Also, his voice was weirdly high. He wasn't entirely incompetent, though the jury was still out on how skilled he actually was. The one thing that was certain was his loyalty to Mogis.

"The dwarves of the Kurogane Mountain Range are calling for us to send reinforcements," Mogis said, not raising his voice.

"Their envoy is a human who says he was a resident of Alterna. It seems you're well acquainted with this Itsukushima fellow."

"Please, let him out of prison." Haruhiro almost added "right now," but managed to stop himself. Maybe his self-control was starting to come back.

Mogis ignored Haruhiro's comment. "Do you believe the dwarves are trustworthy?"

Haruhiro cocked his head to the side. "I don't know any of them, so I couldn't say."

"You spoke to Itsukushima."

"Yeah, but only a little."

"He says that the dwarves of the Kurogane Mountain Range have fielded a new weapon. You've heard, yes?"

"Vaguely."

"I'd like to learn what it really is."

Mogis tapped the armrest of his chair two, three times with his left index finger. That finger was adorned with a ring. The accessory wasn't small, but it wasn't that large either. Its head was made of gold and held a blue stone—a bright whitish blue, with some shapes just under its surface: two petals, floating in the brilliant light-blue gem.

Two.

Haruhiro feigned indifference as he looked away. He slowly exhaled through his nose.

He was sure of it. There were only two petals. Two shimmering petals on the stone. *Weird.*

There were three before.

At least, I think so. Could I be misremembering?

The last time he'd gotten a proper look at the ring, which they believed was a relic, Haruhiro had still been missing his memories. Not anymore. They had come back to him just a little while ago. Everything, probably. That had to be why. His mental timeline was a mess. He had to think hard to distinguish reality from things he'd imagined.

That ring's a relic. That much I'm sure of.

Jin Mogis had used the power of that relic to curb stomp the party. He hadn't had it when they first met him. This was just an educated guess, but he'd likely gotten it from the master of the Forbidden Tower.

There were three petals in the gemstone...I think.

Now there're two.

It's dropped to two.

There's one less.

What's going on here? What does it mean?

"Itsukushima won't talk about the dwarves' new weapon." That was why he'd been jailed, Mogis explained. "Would you people be able to get something out of him? I'd like to settle this as peaceably as I can and keep sacrifices to a minimum. I mean that sincerely."

If Itsukushima wouldn't talk, he'd be injured, tortured, or possibly even killed. So they should go make him spill his guts. That was likely what Mogis was trying to imply.

"I'll try talking to him..." It was the only answer Haruhiro could give.

Smiling faintly, Mogis told Haruhiro, "You may go."

If Haruhiro were to say being dismissed like that didn't rub him the wrong way, he'd be lying. *Does he think he's a king or something?*

There was no choice. Haruhiro explained the situation to his comrades and headed down to the dungeon with Yume. A black cloak guard and Neal the scout were waiting for them by the cell. There to keep an eye on them, no doubt.

When Haruhiro explained why they were there, Itsukushima looked like he felt a little awkward about it.

"Of course it's about that, huh? I shouldn't've said anything about the dwarves having a new weapon. When I got carried away and let that slip, I could see the light in Jin Mogis's eyes change. I knew I'd messed up."

"He must have had all kinds of questions for you. And you didn't give him anything."

"Call me a contrarian, but the thought of having to tell him turns my stomach."

"Nuhhh?" Yume cocked her head to the side. "Master, y'know, your stomach's real hairy, but it's always been straight up and down. What's it look like when it's turned?"

"N-no, that's not what that saying means. And you don't need to mention my hair…"

Itsukushima seemed embarrassed. Haruhiro couldn't have cared less.

"You haven't given us any details about this new weapon either, right?" Haruhiro said with a glance at Neal, who was smirking a short distance away. "Do you think you could, please?"

Itsukushima brought his face closer to the bars. Haruhiro did likewise. Yume had hers pressed right against them.

"You know what that piece of crap is trying to do, right?" Itsukushima said in a hushed voice. "He must be planning to negotiate with the iron king. 'If you want our help, give me your treasure.' That kind of thing."

Haruhiro nodded. He didn't know what the new weapon was, but if it was able to hold back the Southern Expedition, Jin Mogis was going to want it.

"Are they going to be willing to strike a deal?"

"Who knows? Not me."

From the sound of it, it was possible they might turn over the new weapon, which meant it wasn't something they only had one of, and it wasn't immovable either.

"This is just a possibility, but..." Haruhiro let Itsukushima in on something that had just crossed his mind. "Mogis may try to switch to a different negotiating partner."

"Hmm," Itsukushima said, thinking. "If he can't strike a deal with the iron king, he'll talk to the enemy, you mean? I don't see how he'd be able to. Not with orcs and the undead..."

"There's humans too," Yume interjected. "'Cause they've got Forgan with them."

Itsukushima frowned.

"I see... So I'm bait, then, huh?"

"What are you talkin' about?" Yume asked, pursing her lips. Itsukushima turned to Yume. His gaze was endlessly gentle when he looked at her.

"Because I'm an envoy of the iron king. If he hands me over to the enemy, that will at least get him to the negotiating table."

"Yume's not gonna be lettin' him do that, though, okay?"

Yume put her fingers through the gaps in the bars. Itsukushima touched them, seeming a little hesitant.

"Don't worry about me."

"Not worryin's not an option. 'Cause you're Yume's master, okay?"

"Yeah..."

Had Itsukushima accepted that whatever happened to him was going to happen, and there was nothing he could do about it, so he'd deal with it when the time came? Whether or not that was the case, he clearly couldn't stomach the idea of caving in to a man like Mogis. Was that making him act stubborn?

"You should have kept quiet about the new weapon, huh?"

When Haruhiro said that, Itsukushima frowned.

"I'll acknowledge that. It was a mistake. This was always going to be too complex a task for someone like me who barely ever interacts with other people."

"You were praising the iron king before, right?"

"What are you getting at?"

Itsukushima had been given this important job because he had the iron king's trust. And yet he'd carelessly let word of the new weapon slip, and he was on the verge of failing in his task. He'd done the king a great disservice. Was he thinking he couldn't possibly go back after this? That was why he couldn't obey Jin Mogis. He wanted to resist, no matter what.

"The way things are going, it looks like the only way we'll be able to rescue you is to kill or maim those guys over there and then escape from Alterna. It's going to be pretty hard to get the Volunteer Soldier Corps to take us in after we do that. They've got their own reasons for cooperating with the Frontier Army, after all. It's the same for us. One of our comrades has been taken hostage, so we're not exactly sticking around here because we want to. We just don't have a plan for saving her yet."

Itsukushima broke eye contact.

"Forget about me."

Yume wasted no time in wrapping her fingers tightly around his.

"That's not happenin'."

"Yume..." Itsukushima started to say something, but the words didn't come out.

"No matter what happens, Yume isn't going to abandon you," Haruhiro said as plainly as he could. It was pretty embarrassing, stating the obvious like this. "What Yume decides goes for all of us. If you keep acting stubborn, I think this scenario is going to play out like I just told you."

"You're saying I'm being stubborn?"

"I'm not wrong, am I?"

Yume nodded in agreement. "Master can be real bullheaded, y'know?"

"R-really...?" It seemed Itsukushima couldn't talk back to Yume. "Okay, maybe you're right. There's nothing cool about being stubborn. I messed up. I wanted to play it off somehow, cancel out my failure that way."

"Wow, Master. It ain't easy, ownin' your missed takes like that, y'know?"

"Owning up to my mistakes, you mean..." Even as he corrected her mistake, Itsukushima was looking at Yume with an expression that said, *Aww, she's so cute; she can't help it.* But he moved on, possibly because Haruhiro was there.

"Anyway, I get it," Itsukushima said, clearing his throat and putting on a serious expression. "I'll tell you about the new weapon. But it's not like I've used one myself, and I only know roughly how many the dwarves have."

"For reference, what *is* the new weapon?"

"Guns," Itsukushima revealed.

"Guns," Haruhiro parroted back at him.

Yume blinked. "Guhnz?"

"Firearms..." Haruhiro murmured.

Momohina of the K&K Pirate Company, based out of the Free City of Vele, had been carrying one—and the company supposedly had a few more.

"I'm not a fan of them, but..." Itsukushima furrowed his brow. "The dwarves of the Ironblood Kingdom can make guns. They must have hundreds."

Grimgar of Fantasy and Ash

6 | It's All in How You Say a Thing

Jin Mogis had Itsukushima released at once. He apparently invited the hunter to dinner right after that and even apologized. However, what he didn't do was bow his head. Itsukushima said dining with the man made him hate the guy even more. Mogis probably didn't care. The man was shameless.

Mogis decided to send a delegation to the Kurogane Mountain Range while the Frontier Army prepared for the campaign. One of the black cloaks, Bikki Sans, was chosen to lead them as chief delegate in the commander's place. Itsukushima would be going too, of course. The party was ordered to join them. Oh, and Neal the scout was also going. He'd be serving as Bikki Sans's second-in-command and also keeping an eye on Haruhiro and the party, no doubt.

Mogis had a horse prepared for each member of the delegation, brought over from the mainland. They weren't large, but they were well built, and their faces looked mild-tempered. They actually were obedient, and Haruhiro was told they could be used for both riding and pulling.

"You set out tomorrow. Spend your time as you please until then."

That was what Mogis said after summoning the members of the delegation to the grand hall. He made it sound like he was a generous liege, doing his subjects a favor.

Itsukushima said he was going to take the wolf-dog he'd brought with him from the Kurogane Mountains around to visit the hunters' guild building and some other places before meeting back up with them the next morning.

The party decided to spend the night in the volunteer soldier lodging house. It was beyond ruined, but it still had a roof, at least. There were lots of rooms there. If they just got some fuel together, they could keep warm too. They could even use the bath. It'd be a lot more relaxing than staying in Tenboro Tower.

Haruhiro was concerned about Merry, of course. But, honestly, he didn't know what to do about it. He left his comrades at the lodging house and headed for the thieves' guild in West Town.

Mentor Eliza was at the guild. She refused to show her face as per usual, though. They exchanged information, and without meaning to Haruhiro told her that his memories had come back. They talked a bit about Barbara. It really hurt, losing her. Right now, he wanted Barbara-sensei here more than ever.

In addition to Eliza, there were two other surviving mentors, the brothers Fudaraku and Mosaic. They were supposed to be following the Southern Expedition, but they hadn't come back yet. If even one of the brothers was still alive, they might try to contact Haruhiro and the party as they headed to the Kurogane Mountain Range. Just to be safe, Eliza taught Haruhiro the code to check if the person he was talking to was a mentor of the thieves' guild.

"But I'm sure it won't be of any use." Eliza apparently didn't expect much of the brothers. "If they're alive, they're lying low somewhere waiting for the heat to die down. That's how those two are."

Haruhiro returned to the volunteer soldier lodging house. They could have split up into the boys' room and the girls' room like they had in the past, but with Merry's current issues to consider, they decided to each take one room for themselves.

Haruhiro chose a room with two bunk beds packed full of straw. He lit the lamp on the wall and took off his cloak, sitting on the lower bunk of a bed.

Back when they were volunteer soldier trainees, they'd rented this room for ten copper a day. It was a real trip down memory lane. Ranta had slept in the top bunk of one bed, with Moguzo on the bottom, while the other bed had been Haruhiro on top, Manato on the bottom.

"We went and peeped on the girls in the bath... I know it was Ranta's idea, but that was pretty awful of us, huh?"

This bed, the one that Haruhiro was sitting on now, had been Manato's. Next to it was Moguzo's. They were both gone now.

Barbara-sensei had died too.

Come to think of it, Team Renji had also lost Sassa on the Red Continent.

Haruhiro sighed.

I wish I could just sigh away all these heavy emotions, but it's probably not gonna happen, he thought. He wasn't good at changing gears. He'd forgotten all this stuff, even though he hadn't meant to. But now he'd remembered it all. Maybe everything was back to the way it should have been all along.

Someone knocked at the door. He'd heard their footsteps before that, so Haruhiro wasn't surprised.

The door opened before he could answer.

"Heh." It was the masked man. "Boy, that face is depressing. You're gonna affect morale, you idiot."

"Sorry, man. This is the face I was born with."

"I know you can't change that, but pull yourself together. You know what I'm trying to say here." The masked man came in and plunked himself down on Moguzo's bed. "You remember it all now, huh?"

"Well..." Haruhiro sighed. He felt like he was sighing a lot, but that was nothing new. He always had. "Probably, yeah."

The masked man bared his face and sprawled himself across the bed. "You're so noncommittal. Memories or no memories, you always have been."

Haruhiro forced a smile. "Yeah, I guess."

"As for Merry..." Ranta said in a low voice, "I've got Yume keeping a subtle eye on her."

IT'S ALL IN HOW YOU SAY A THING

Normally, maybe Haruhiro should have given some directions, orders on what to do about Merry. He'd ended up leaving it to Ranta. That was an oversight on his part, but whatever. Haruhiro decided to accept it for what it was.

Did Haruhiro need to shoulder everything himself? No. He could let Ranta take some of the burden, and Yume had become so reliable she was hardly recognizable. Setora's head was built differently from Haruhiro's too. And as for Kuzaku, he was well above average when it came to putting his body on the line.

"Hey, Ranta."

They'd lived a hand-to-mouth life here in this room.

Time went by.

So many things had happened. More than could ever be told.

Haruhiro and the others had changed. None of them were able to stay the same.

"Back then..."

"Huh?"

"I never would have thought things would turn out like this."

"Yeah, I'm all-powerful," Ranta said with a laugh, "but, sadly, I'm not all-knowing. I can't predict the future."

"Yeah... It's all so hard..."

Haruhiro was venting to the wrong person. Knowing Ranta, he'd mock and insult Haruhiro.

"In the end, everything's just a load of shit." Ranta loosely crossed his legs, put his hands on the bed, and sat up. Uncharacteristically, he didn't belittle or make fun of Haruhiro, even though he *was* Ranta. "Is there that much in life that's not shit? I mean, think about it. We started this life with the shit condition of not knowing anything but our names. But even if that weren't the case, I'd still say it. Once you're born, it's eat, sleep, shit, eat, sleep, shit, eat, sleep—and so on and so forth, until one day you kick the bucket. It's more or less the same for every living thing. Basically, all we do is eat, shit, and sleep!"

"You don't mince words, huh?"

Haruhiro laughed just a little. Not because it was funny, but because what could he do but laugh? It was about the only option he had.

"But that's not all life is, is it?"

"Well, no," Ranta was quick to admit. "There's always more living things born before the current ones die. We're born to give birth and die, so when you think about it that way, procreation's important."

"Yeah, I guess."

"Hey, man, you wanna screw women too."

"...I'm not gonna deny it."

"Why've you gotta be so noncommittal? If you wanna do it, even if it's just occasionally, what's wrong with just saying that you do?"

"Okay, sure. I do."

"Though, even that impulse, it's just a system put there to make us animals leave behind offspring."

"If you put it that way…maybe it is, yeah."

"I'll bet, once you've got a kid of your own, even a noncommittal guy like you would adore them so much it'd make me want to puke."

"I've never thought about it."

"I'll say it definitively. You're the shittiest of shits, and you'd adore your brat to puke-worthy levels."

"Adoring your own child isn't that bad, is it?"

"It wouldn't be, if it weren't all a big setup to make you feel that way."

"Oh... You're saying, as living beings, we're wired to adore kids who carry our blood?"

"Of course, there's shitty parents out there who can't love their own kids. But in general, things are set up so we care about them. If they weren't, the whole procreation thing wouldn't work. So, knowing it's all a setup, doesn't that kill your enthusiasm?"

"Nah, not really..."

"It kills mine. It's total shit. Everything's shit. Seriously. Seriously..."

Ranta told him about the time when he was alone in the deep forest with no one else around. Absolutely no one. It felt like he was the only person in existence. No matter what he did, where he went, how much time passed, he never met anyone. He was sure he'd never see anyone again.

He even hoped he'd be attacked by a wild beast and devoured.

He considered not eating or drinking, just waiting to waste away.

Despite that, he made an effort so that he could escape the deep forest someday. No matter how much he yearned to, could he actually get out? He didn't know if it was possible. It might not have been. He might be devoured by wild beasts in the forest, or wander lost until he died without anyone ever knowing.

In the endless silence, a voiceless terror strangled him.

He felt like he was going to suffocate, but he never passed out.

His feet were leaden.

His whole body felt as heavy as it possibly could.

Try as he might, he couldn't take that one first step.

Even so, he would do what he could to eventually escape that deep, deep forest.

"It wasn't just once. I went through that countless times."

Ranta was smiling faintly. His eyes were half open. His lips and jaw seemed to quiver. It must have been terrifying for him to think back on it. But he didn't intend to run from those memories. Even if he was just trying to act strong, if he could keep it up long enough, it would eventually become genuine. That was Ranta's style.

"It was like, 'I'm seriously all alone.' It forced me to realize that. If I wanted someone to talk to, I had to imagine them in front of my eyes, or inside my head, and mumble to myself. It was seriously shitty. Even now, just occasionally, I have dreams about that time. Like, 'Aw, not this again.' Sometimes, I think that's what dying might be like. And if so...I don't wanna die slowly. One good, clean shot is the way to go. Man, it's such shit. That's ultimately just how life is."

"I don't really get it, but...what do you mean, that's ultimately how life is?"

"Are you a moron? Figure it out, man!" Ranta clicked his tongue. "Listen, Parupiro. No matter how good a time you have, it's all the same in the end. Even if you have three thousand kids with genes as incredible as mine. Either you die instantly, not knowing a thing, or you go out writhing in agony, thinking, 'Wow, this sucks,' but either way, you turn into a corpse that's practically—no, that's *actually* shit. That's our life. That's the one truth, isn't it?"

"I don't see it that way, though."

"You do you. That's your freedom. I think everything's shit. That's my freedom."

"We just don't get along, huh?"

"We've known that a long time, haven't we?"

"Yeah, kinda."

"Everyone's shit."

"Yume too?"

"No exceptions. I'm shit, she's shit, living's shit, dying's shit. But I still want to hold her tight and treasure her until the day I die. You could say that I had an epiphany out there, alone in the forest. I figured it out. The important thing isn't whether she's shit or I'm shit."

If Haruhiro were to interpret, here's what Ranta was trying to say:

The value of everything is just for show. Everything is worthless. You have to strip the value away from everything, even the things that seem like they can't possibly be without it. Then it's just a matter of treasuring whatever's left.

"Haruhiro, do you think there's some sort of special reason that these shitty events keep on coming?"

There isn't, was what Ranta was implying with total confidence.

"From the very beginning, it's all been shit. You included. Of course all the events are going to be shit too. You're shit, so don't complain like you're something else. Learn to live with things being shit. Because you're shit."

That's a pretty awful thing to say, Haruhiro thought. But he didn't get pissed off.

Time had gone by, and he had sensed that he was no longer his old self. So why was he still being tossed about at the mercy of every little thing life threw at him? Wasn't there some way he could make better decisions and get them out of this awful situation? Ranta had seen Haruhiro thinking that way, so the dread knight had come to say, *Don't be conceited.* Haruhiro and the gang had been like this all along, so it wouldn't be strange if things carried on the same way forever.

I hope not, but I can't give up either way. I've got to look for a way out of this deep forest. And unlike Ranta's situation back then, I'm not alone, so I have it much better.

7. Not So I Can Remain Myself

IN THE DIM LIGHT of early morning, before the first bell rang, Shinohara and the members of Orion showed up in front of the north gate where the Frontier Army's delegation was assembling to see them off. There was mist in the air, giving the whole thing an ambience like they were inside a dream as they prepared to leave. Not a good dream, though. If anything, it was a nightmare.

"Sorry to trouble you..." Haruhiro said meekly, but Shinohara laughed it off, telling him not to act so reserved.

"I wish we could join you, but unfortunately we can't. Watch yourselves out there. I'll be praying for your safety."

This man had just lost his friend and confidant, Kimura, the other day. At the time, he'd been beside himself with grief in a way that felt uncharacteristic of him, but now he was just fine. There were still suspicions about him and what involvement he might have with the master of the Forbidden Tower, so the way he was acting looked kind of dodgy.

If Haruhiro were to list the senior volunteer soldiers who'd helped him out, Shinohara's name would be at the very top. Haruhiro respected the guy, and had always thought of him as good-natured and trustworthy. Was he just a poor judge of character?

"Thank you... Well, anyway, we should be going."

As Haruhiro bowed his head, Shinohara raised a hand.

"Orion!"

Immediately, Hayashi and the other members lifted their weapons over their heads in unison.

"Whoa! That's so cool..." Kuzaku was honest with his emotions, kind of a simple guy. Ranta, on the other hand, just clicked his tongue with distaste behind his mask.

"Time to go!" Bikki Sans declared loudly. He, Neal the scout, and Itsukushima were all on horseback. Haruhiro and his party hadn't mounted up yet. They had put their luggage on the horses and were leading them by the reins.

"Poochie!" Yume called the name of Itsukushima's wolf-dog and the animal rushed over to her. Poochie had been raised by the hunters' guild, and it wasn't just Itsukushima he was attached to; he was friendly with Yume as well.

The Frontier Army's delegation—nine people, nine horses, and one wolf-dog—set off north from Alterna. By the time they entered the Quickwind Plains, the fog had totally cleared.

Soon the sun rose and it started getting warmer. There weren't many clouds in the sky and, despite the name of the area, the wind wasn't all that strong. The weather was just right.

Haruhiro and the others were practicing their riding so that they were prepared for anything that might come up. Yume, who had apparently been on a horse before, improved rapidly, while Haruhiro, Ranta, Merry, and Setora could handle themselves at regular speeds. Kuzaku's horse didn't like being ridden.

"Well, I am a big guy and all. Maybe I'm heavy?"

The horse didn't seem to mind it when Kuzaku stroked its mane, so it wasn't like it hated him or anything.

"To think you'd be unable to ride a horse. Useless."

Despite his harsh words, Chief Delegate Bikki Sans, a hairy fellow with a full unibrow, proceeded to teach Kuzaku everything he needed to know. It turned out he was from a family of equestrians and had worked as a groom back in the mainland. Thanks to his careful instruction, Kuzaku was at least able to get on the horse.

"Ooh. He's walking. Horse-kun's walking for me. Thanks, Bikki-san."

"Don't thank me, thank your horse. You dolt." Despite the insult, Bikki Sans's face was a little red. He must have been embarrassed. A weirdly nice guy, considering he was one of the black cloaks.

If they continued for another three hundred kilometers across the Quickwind Plains, they'd come to the Shadow Forest. From there it was a hundred and fifty kilometers east to the River of Tears, the Iroto. The source of that river was in the Kurogane Mountain Range. They just had to follow it a hundred and some kilometers upstream to reach their destination. This was the simplest route, but they would have to make detours.

They would start by heading toward the Crown Mountains, a mountain range in the middle of the Quickwind Plains. Obviously, they wouldn't be climbing them. They would travel through the foothills, heading northeast until they ran into the Iroto. Then they just had to follow the river to the Kurogane Mountain Range.

That was just the plan, though. There was no telling where they might encounter the enemy. It was going to be harder to remain undetected as a group than if Haruhiro were acting alone. There was extremely little cover in the Quickwind Plains, so you could see things from really far off. He didn't know what was going to happen, but he'd have to respond flexibly as the situation demanded. They had Itsukushima and Yume—experts at operating in the wild—working with them. Itsukushima seemed to know the Quickwind Plains well too, so it was fair to say they had the terrain advantage.

It was apparently about three days' travel to the Crown Mountains. And yet, even at this distance, you could see the outline of the mountains on a clear day, so they served as landmarks.

Things went well on the first day, but just after noon on the second, Yume found something.

"Fwooo. Master, hey, lookie, lookie."

Yume was on horseback, pointing a little to the west. Itsukushima stopped his horse and squinted in that direction.

"Hrm, that's..."

Haruhiro's eyesight wasn't as good as that of hunters like Yume and Itsukushima. Despite that, he could immediately tell what she was pointing at. Actually, everyone could.

"Huh?" Kuzaku muttered, cocking his head to the side as he stroked the neck of the horse he was riding. "That's a tree, right?"

"You moron!" Ranta shouted, unmasking himself on horseback. "No tree on the Quickwind Plains grows that tall. It *is* pretty gangly, though..."

"It appears to be moving," Setora noted as she deftly controlled her horse. She could make it stop and go as she pleased.

"Seriously?" Neal the scout grumbled, clicking his tongue. His horse looked left and right, flaring its nostrils. If Haruhiro recalled correctly, that was a sign it was feeling uneasy.

Looking down, he saw his own horse was twitching its ears. He'd been told saying "whoa" and petting it was supposed to help if that happened. Come to think of it, Kuzaku was already stroking his horse. Haruhiro decided to imitate him.

"There, there..."

"And?" Bikki Sans asked, sitting tall on his horse, which made him look a good fifty percent more impressive. No, make that twice as impressive. "What is that tall, thin thing?"

"A Quickwind Plains giant..." Merry mumbled.

Bikki Sans's eyes bulged. "Did you say 'giant'?"

Poochie the wolf-dog started howling.

"Poochie!" Itsukushima scolded him and the wolf-dog immediately stopped.

Neal blinked repeatedly. "It looks pretty far off to me... Isn't it awfully big, considering?"

"Heh," Ranta snorted. "They call 'em giants for a reason."

"How big is it, actually?" Bikki Sans asked Itsukushima.

The hunter shook his head. "I couldn't tell you exactly. I've seen them at a distance a number of times, but never tried getting close to one. A good ten meters, at least, I'd think."

"So we just have to keep our distance, then." Bikki Sans was surprisingly calm.

Itsukushima nodded. "Yeah, that's right."

For the moment, they decided to keep going and not pay too much mind to the gangly giant. It remained visible until the sun had set and darkness fell, which was unsettling, but it didn't seem to be approaching them. The group took turns on watch as they got five or six hours of sleep. Haruhiro woke as the sky began to brighten.

"And it's still there..." *Off to the north. The gangly giant. I dunno if it's moving or not. But it's there. That's for sure.*

"I feel like I had a really weird dream. Was it this...?" Kuzaku said as he got up, still half asleep.

"We should set off quickly," Itsukushima said, hurrying them all along. No one objected.

Once the sun had fully risen, the members of the delegation felt a much greater sense of urgency.

"Mew..." The first one to spot it was Yume, of course. She pointed to the northeast while skillfully controlling her horse. "It looks like there's another one, huh?"

The northeast was the direction of the Crown Mountains, which they were heading toward. But between the mountains and the delegation stood another gangly giant-looking figure. It was a little hard to see, as it blended in with the outline of the terrain, but if Haruhiro looked hard enough, even he could make it out.

Itsukushima looked at Yume, his nose twitching.

"Yume, you can see even farther than me now, huh?"

"Is now the time to be impressed?" Ranta quipped listlessly.

Bikki Sans's unibrow raised in a V-shape and he turned his eyes toward Neal the scout. "What do you think?"

Neal shook his head. "I dunno..."

"The issue is if it is coming toward us or not," Setora said, stating the obvious. When people were uneasy or frightened, things that should have been obvious sometimes stopped feeling that way.

"Nuhhh..." Yume looked from one gangly giant to the other. "This could be tough."

"I've had them get this close a number of times. Let's continue as planned for now, and keep an eye on how far away they are."

As Itsukushima said that, Poochie the wolf-dog barked twice.

Yume smiled. "Poochie's sayin' that'll work too. Aren't you, boy?"

Bikki Sans was quick to accept Itsukushima's proposal. He was a good listener, and could be decisive. It also took a lot to unnerve him. Did that mean some of the black cloaks were actually decent?

The delegation headed toward the Crown Mountains while keeping a careful eye on the gangly giants. The sun was beating down mercilessly as the violent winds tried to blow them all away—just another afternoon on the Quickwind Plains.

The area around Alterna at the foot of the Tenryu Mountains had something resembling four seasons, but the Quickwind Plains were more or less the same throughout the year. It was unbearably hot on days with clear skies when the winds were weak, but when they were stronger it was more tolerable. Once the sun went down, it got really cold. When the weather was bad, it hammered you from every direction.

Haruhiro had heard there was a type of heavy thunderstorm unique to the Quickwind Plains. The clouds would rise up to blot out the sun as you watched, and powerful winds would rage as lightning poured down like rain. In a heavy storm like that, you could be electrocuted even if you were clinging to the ground, so it was difficult to survive.

We're being blessed with fair weather, but how's our luck otherwise?

Yume spotted a third gangly giant shortly after noon. It was in roughly the same direction as the second, but farther away.

That meant there was one giant north-northwest of the delegation, and two more in the direction of the Crown Mountains to the northeast and north-northeast.

"We have to assume they're stalking us," Itsukushima concluded. "It would be a bad idea to keep heading toward the Crown Mountains. We'd be narrowing the gap ourselves."

"Do we turn back...?" Neal asked anxiously, looking at Bikki Sans. The chief delegate shook his head with determination.

"No. We have to make it to the Kurogane Mountain Range

and deliver the commander's letter to the iron king. No matter what. Turning back is out of the question."

"Yeah, I know. I was just saying it," Neal said with an awkward frown. "So? What do we do?"

Even if returning wasn't an option, running straight into the gangly giants was obviously a dumb idea.

"If we head east from here, we'll still run into the Iroto. Yes?" Bikki Sans asked Itsukushima. The delegation's destination was the Kurogane Mountain Range. So long as they followed the Iroto upstream, it would take them there.

"That's right," Itsukushima said, nodding, and Bikki Sans made an immediate decision.

"Then east we go."

With that, the delegation changed direction to head due east.

Kuzaku had gotten pretty used to riding at this point, or at least had gotten his horse to tolerate him.

They wanted to get away from the gangly giants as soon as possible. But no matter how far they went, they couldn't shake their three gargantuan pursuers. They might not have been getting any closer, but they weren't getting any farther away either.

"This has never happened to me before." Even for Itsukushima, who was familiar with the Quickwind Plains, this development was beyond his expectations.

"The giants may be reacting to any major intrusions into the Quickwind Plains. Lately, they've had armies of orcs and undead marching through here like they own the place, after all."

The humans hadn't settled the Quickwind Plains, instead building cities like Damuro at the foot of the Tenryu Mountains. The elves had lived in the Shadow Forest, which spread out nearby. That was in part because the climate of the Quickwind Plains was forbidding, but Itsukushima said there were other reasons too.

The towering giants of the Quickwind Plains terrified human, elf, dwarf, and orc alike. There were countless stories of the giants. However, the humans had lost most of their kingdoms, and even the Kingdom of Arabakia had been forced to flee south of the Tenryu Mountains. Thanks to that, tales about the giants were gradually being forgotten.

"I know some of the legends the elves and dwarves tell about giants. Humans take the giants of the Quickwind Plains too lightly. The same is probably true for orcs. We need to keep in mind who the true masters of these plains are. It's not us. That's for sure. And it's not the orcs or undead either."

Once night fell, they obviously couldn't see the gangly giants anymore. However, their pursuers had been within visual range for as long as the light lasted, so it would have been a huge mistake to think they'd escaped.

The delegation decided to keep moving through the night.

Itsukushima and Yume set their course by the stars. The darkness was terrifying—so dense it rendered the moonlight practically useless, making it impossible for anyone to see the person next to them—but they pushed onward and onward to the east. Aside from the times they stopped to let the horses rest or eat grass, all they did was push eastward.

"Wait." It was just before dawn when Itsukushima called for them all to stop.

He dismounted to crawl on the ground. What was he doing? Yume did the same thing.

"You can feel them," Itsukushima said and Yume immediately agreed.

"Yeah. They're gettin' pretty close, aren't they?"

Bikki Sans got down off his horse and asked Itsukushima, "What's going on?"

"Hold on a moment," Itsukushima said, raising a hand to stop Bikki Sans. He wasn't just crawling around. He had his head—or his ear, rather—pressed to the ground. The hunter changed places a number of times.

"This is bad..."

Poochie suddenly started barking.

"Poochie!" Itsukushima shouted and the wolf-dog immediately quieted down.

By that point, Haruhiro had already started sensing something. No, describing it that way was too vague. It was a sound. Heavy and low. And it was probably coming from the east. The sound was in the direction they'd been headed.

"Something's coming..." Ranta said in a quiet voice.

The horses started whinnying and twisting their bodies around.

"Wh-whoa...!"

It was too dark for Haruhiro to see, but that was probably Kuzaku struggling to control his horse. The thief wasn't doing much better himself.

"Whoa, whoa!"

He stroked his horse's head and neck to try to calm it, pulled back on the reins, and squeezed the animal's sides with his legs, but the horse kept on freaking out.

"This is ridiculous!" That was Neal the scout's voice. It was followed by the pounding of hooves.

"He's running away!" Setora shouted.

"Neal...!" Bikki Sans loudly called his name, but Neal didn't respond.

Poochie started barking again. Itsukushima didn't stop him.

"Everyone, get your packs off the horses and let them go! Hurry! We have to act fast!"

"Right!"

That was probably Merry, reacting faster than any of them. Kuzaku fell off his horse before he could dismount on his own.

"Whoa?!"

"You okay, Kuzaku?!" Haruhiro called out as he unfastened his luggage from the saddle. He dismounted, then slapped his horse on the butt. "Go! And stay safe...!"

The horse didn't need some human to tell it that. It was already running.

"What do we do?!" Bikki Sans shouted, seemingly still on his horse. The horse was pretty restless, but it hadn't thrown him from the saddle.

"We can't do anything with it being so dark..." Itsukushima said, then raised his voice to shout, "It's all or nothing! Get us some light...!"

"On it!"

In no time, Setora retrieved a square hand-lantern from inside her luggage and lit it. Everyone but Bikki Sans had ditched their horses, and their luggage was scattered all over. Neal was, of course, nowhere to be seen. Ranta had already unsheathed his katana. Exasperated, Haruhiro thought, *You're gonna fight?*

Yume pointed to the east. "Thataway!"

Setora turned her lantern eastward. It didn't have a reflector for focusing its glow, so its range was limited. The darkness outside the bleary circle of light it cast on the ground seemed impenetrable. It was so dark. Too dark. Maybe Yume's eyes let her see some semblance of what was around them, but for Haruhiro it was pitch black. For now, at least.

Even if he couldn't see, he could sense them. The sound—the vibration—was getting closer.

"Grab all the stuff you can carry!" Haruhiro ordered as he gathered up his own luggage. Fighting would be reckless, or flat-out impossible. Shouldering his pack, he asked Itsukushima, "If we're going to run, where do we go?!"

Itsukushima looked at Haruhiro and was about to say something, but then he immediately turned to the east.

Ranta shouted, "Here they come!"

"Mmmew!" Yume let out a strange cry.

Bikki Sans pulled back on his reins hard, making his horse turn as he shouted, "R-retreat...!"

"Everyone, go on ahead!" Kuzaku shouted, charging into the darkness. What was he thinking? "I've got this!"

"Wait, you imbecile!" Setora tried to stop Kuzaku, but she didn't move from where she stood. She just called after him. Simply telling him not to go wouldn't stop Kuzaku. Setora had to know that, but chasing after him in this situation was too dangerous.

The darkness is moving, pushing in toward us. No, not just the darkness.

Haruhiro saw something else. It was much higher up. Some sort of round object, vaguely shining. There were two of them aligned horizontally. *What're those?* he wondered.

"Ahhh...!"

He heard Kuzaku's voice. It came from the overwhelming darkness up ahead. At the same time, there was the sound of two hard objects colliding.

Yume's gaze turned up. Then her head snapped around to look behind her. Ranta looked behind himself too.

"The hell?!"

There was an unsettling noise from that direction. Haruhiro screamed, "Kuzakuuuuuuuuuuu!"

"I'm here..."

The voice was weak, but he definitely heard it.

He's alive. At least, he's breathing for now. Kuzaku's the toughest guy on the team, he's not gonna die that easily. I won't let him do that to us.

"Merry!" Haruhiro called her name, but Merry was already on the move.

He couldn't hear very well, but he had a feeling she said something like "Leave it to me!"

"Will it reach?!"

Itsukushima was holding his bow at the ready in a position that had him almost bent over backward. What was he planning to do? That much was obvious.

Itsukushima meant to shoot. At those two objects, vaguely shining high up above them? Haruhiro had some idea what they were. Eyes, probably. Did these gangly giants have eyes? He wasn't sure, but that was probably the function those organs served.

Basically, the giant's head was that high up, and it had something resembling eyes. Itsukushima was trying to attack them. Yume nocked an arrow.

"Yume too!" she shouted.

"Wait, that's not gonna—!"

Itsukushima loosed his arrow before Ranta could complain. And it wasn't just the one. He shot several times in rapid succession. Yume followed suit. It was an incredible feat of speed. The two hunters fired shot after shot at what had to be almost a ninety-degree angle. Haruhiro couldn't see the arrows' paths very well. But the arrows *were* flying. That was all he knew for sure. The sound and vibrations soon stopped. No, there was an echoing noise. A different one.

"Mmoooooooooooo. Mmmmmooooooooooooooooooo."

It was like the lowing of a massive cow. He heard it coming from the sky. Up above them. Was that a voice? If so, it might have belonged to the gangly giant.

"I-It's working...?!"

Ranta's question was a hard one to answer. Was it working? Haruhiro wanted to know too.

"Okay, now's our chance...!"

Bikki Sans had been on the verge of setting his horse to flee, but seeing how Itsukushima and Yume were desperately firing arrows, he reconsidered.

"Nngh...!"

Without the hunters holding off the gangly giant, they couldn't run. That meant that if the delegation were to take this chance to flee, they'd have to sacrifice the two of them. Haruhiro felt something resembling affection for Bikki Sans when he didn't order them to do so.

Is he a pretty decent guy?

That still left the question of what exactly they were going to do instead, though.

"Let me borrow that!" Haruhiro yelled as he snatched the lantern out of Setora's hand. If they couldn't see the enemy properly, they couldn't do anything.

Haruhiro had a vague expectation of what the gangly giant would look like as it was slowly revealed by the lantern's light, but he was totally wrong.

"Mmoooooooooooommmmmmmooooooooooo."

It happened so suddenly. A wall rose up in front of Haruhiro. What was it made of? It wasn't smooth, didn't glisten. Was it rock? It looked like it could have been wood too. But it didn't have the texture of a plant. What was it, then? Haruhiro didn't really have the words. He'd never seen anything like it before.

It was hard to identify the color too. No, not just hard—impossible. What was he supposed to call this color? It wasn't white. It wasn't black. Wasn't red, blue, yellow, green, or brown. It probably didn't even have a name.

Haruhiro raised the lantern. The wall continued up and up. Tall. It was a really tall wall.

Something fell toward him. Haruhiro instinctively dodged, and it hit the ground.

It's an arrow.

It had to be one of Itsukushima's or Yume's. That was the only possibility.

The arrow had fallen vertically. One of them shot it upward and it bounced off something. Then, by pure chance, it fell down toward Haruhiro. That was probably it.

So? What do we do? Think. No, it's no good. I don't have time to mull things over. I need to decide fast.

By the time he'd thought that, something else was already happening.

The wall rose up. Not super fast, but not slowly either. It didn't make much noise. Haruhiro's jaw dropped. He turned into a bystander without meaning to. It was careless, yes, but he couldn't help staring. He was entranced, overwhelmed.

"Oh, shi—"

How high had the wall risen? It was temporarily out of sight. Then, immediately after, it came back down again. Wait, something was weird. Before it rose, the wall had been in front of Haruhiro. Now it was falling again. From above him. Directly above him.

He couldn't call it a wall anymore. Some huge mass, a part of the gangly giant, likely a foot, was coming down on Haruhiro's head.

Haruhiro turned tail and booked it out of there. Thoughts like, *Oh, crap, I'm about to get stepped on. It'll crush me. I can't let that happen. I'd die*, raced through his mind.

His body was lifted up into the air before he felt the impact. Normally, it should have been the other way around. But for whatever reason, that was how Haruhiro experienced it.

"Oh...!"

Haruhiro wasn't the only thing that had been lifted into the air. There was dirt too. No, not lifted, he'd been kicked up, together with a ton of sand and pebbles.

Hadn't he been stepped on? It hadn't crushed him, so he must have avoided a direct hit. Haruhiro flailed around desperately in the middle of that flurry until, somehow, he managed to land. He turned to look behind him, but the wall—no, the gangly giant's foot was nowhere to be seen.

"Huh?! No way...!"

"Ruuuuuun!" someone screamed as if they were trying to destroy their vocal cords. Was it Ranta?

At that moment, it occurred to Haruhiro that the gangly giant might be about to do the same thing again. Ranta had just shouted for him to run away.

Oh, right. I'd better run. Run away. Or this time it'll crush me for real. I've gotta run through the dust cloud. Run.

Haruhiro was holding the lantern tight. Even with a light in his hands, he didn't have time to look behind him or above his head. While it might not have been anything more than an emotional crutch, having a light source close at hand made a pretty big difference for him. It was really revitalizing.

"Ah...!"

He felt an impact and the sensation of being lifted up simultaneously. It had been a much narrower shave this time. A stone or something struck the lantern, breaking it. The light of the flame inside flickered wildly. Haruhiro felt his body taking a lot of hits too. They didn't hurt, but his feet weren't on the ground, so it sure felt like he was getting put through the wringer. *I'm in serious trouble, aren't I?*

He couldn't brace himself for the landing. He didn't have any sense of how far up he'd flown, or any idea what kind of position he was in, so he didn't know how he'd hit the ground. The lantern was gone. Haruhiro was in darkness.

He wasn't dead. He was still alive. That much he knew for sure.

Haruhiro got up and tried to keep going. He never thought, *Is this the right way?* What caused him to make his decision? Whatever it was, he followed an intuition that said, *This way.* Did Haruhiro crawl forward? Was he walking? Did he run? Jump? He couldn't even tell, but only a moment later, there was another impact, and he was showered with more dirt. Still, Haruhiro wasn't dead yet. He'd avoided getting stepped on.

Am I in the air again, maybe? I'm not on the ground, at least.

Haruhiro was driven by some kind of premonition. Call it instinct. He drew his dagger with his right hand. Or more like, even without his meaning to do so, the dagger drew itself.

I'm going to hit it. No, cling on to it, Haruhiro willed himself.

To elaborate, Haruhiro had this mental image that he was about to collide with an unimaginably large solid object, and he had to grab on to it just before he did, then stab it deeply with his dagger so he wouldn't fall. Also that if he moved his hands, feet, and waist in a particular way, things would more or less work out. He knew this from experience.

"Urgh...hhh...!"

He couldn't see a thing. Had he gone deaf? He could hardly hear either. It was hard to say anything for certain, but maybe things had gone just as Haruhiro thought they would?

There was incredible motion up and down. Rising, then falling again. An impact. Another rise, another fall. An impact. It was amazing he hadn't been thrown off. Thank goodness the dagger had sunk in. And just as impressively, he'd been able to find something sticking out of the giant that he could grab with his fingers without even a moment's notice. He lost his grip, but got it back. Lost his grip again, and scrambled desperately to get it back. Not to toot his own horn, but he was putting in a pretty good effort here. He had to, or he'd be thrown off in no time.

He was concerned for his comrades. Were they okay? What were they doing? But right now he had no choice but to focus on himself. *Ranta's with them, Yume's with them, Setora's with them, and even Itsukushima's with them. They'll be fine,* he thought. His comrades would get through this. For now, he needed to think about surviving and getting back to them.

Hold on, isn't it moving...?

The gangly giant that Haruhiro was desperately clinging to had probably been stomping its feet before. Things seemed different now. The up and down motion was more relaxed. The impacts, much smaller.

Could the gangly giant be walking?

Walking away from that spot?

Or is it chasing the rest of the group as they run away?

Considering Haruhiro was now able to ponder these things, the gangly giant had to be walking at a sedate pace.

Even so, he couldn't relax. It's important to remember that incaution is our greatest enemy. Even though we know that, we humans are prone to getting careless, and it often leads to failure.

That was why he looked around, cautiously, without letting his guard down. He didn't see anything. It was dark. Just dark. He couldn't even make out the moon or the stars. Just a world of darkness spread out before him.

The way he saw it, Haruhiro was clinging to the gangly giant's leg. That was more or less certain. The leg. Where, specifically? Just how long were the giant's legs? What part was Haruhiro clinging on to? The giant had been stomping its feet. It probably had joints, like the human knee, which bent. Haruhiro figured he was on a lower part. Like the shin. Or maybe the ankle, or the calf. He couldn't be that high up. Maybe two, three meters. It was pitch dark, so he had no clear idea.

Seriously, not knowing was a real problem. It made it hard to decide whether to risk letting go. The moment he did, he might get kicked or stepped on, or he might be higher than he'd expected and hurt himself badly. He might fall to his death.

He couldn't help but think of his comrades. Why had the gangly giant started walking in the first place? It might be that it had already trampled all of them, so there was no point in it staying there anymore. If so, Haruhiro was alone. He'd be the sole survivor. Oh, but what about Merry? Merry, who'd died and come back.

Hadn't Jessie said it?

"It did get harder for me to die once I came back, though."

Haruhiro seemed to remember him saying that. Would it be the same for Merry?

The gangly giant kept walking. Haruhiro shook with each step. But his heart was being shaken even harder.

Again and again, he thought about it.

Enough. I should just drop down. I'll either live or I'll die. What's it matter which it is? My comrades might be dead. Or someone might have survived. Like Merry. But it's hard to imagine all of them did. I'm just exhausted. Haven't I done enough? I don't need to try anymore. It's time to give up.

Haruhiro was weak. He was mediocre. It didn't take much to make him want to throw everything away. There was nothing to be done about that. The question was, once he'd acknowledged that weakness, what could he do?

Hang on. That was all.

Oh, I hate this. I can't take it. It's ridiculous. I can't do this, I can't do this, I really can't. I'm at my limit. I'm way past it. What am I doing? I'm tired. Enough of this. I don't want to keep trying. Let me just stop already.

He complained, and complained, and complained until he was sick of it, but somehow he managed to hang on, no matter how much he wanted to give in to despair. *I know how you feel,* Haruhiro thought. It was weird to be sympathizing with himself, but clinging to a sense of desperation actually made this easier on him. If he acted without caring what happened, he'd at least get some result. Even if it was a bad one, he'd be able to end things.

But, well, you know...? It's not like I saw my comrades die with my own eyes. Maybe nobody died.

If they'd already lost someone, that would be incredibly painful for him, but if just one of his comrades was left alive, he had no choice but to persevere. Actually, as long as that was how he felt, even slightly, it was the right choice for him to keep hanging on. Because until he was no longer able to think that way, try as he might, he wouldn't be able to give up.

"Ungh..." he groaned.

It had gotten brighter, if only a little. The sky was starting to take on color. The moment morning twilight arrived, the black of night beat a hasty retreat.

Low. Haruhiro was at a really low point on the gangly giant's leg. That was more or less as he'd expected. He'd be maybe two meters from the ground when the giant's foot was touching it.

This might seem like an obvious thing, but the gangly giant had two legs. Haruhiro was clinging to the outside of its left one.

It looks like I can make this work, he thought. It would have been dangerous if he'd been on the inside or front of the leg, but the outside seemed comparatively safe.

Still, the gangly giant was huge. Gargantuan. So massive it was hard to even estimate its size.

Was this its skin that Haruhiro was clinging to? It was weird. And not just because it was hard as a rock. It had a unique elasticity to it, and a slight moistness, though he wouldn't have called it wet. It must have been chilled by the night air of the Quickwind Plains, but it didn't feel cool at all. Well, considering they could move, the gangly giants were obviously living creatures. Did they have body heat?

"That's insane. How can a creature like this actually exist?"

Haruhiro waited for the gangly giant's foot to be touching the ground before pulling the dagger out of its skin. *Sorry for stabbing you,* he apologized in his head. Could the giant feel pain? Whether it could or not, Haruhiro's dagger probably hadn't even registered as a pin prick to it. Haruhiro was beginning to develop a sense of awe. Humans, elves, and orcs needed to learn their place. They should have been grateful if the giants left them alone when they entered the Quickwind Plains. And anything that might have angered them ought to have been strictly forbidden.

Haruhiro rolled as he landed. After several rolls, he darted away. By the time he got up, the gangly giant had already put dozens of meters between them.

"It's huuuge..."

He stared in renewed awe.

The eastern sky had turned somewhat whitish as dawn approached the Quickwind Plains, providing enough light to make out the shapes of bushes and patches of grass. The gangly giant behind Haruhiro couldn't be more than a hundred meters away yet. But even from this distance, he couldn't tell what it was. Well, no, he knew it was a giant. It had two arms, two legs, and something resembling a head. But he couldn't bring himself to think of it as a massive humanoid creature for some reason. Even though he could see it properly, it seemed as if he couldn't make out the details.

The sounds of its massive footfalls sent tremors through his entire body. It was a being on a scale so incredible it felt like some sort of illusion.

Haruhiro had the strange feeling that perhaps the gangly giant had no physical form and that he was only seeing it in a dream.

"I'm alive...?"

Haruhiro sat on the ground, exhausted. Once he did, he couldn't resist the urge to lie down completely.

"Ohhh, it's cold..."

He wouldn't say that grass glistening with the morning dew was the best bed he'd ever had, but it beat sitting up. Haruhiro lay there awhile, figuring out which way was which.

I know where the east is. The sun'll be coming over the horizon soon. So west is the opposite of that, which makes that way north, and the other way south.

"Which means..."

He could see what looked to be the Crown Mountains to the southeast. The gangly giant was heading northwest.

"Whoa... I'm way up north..."

Considering how gargantuan it was, the gangly giant walked at speeds a tiny human couldn't possibly compare with. It might have covered over a hundred kilometers in the last few hours.

"I'm lost... Totally lost..."

Haruhiro gazed up at the purple sky. This wasn't funny. There was nothing humorous about it. But he couldn't help but laugh.

"Now what...?"

Haruhiro shut his eyes. He couldn't think of anything. He was exhausted, body and soul. Even if he forced himself to think in this state, he wasn't going to come up with anything decent. *Fine,* Haruhiro told himself. *I don't have to think. I'll rest. Not for long. I'm sure I won't be able to sit still.*

Haruhiro was right. Once the sun had fully risen, he got up.

The next thing he knew, he was thinking all sorts of things, such as, *Looks like clear skies again today,* and, *I'm glad there's not much wind,* and, *There don't seem to be any dangerous animals nearby.* He was feeling depressed, but it still could have been a lot worse.

"South," Haruhiro said, deliberately emphasizing the word.

"I'll head south..."

He kept mumbling the words to himself. No, he wasn't brimming with confidence. He wasn't Ranta. It was impossible for him to become someone he wasn't, and he thought that was okay. In a situation like this, the bigger question was whether or not he could remain himself.

"Probably, at least..."

He had a water bottle in his pack. Portable rations in dumpling form too. Haruhiro ate one of them between sips of water. Then he started walking south.

He wouldn't act optimistic. He wouldn't act pessimistic. He'd keep an eye out around him, perk his ears up, and occasionally glance at the gangly giants in the distance as he walked at a fixed pace.

It was maybe three hours after he'd started walking that he saw it.

"Huh...?"

At first, Haruhiro saw it as a pea-sized figure in the distance.

Is that an animal?

It was coming toward him from the direction he was walking.

The sun was really strong. He shaded his eyes with one hand and squinted at it. Haruhiro was sure now. There was a creature of some sort heading in his direction.

Should I run? Haruhiro quickly thought about it. But the area was flat as far as the eye could see. There was no copse of trees he could hide in around here. *Aw, shoot,* he thought, letting out a small sigh. Was he going to have to do something about this without running and hiding? Well, if there was no other option, he would.

Just as he was thinking, *I should have my dagger ready...*

Woof, woof, woof! Awoooooooooooo!

"Huh? Wait..."

Wasn't that some kind of wolf or dog barking and howling? That was what it sounded like.

"It can't be..."

He was hesitant to believe it, and frankly Haruhiro didn't know what to believe anymore. But as the animal approached, he started to get a clearer view of it.

It had tough-looking fur—gray and brown with yellow patches.

That's a wolf.

No matter how I look at it, all I see is a wolf.

"No, it looks like a wolf, but it's not. A wolf-dog?"

The wolf-dog came to a stop five meters from Haruhiro, barking twice. It didn't look like it planned to get any closer. They didn't act overly friendly with humans they didn't know well.

"Poochie."

Haruhiro couldn't help but laugh. His eyes felt a bit leaky, but thankfully they weren't so leaky that he ended up crying for joy.

Poochie the wolf-dog turned his tail toward Haruhiro. He walked two or three steps, then barked again.

"You want me to follow you...?" Haruhiro asked and Poochie gave a short bark in response.

"I'm gonna owe you for this, Poochie. You're a real lifesaver..."

It wasn't clear if Poochie heard Haruhiro's mumbling or not, but he started picking up the pace.

Haruhiro hurried too. It would be a shame to get left behind after Poochie had gone to all the trouble of finding him. Surprisingly, it turned out not to be that big of a strain on Haruhiro. The pace was manageable for him—just right, in fact.

"Thank goodness for Poochie..."

8. For Now

That he was able to rejoin the group in only a day had to be considered good luck.

The Frontier Army's delegation had lost four horses. However, Bikki Sans had incredibly stayed mounted through the whole debacle, and Itsukushima, Yume, and Setora's horses hadn't gone far, so they were able to catch them. Neal the scout, who had run off on his own, came back too. The most important thing was that they hadn't lost anyone. They'd been really lucky.

"This is on me. I might not have been paying the Quickwind Plains the respect they deserve," Itsukushima apologized, reflecting on his failure. "I normally come to the plains by myself. I might have dogs with me, but since I'm the only person around I hardly ever let my guard down. Maintaining maximum awareness of my surroundings is a must. But this time..."

People can't help but feel more confident in a group. Three people will behave like they're a group of ten, and ten people will act with the audacity of a hundred. It's how humans are. That was Itsukushima's view, and though it may have been a little extreme, Bikki Sans nodded repeatedly in agreement.

"When humans are born and raised in a town of stone, the more solid walls and buildings we construct, the bigger we mistakenly think we are. We tend to forget that once we take one step out of our towns, we're weak creatures with little ability to defend ourselves. We need to be humbler."

Neal was ignoring all this talk, looking fed up with it, but perhaps it was fortunate that a man like Bikki Sans had been chosen as chief delegate. If the leader of the delegation had been incompetent or had a horrible personality, you could bet that nothing good would have come of it. Neal was unquestionably a piece of trash, but Bikki Sans was decent. Just knowing that alone was pretty comforting.

The delegation continued their advance across the Quickwind Plains, now with even greater caution than before. It looked like there were a lot of gangly giants in the area around the Crown Mountains. Maybe that was one of the places they lived. Itsukushima didn't know, so there was no way to be sure, but it was probably best, for the time being, if the delegation were to give them a wide berth, diverting toward the northeast as they headed for the Iroto.

"For the time being" was the key phrase here. Should a problem arise, it would be too late to act at that point. If anything felt off, if anyone had a bad premonition, they needed to share it and discuss. If a change of plans was required, then they couldn't hesitate.

Itsukushima said it was incredibly rare to run into danger while operating on the Quickwind Plains alone. That was because he would always make avoiding danger his highest priority, and never had any qualms about changing course.

However, operating in a group with a fixed destination, it wasn't so easy to do that. On this expedition, they were trying to take the shortest possible route to the Kurogane Mountain Range. Following the optimal routes didn't afford them much room for deviation, so that made it difficult to respond flexibly to emerging threats.

Bikki Sans ordered Itsukushima to act as more of a leader than a guide, making it official that Itsukushima and his experienced wolf-dog, Poochie, would be the ones choosing the route they took, and the rest of the party just had to follow them.

It took three days of travel before they reached the north side of the Crown Mountains. No day passed without them spotting a gangly giant in the distance, but Itsukushima changed direction as necessary to avoid getting any closer. They managed not to agitate the giants that way.

From there, the delegation advanced in a northeasterly direction. After about a day and a half, they started to see more groves of trees and hills covered in shrubbery. The ground wasn't level, making it hard to see far, but they could tell that the woodlands stretched out to the east and northeast. Itsukushima said the Iroto wasn't far now. There were no gangly giants anywhere to be seen and it was about time they bedded down for the night.

"How's it look?" Bikki Sans asked Itsukushima. Since the giant's attack, Bikki Sans had only been riding his mount occasionally. It and the other horses were primarily being used to carry luggage now. Neal was the only one who stayed on horseback, constantly looking down on all of them.

"Seems fine to me," Itsukushima said with a nod. "Let's get a fire going and camp here for today. We'll finally reach the Iroto tomorrow."

"Aw, yeah!" Ranta said, jumping for joy. "It's campfire time! Seriously! Seriously, seriously! I've been missing a good fire! Fire is righteous! No, it's evil! Praise Skullhell!"

Haruhiro's party went around gathering kindling, then started a fire under the trees where Itsukushima told them to. Yume and Poochie went out and caught some big fat plains mice as well as a long-tailed fox with a spectacle pattern around its eyes in a little over an hour of hunting. Itsukushima and Yume butchered them with great skill, offering a part of their catch to the White God Elhit, then cooked the rest. They only had a little salt and herbs to season the meat, but they gave everyone a bit of everything, even the somewhat bitter offal, and it was all delicious.

Once he was finished eating, Bikki Sans started looking after their five horses. He'd brought a brush with him on this trip. Whenever he found time, he'd brush the horses, talk to them, and touch their bodies all over, checking for anything that might be wrong. He probably loved horses so much he couldn't help himself. It seemed the horses reciprocated that affection.

Kuzaku went over and said to him, "Horses sure are cute, huh?"

Bikki Sans broke into a grin so wide you'd think that the compliment had been meant for him. His distinctive unibrow gave him a rather unique smile. It looked a bit comical, but also showed how good-natured he was.

"You get it, huh? The more affection you show them, the more horses'll love you back. Unlike people. They're truly adorable creatures."

"I see what you mean. That makes sense... I mean, they've got such lovable faces. Like those cute eyes."

"These eyes could never lie to you, right?"

"Ohhh, yeah, I get you. They do feel that way. These beady eyes'd never tell a lie."

"I've looked after more horses than you can count. Some of them were temperamental, some of them were difficult, and some of them were stubborn. But I haven't met one horse that ever lied to me."

"Hmm. So that's how it is. Horses don't lie, huh? Good to know."

"I'm just getting a feeling here..." Ranta said as he crouched near the fire. He had a half-smile on his face. "That guy must've either been tricked by a woman or put through absolute hell by someone and lost his faith in humanity, don't you think?"

"He's an oddball," Neal, who was standing a short distance from the fire, said with a smirk. "Rumor is he screws the horses."

Ranta just glanced at Neal, but didn't say anything. Neal might have thought he'd just told a funny joke, but it was a bit too vulgar.

"What gives, asshole...?" Neal said, clicking his tongue at the lack of response. He might have been about to head off somewhere, but ultimately he decided against it, instead sitting down with his back to a nearby tree.

"Ahhh! Hey, hey, Merry-chan, Setoran!"

Yume took Merry and Setora by the arms, pulling them close while saying things like, "Come on," and, "What's the harm?" The three women were sitting in front of the fire, arms linked. Setora seemed a little put out by this, but she was apparently willing to tolerate it. Merry, meanwhile, looked like she didn't mind at all.

"I'm going to go patrol. You all go to sleep or whatever," Itsukushima said, moving away from the fire with Poochie.

Bikki Sans came back to the fire with Kuzaku, who had been helping him take care of the horses.

"Man, horses're so cute. I could really get into them."

"You've got potential," Bikki said, slapping Kuzaku's back. Kuzaku seemed genuinely pleased.

"Whoa! You mean it?"

"If you train diligently, you'll make a good groom."

"Well, I dunno that I want to train for it, and I'm not really looking to become one, though."

"A good groom can become a good rider."

"Oh! Now that has some appeal to it."

"Listen, you..." Ranta seemed like he was about to say something, but he just shrugged and rolled over onto his side instead. "I'm gonna go to sleep. Wake me if something happens."

"For the first watch—" Bikki Sans started to say, but Haruhiro raised his hand before he could name anyone.

"I'll do it. We'll take shifts from there. Itsukushima-san is out patrolling, so I think that should be fine."

"That sounds about right," Bikki said, satisfied with the arrangement, and took two blankets out of the luggage. He spread one out on the ground, then laid the other over it, with a pack as a pillow. He crawled between the blankets, and turned his unibrowed face toward Haruhiro and the others.

"Good night."

Once Haruhiro and the others had each said good night to him, Bikki Sans nodded and closed his eyes. He knew what he was doing. The man was nothing if not meticulous.

"The rest of us oughta be gettin' to sleep too, huh? Watch out for us, okay, Haru-kun?"

Yume, Merry, and Setora all went to sleep next to each other.

Merry seemed to have gotten a little better. Haruhiro was relieved to see that. He felt like he'd been putting off addressing the problem all this time, so maybe he shouldn't have been taking things so easy. But what was he supposed to do? Not just about Merry. He also had to find a way to get Shihoru back. Haruhiro was thinking about these things, but honestly, he didn't have the foggiest idea how he was going to solve either problem.

Kuzaku let out a big yawn next to Haruhiro. His eyelids were looking pretty heavy.

"Go to sleep," Haruhiro told him.

"Mm, yeah," Kuzaku replied, sounding like he was half asleep already.

Neal was sitting against the tree still, hanging his head. He hadn't moved in a while, so maybe he was actually sleeping. Being a scout, he was probably used to sleeping in odd positions.

"Hey, Haruhiro," Kuzaku said with another big yawn.

Haruhiro stared into the fire as he asked, "What?"

"You remembered everything, right?"

"Yeah... I guess?"

"Glad it worked out this way."

"What do you mean?"

"It's a good thing, I guess. I was just kinda thinking..."

"Yeah."

"Like, rather than me remembering, and you not, it's better that you remember, and I don't, you know?"

"Maybe... You could be right."

"I definitely am. So that's why I'm glad it worked out this way."

"Just go to sleep."

"Yeah. I'll do that." Kuzaku got up, took two or three steps away from the fire, then collapsed like he'd run out of juice. He was already snoring.

"You've gotta be kidding me..."

It was kind of exasperating, but this simple, childish side of Kuzaku—maybe you could call it straightforward, if you were being nice—had been a great support to Haruhiro. He even felt like it had saved him before.

Now that he thought about it, Haruhiro tended to be hesitant about everything, not wanting to stand at the front or above others. Despite that, he'd been able to come all this way thinking of himself as the group's leader. It might well be that Kuzaku had been a major factor in that, second only to Haruhiro's desire to protect his comrades.

Whatever the case, Kuzaku had absolute faith in Haruhiro and supported him. Despite standing a full head taller than Haruhiro, Kuzaku was always looking up to the thief. Kuzaku was the only one who would always act as a follower around Haruhiro, no matter what happened. To Kuzaku, he was more experienced—a leader and an older brother figure—someone he had to respect.

"You weirdo..." Haruhiro murmured, looking back to the fire. It was getting pretty low. He fed it some more dried branches.

Kuzaku had feelings for Merry. There was a time Haruhiro had even suspected they might be in an intimate relationship. It had made him jealous and depressed. Yep, that was a thing that'd happened.

Itsukushima and Poochie returned, but headed out again after letting Haruhiro know nothing seemed out of the ordinary.

Night here was totally different from out in the middle of the Quickwind Plains, that was for sure. There was no wind, for one thing. It wasn't that chilly either. There was no sense that vicious predators were lurking on the other side of the darkness. Lots of bugs were chirping, but it felt quiet. Obviously, he still couldn't let his guard down. He knew that, but he was starting to get sleepy.

Merry woke and came over to the fire. She sat down next to Haruhiro quietly.

"Were you able to get some sleep?" Haruhiro asked and she nodded.

"Yes."

"Oh, good."

"Should I take over for you?"

"Ah..." Haruhiro rubbed his chin. "Nah, I'm still good."

"I see."

"Hnnn."

Merry hesitated a moment. "I'm sorry."

"Huh? What for?"

Merry just shook her head, declining to elaborate.

Someone sighed. It wasn't Haruhiro or Merry.

It was Neal.

"For the love of... What the hell is this garbage?" Neal muttered as he walked over and sat down next to the fire.

Haruhiro and Merry looked at one another. *What the hell is this garbage?* should have been their line.

Neal sighed again. He clicked his tongue, then sighed a third time. To top it all off, he spat on the ground.

"You're in the way."

"What?" Haruhiro wasn't the type to snap easily, but obviously he was going to get mad now. What was wrong with this guy?

"I'm trying to say..." Neal tore up some grass and threw it. "You're in my way, so go take a walk or something. I'll keep watch for you. I'm not gonna be able to sleep right anyway."

He was apparently trying to be considerate of them. It took some time before Haruhiro understood that. Why would Neal go and do that? What was he being considerate of? Haruhiro kind of got it and kind of didn't. But it wasn't totally incomprehensible.

Haruhiro looked around the area, not really for any specific reason. Ranta was sitting up a bit, which startled him a little. The dread knight silently gestured with his chin. Like he was saying, *Go on.*

Haruhiro wanted to think, *Stop trying to be cool when you're just Ranta,* but he couldn't.

"Okay, just for a bit..."

When Haruhiro stood up, Merry followed suit. With nowhere in particular to go, they decided to check on the horses, which were still calm, thanks to Bikki Sans.

Haruhiro couldn't help stealing glimpses at Merry's face.

"It's okay," Merry said, smiling as she stroked a horse's mane. "I'm me right now."

Haruhiro hadn't thought for a second that the Merry he was with wasn't Merry. That said, going out of his way to tell her he hadn't suspected otherwise kind of seemed like the wrong thing to do.

"I can tell," Haruhiro said, petting a horse too. "I dunno how, but I just kinda get it."

"I see," Merry murmured. What was that supposed to mean? Haruhiro didn't really know. He'd just said he got it, but he didn't get this, not one bit.

Haruhiro looked up at the night sky. "Moon sure is bright tonight..."

Merry looked up too. The profile of her face was distinctly visible in the moonlight. Her eyes narrowed slightly. "It sure is."

The next thing he knew, Haruhiro found he was staring at Merry.

He got all flustered as she turned to look at him.

"How about we go for a walk?" he suggested, his voice rising shrilly at the end. It wasn't particularly funny, but Merry smiled a bit.

"Okay."

"Watch your feet. It's dark." Those were just the first words that came to his mind.

Merry nodded. Then, a moment later, she looked down.

She might have been checking to see if she could see the ground. No matter how big and clearly visible the red moon was in the sky, no matter how many countless stars were shining without twinkling, the darkness was deep here on the Quickwind Plains. Merry took a step forward, but she must have stepped on a rock or something because she stumbled, even if it was just a little.

Haruhiro instinctively grabbed her arm and supported her.

"Thanks," Merry whispered, her voice incredibly close.

"Your hand." Now this was a surprise. He hadn't expected himself to say that. Without waiting for her reply, he moved the hand holding her arm down. He never would have thought he had it in him. Haruhiro held Merry's hand.

Merry looked down and nodded. Then she gripped his hand in return.

The two of them walked through the darkness, hand in hand. Haruhiro couldn't navigate by the stars the way Itsukushima or Yume could, but he could see their campfire in the distance, so there was no risk of getting lost.

The footing here was solid, and there was a small hill that looked like it would be easy enough to climb. He saw some trees growing at the crest. Haruhiro led Merry by the hand and began walking up the hill. Getting to the top was as easy as he'd expected. It was a bit breezier up there.

"You're not cold?" Haruhiro asked, and Merry shook her head. "Okay then."

It was times like this that made him resent how poor a talker he was. He wished that, even if it was just once, he could be like Ranta and ramble on for hours when he felt like it.

"Inside me..."

Ultimately, Haruhiro stayed silent until Merry started talking by herself.

"Inside...you?"

"There's someone...something inside me that's not me. You must already know that, though."

Haruhiro tightened his grip on Merry's hand a little.

"Yeah."

"It..." Merry said, referring to the thing inside her. "It's not always trying to push me aside and come out... I don't know how to describe it. It's not me. But it's not entirely someone else.

I feel it. It's always there, existing. Watching, or pretending not to watch. There are times I think it's trying to help. But it may not be... There's several people in there."

"It's...not just one person?"

"No." Merry shook her head, then nodded. "It's multiple people. I'm sure they were all individuals at one point."

"Is Jessie...one of them?"

"Yeah."

"'He's not here.'"

Not Merry, but the thing inside her had told Haruhiro that.

"Right." Merry nodded. "Jessie's memories were broken."

"When we came back to Grimgar, the master of the Forbidden Tower gave us some kind of drug. Were you...Jessie then?"

"I ran away. I fled into myself. I didn't want to come out."

"Is that why you don't remember Parano very well?"

"It's rather vague, so I only have a hazy sense of what went on."

"Jessie's gone..."

There were multiple people inside Merry. Haruhiro had witnessed the contents of Jessie being poured into her. Jessie hadn't been one person either. He'd had multiple others inside him too. Merry had inherited them.

Some person, or some *thing*, had to be the originator. Let's call them A. A went inside B. At that point, A and B shared B's body.

Next, B entered C. Now C had both A and B inside them.

Was it okay to ask about this? Haruhiro hesitated for quite a while, but he ultimately decided to go ahead. "How many of them are there? Do you know?"

Merry didn't answer immediately. Instead she said, "Would you mind if I sat down?"

"Of course not."

Haruhiro found a dry rock that looked good and sat on it with Merry. He never even considered letting go of her. As they sat hand in hand, their shoulders naturally ended up touching.

"The ones I know distinctly are...a woman—a volunteer soldier. She had a lover. And comrades... All of them died. She was the last one left. Nearly dead herself... And then she stopped breathing. Her name was Ageha."

"Was she...uh, the one before Jessie?"

"I think so. Before her was...a mage. He was a volunteer soldier too. Yasuma... He was learning from a wizard in the mage's guild: Sarai. If I remember, Shihoru's wizard was called Sarai too."

"He's not from that far in the past, then."

"Sarai joined the guild at a young age and went on to lead them. I think it must have been twenty, thirty years ago that Yasuma was apprenticing under him."

Before that had been a man from the Hidden Village, surprisingly. His name was Itsunaga. He broke the code of his people and was exiled with his mother at a young age. After that, his mother passed away, and he'd been left all alone. He held a deep grudge against the villagers, and he had wandered for a long time to many disparate places.

He kept himself alive by working as a bandit, and also as an assassin, but he who lives by the sword dies by the sword. After failing to kill the leader of a band of thieves, he ended up with others seeking his life. He ran, and he ran, and eventually he got into a stupid fight that left him mortally wounded. As he lay dying, an orc appeared before him.

Diha Gatt.

That was the orc who'd revived Itsunaga.

"I don't know much about Diha Gatt. He doesn't come out much. He seems to have traveled all over, though."

Haruhiro counted them off on his fingers.

Merry.

Jessie.

Ageha.

Yasuma.

Itsunaga.

Diha Gatt.

Six people.

"Is that...everyone?"

The question in Haruhiro's mind now was, *Who was that?* In front of the Forbidden Tower, it had spoken to Haruhiro out of compassion for Merry, telling him that she was not responsible for this. She did not choose it. It had followed that up by also saying this:

"Nor was it I who chose her."

Normally, he would have assumed it was Jessie speaking. He was the one who'd revived her, after all. But Jessie was gone. So who was "I" in this case?

This is just a vague sense I get, but the way it talked makes me think it wasn't a woman. It probably wasn't Ageha. Was it the mage

Yasuma, then? Was it Itsunaga of the Hidden Village? Or maybe the orc, Diha Gatt?

"Everyone..." Merry mumbled. "No... It's not."

"There's still more?"

"I...think so."

Merry hung her head, shuddering. It looked like this was hard for her. She gritted her teeth, breathing only through her nose. *I want to do something for her,* Haruhiro felt strongly. But what could he do? Haruhiro was holding Merry's left hand in his right. He placed his other hand over the top of hers too. Then Haruhiro let go with his right. He felt nervous, but he put his now empty hand around her back, or rather her waist. Haruhiro began to wonder whether he was doing this for Merry's sake or because he wanted it himself. He couldn't deny it completely. But Merry's mouth opened and she exhaled. He felt her relax a little.

"A rat," Merry said.

"A rat?"

"Yes... I don't know much about him. But...I think, probably, he was a rat. Inside...a rat."

"Who was inside a rat?"

"It was..." Merry's breathing grew ragged. Haruhiro rubbed her back.

"You don't need to force yourself."

"I mustn't...go back...any farther."

"Huh?"

"Mustn't look... Mustn't hear... It's better not to know... I shouldn't know... Something's...trying...to stop me..."

Merry kept repeating herself.

"I mustn't go back any farther."

She repeated it again and again.

"I mustn't go back any farther... I mustn't go back any farther... I mustn't go back any farther... I mustn't go back any farther. I mustn't go back any farther. I mustn't go back any farther mustn't go back any farther mustn't go back any farther mustn't go back any farther mustn't go back any farther mustn't go back any farther mustn't go back any farther mustn't go back any farther mustn't go back any farther—"

Merry repeated that mantra faster and faster. How did she not get tongue-tied? It was a mystery. And obviously not one Haruhiro had time to be puzzling over right now.

"Stop it, Merry. That's enough. This isn't working. You don't need to keep thinking about this. You clearly shouldn't. Merry. Merry."

"No. No. No. No. No. No, no, no, no, no, no...!"

Merry shook her head around, messing up her hair. Haruhiro was terrified. This wasn't necessarily the fear of the unknown. He had no idea what, or who, lay beyond the point Merry was talking about. In that sense, it was an unknown to him. But Haruhiro's fear was of something more concrete. If this continued, Merry might end up like before. That was his worry. Basically, that she might be unable to maintain her sense of self. The result would be that she would retreat, or sink away, and that other "I" would emerge again in her place.

"Merry."

Haruhiro grabbed Merry's shoulders tight, turning her body toward his. Merry reacted to his touch as if she disliked it, but it might have been reflexive. Even so, Haruhiro refused to let go.

"Merry, look at me. Merry. Merry. Merry!"

"Haru..."

"That's right. It's Haruhiro. Merry, you know me, right? Look at me."

Merry nodded a few times, her jaw quivering.

"Breathe in... Breathe out. Gently. Yeah. Breathe in... And out."

Merry adjusted her breathing as Haruhiro instructed. It seemed to help her to calm down somewhat.

"So long as I keep it together, that thing won't come out. It's probably up to me."

"That's not true," Haruhiro countered instantly.

Merry blinked at him two or three times. "Huh...?"

"It's not, Merry. You have us. You have me."

"I have...you."

"Yeah. This isn't all on you. We won't make you carry the burden all alone. Me, I'm not the same person as I was back when I first invited you to be our comrade. It may be weird for me to be pointing it out myself, but I think I've changed a lot. I'm not as unreliable as I used to be."

"I've never thought you were unreliable."

"Well, you're welcome to rely on me more. I want you to. Listen, Merry..."

"Okay."

"I owe you an apology. For letting you die, and for bringing you back afterward. I decided that on my own, without asking."

"Yeah, but..."

"Listen."

"Okay."

"But I still don't regret it. No matter what it took, I wanted you to come back. I couldn't bear the thought of never seeing you again. I want to be with you. I know we'll have to part someday. No matter how precious something is, we always lose it in the end."

"Yes. I suppose...that's something we know all too well."

"Yeah. But still. I want to be with you. Even if it's just for one minute or one second longer. I'd do anything for another moment with you. That's just how important you are to me."

Had Haruhiro meant to say all this to her face?

"Because I love you, Merry."

Haruhiro was shocked when those words left his mouth. But for all his surprise, there was a part of him that wasn't really losing its head over this. He even thought, *Yeah, go figure.* Haruhiro's feelings for Merry had been beyond clear for a long time now. Provided she wasn't unbelievably dense, she knew by now without him saying anything.

Haruhiro had been harboring feelings for Merry for quite some time. By this point, he wasn't sure if it was her beautiful face, the kindness hidden behind her thorny exterior, or her straightforward sincerity that he'd fallen for. Whatever it was, the more they were together, the more important Merry had become to Haruhiro.

Even when Mimori and Setora had made their romantic intentions clear, Haruhiro's heart had never wavered. Not one bit. He had great affection for both of them as fellow human beings. But he felt that that was something entirely different. Haruhiro loved Merry. From the bottom of his heart. There was no way he could love anyone else when he already loved her so much.

"I really love you. Everything, everything about you. I don't think my feelings will ever change. No, I know they won't."

"Haru." Merry closed her eyes. Tears streamed from both of them. She might have been trying to hold them back. But they wouldn't stop.

"I...love you too. I love you, Haru."

"I'll never," Haruhiro said, holding Merry close to him, "let go of you again."

Merry wasn't petite. But when he held her like this, she seemed incredibly delicate. Merry was so soft it was mind-numbing. Beyond that, though, there was a definite weight to her, so it wasn't like she was going to crumble apart. As Haruhiro hugged Merry tight, a sigh escaped her lips next to his ear. Merry hugged Haruhiro back. Then she nuzzled up to him like a cat, rubbing her head against Haruhiro's cheek and jaw. It felt so fulfilling. He was already satisfied enough. There was an impatience there too. He couldn't just stay still, holding her like this. Haruhiro kept stirring, and Merry did too. Soon enough, their cheeks touched.

Merry's cheeks were wet with tears.

If he turned his face a little, it felt like something would happen.

But he couldn't do that. He couldn't possibly, and yet that was exactly what Haruhiro did.

A slight turn of his face and Haruhiro's lips brushed, however faintly, against something incredibly, exceptionally soft.

I should pull away, he thought.

Honestly, he was hesitant.

He didn't even know how he shook free of his indecision.

Haruhiro pressed his lips against Merry's.

If you put it into words, it was just a mouth touching another mouth, so why did it feel like this? What was this sensation?

I think I love Merry.

I love her so much that my chest could burst, and my body might fall to pieces.

Merry's the only one who could sew my chest back together, reconnect all my broken pieces.

Because she's so dear to me.

Merry pulled her face away. Their lips parted. But only for a moment. Merry immediately pushed her lips against his of her own accord.

Haruhiro couldn't tell who ended the kiss, or how. He didn't remember.

Whatever happened, they were still holding one another. They'd been doing so all this time, so he'd gotten pretty used to it. They were both getting good at hugging each other in a way that minimized the space between them.

"I love you," Merry said. It felt like he was dreaming. But Haruhiro knew that this was no dream. "Haru. I love you. Don't let go of me."

9. Wild Nature

Once dawn broke, the Frontier Army's delegation pushed on toward the Iroto.

"So?" The masked man elbowed Haruhiro lightly in the ribs before whispering, "Did you two do it last night?"

"Huh?" Haruhiro rubbed his mouth with the back of his hand.

There was a sparkle behind the mask's eye holes—*I think.*

Obviously, nothing actually flashed. It was his imagination.

"No...way. Parupi—you...!"

"What's a Parupi?"

"You bastard! I figured you were so spineless you wouldn't do anything, but I was wrong, huh? You went and did it, you little snot? Seriously? *Seriously?* Are you serious? For real? You gotta be kidding me. Don't you try and pull a fast one on me, bud. You're just Parupiiirooo, so you've gotta be faking it, right? I mean, you could be. You could. You totally could. Yeah, that's it. It's seriously the only thing I can think."

The masked man kept rambling on in a whisper. He threw his arm around Haruhiro's shoulders and pulled him close. "Did you put it in? Your tongue, I mean. Did you slip her the tongue? You did, right? You must've given her some sloppy kisses, right? Damn it, you did?! How far did you two go? I'm asking how far you went, you bastard!"

Haruhiro kept silent. He wasn't going to disclose anything. He was heading into a battle of wills against the tenacious man in the mask, and it wasn't one he had an advantage in. Even so, Haruhiro had reason to fight. Not only to fight, but to win. If he revealed anything, the masked man would only push harder, and pump him for every last detail.

Ultimately, Haruhiro proved victorious. He ignored all the masked man's tricks and finally got him to back off.

Still, he couldn't rest easy. He knew who he was dealing with. The masked man would look for a chance to press the attack again later. This battle would continue. Perhaps it would never end. He might give in at some point, reveal some of what had happened.

Talking about it would be easier. Haruhiro had a certain vague desire to be open about it too, though he couldn't figure out why.

Do I tell him? Ranta, of all people?

No. Not a chance. If he talked, he was finished. That was the sense he got. But if he found himself alone with Ranta, and the chance to tell him came up, his tongue might slip. Did Haruhiro want to talk about it? No, he didn't. He shouldn't have, at least.

After they'd crossed a number of small hills, a sparkling river came into view up ahead. It wasn't noon yet. The surface of the water was shining brilliantly in the morning sun. The Iroto was like a massive snake wreathed in light.

The delegation stopped there for a time.

"If we follow the Iroto upstream, it will take us to the Kurogane Mountain Range. There's no way for us to get lost now," Itsukushima said as he patted Poochie the wolf-dog on the head. "But we shouldn't get any closer to the river than this, except when we need to refill our water."

The Iroto was the longest and largest river in the frontier. Fertile land extended throughout its basin. And yet, despite that, no one had settled there—not the humans, nor the orcs, nor the elves. They couldn't have, even if they'd wanted to.

According to Itsukushima, the Iroto was home to the small but vicious river shark and the black-and-white spotted river snake, which had a powerful neurotoxin.

The smell of blood drove river sharks into a frenzy, and they would swarm their prey, tearing whatever it was to pieces. As for the black-and-white spotted river snake, its bite rapidly paralyzed the victim, killing them via asphyxiation. The snakes were even able to come out onto the riverbanks. And regardless of how shallow the water was, the slightest cut—say, from a rock—would instantly draw a shiver of sharks. Something as simple as trying to draw water from the river became a fairly risky task with them around.

Furthermore, in the area around the river there were long-toothed river otters, which could grow to three meters in length; the Iroto crocodile, a species with males that grew up to five meters long; and the long-tusked hippopotamus, which formed pods with dozens of members. These creatures were all carnivores or omnivores, and they preyed on each other. Evolution had made them all vicious.

It goes without saying, or maybe it doesn't, that the long-toothed river otter didn't exclusively eat the Iroto crocodile, and the Iroto crocodile didn't have a preference for the long-tusked hippopotamus. They would eat whatever filled their bellies. To their eyes, humans looked like weak, easy prey.

"They eat anything that comes to drink from the Iroto. You'd best assume there's no way to fight them near the waterside."

"Yume wouldn't mind seein' them, though," Yume said, puffing up her cheeks.

"We'll have to refill our water eventually," Itsukushima replied with a shrug. "When we do, the two of us will definitely have to be on the team. I'm hoping we won't encounter any animals at all, but I wouldn't count on us being that lucky. Long-tusked hippos are huge, and they move in pods, so I suspect you'll have an opportunity to catch a glimpse of some."

Two days of traveling up the Iroto later, that opportunity appeared.

Itsukushima, Poochie, Yume, Haruhiro, and Ranta left Chief Delegate Bikki Sans, Scout Neal, Kuzaku, Setora, Merry, and the horses behind as they embarked on an operation to replenish the delegation's water supplies. While everyone still had a little drinking water left, they wanted to replenish their stock before the situation became dire.

"Make sure to be careful out there," Bikki Sans said with genuine concern. You could tell from his tone of voice and his unibrow.

"I wish I could go too..." Kuzaku said, sounding dissatisfied.

The masked man kicked him in the butt. "Shut up! You're too big! You'd just be in the way!"

"Man. That didn't hurt. I didn't even feel it."

"What was that, you ass?!"

"Stop fightin', you two," Yume said, putting herself between them. "Enough's enough. You're gonna get me hoppin' mad!"

Neal burst out laughing for some reason. He turned his ruddy face to look the other way.

Kuzaku's expression had melted into a goofy grin. "Yume-san... That was cute, just now."

Yume tilted her head to the side and blinked. "Fwuh?"

"I can see why you'd think that," Setora agreed with a nod. "She doesn't even realize she's doing it. I'd like to keep her as a pet."

"Not sure what you mean, but maybe bein' your pet'd be nice, Setoran. You'd take real good care of Yume, wouldn't you?"

Haruhiro could understand Merry smiling at Yume. He could even understand the warm look Bikki Sans was giving her, given the kind of guy he was. But Neal? Looking at her sideways and clutching his chest? That was unexpected, and he wondered what the scout could be thinking.

"Take care," Merry said, subtly grabbing Haruhiro by the left wrist. If they'd been alone, he wouldn't have been able to leave. He might have embraced her. It made him kinda uncomfortable that his thoughts were running off like this, but he also figured it was inevitable that they would. Haruhiro loved Merry, after all. More yesterday than the day before. And more today than yesterday. He couldn't help himself.

And so, the team left to draw water.

"So?" Suddenly, the masked man went on the attack again. "Did you do something again last night? How far did you go?"

"Man, you're annoying..."

"Same as a moment ago, you two were clinging to each other like it was natural. What are you, a married couple? You think you're married already? Are you drunk on love? You are, aren't you? Well? Huh?"

Haruhiro looked at Itsukushima, who was taking point with Poochie, and Yume, who was at the rear. *Um, this guy's being a pain, you know? He keeps on whispering at me,* he thought. He wanted them to tell Ranta off, but they had more important things to focus on. They were already in dangerous territory.

"This is what I hate about you. You can't just be clear about things. If you did her, say you did her. 'I did this. I did that. I went this far.' Why not? Tell me, you moron. Let's share intel here. We're comrades, aren't we? We've been together a long time. Right?"

Ranta was whispering a lot, but his volume control was perfect. He stayed really quiet. And yet, at the same time, Haruhiro could hear him perfectly. Being a thief, Haruhiro had good ears. Ranta had factored that in when deciding what volume to use. The guy was shrewd.

"What about you…?"

There was nothing else for it. Haruhiro whispered back at Ranta, launching a counteroffensive.

"Huh? Me? What about me?"

"How are things with Yume? Any progress?"

"Progress? What do you mean? Ohhh. That, huh? Progress, huh? Like forward movement, right? Hmm…"

"What're you dodging the question for? Did you tell her? Or are you not gonna?"

"Wh-what'm I supposed to tell her…?"

"That you love her."

"D-d-d-did you say it?! I know you. I bet it was vague, like you kind of did, and kind of didn't…"

"I told Merry."

"Wha—"

"I came out and said it, like I should."

"You…did? You mean, you confessed your feelings?"

"Yeah, that's right."

"That's a lie. A dirty lie. You're lying. You've gotta be. I don't believe you. I mean, you're Parupirurun!"

"Honestly, it was just a matter of telling her how I felt. Even I could manage that much."

"Even though you're Parupororon?"

"Even I managed it, so…"

"And then you kissed her, huh?!"

"No comment. I don't think it's worth coming out and saying."

"Quit trying to act all mature!"

"Maybe I'm just not as much of a kid as you."

"Urgh!"

He didn't think, *That was payback. Serves you right.* Instead, he felt something akin to pity. Ranta was so forward with most people that it was really over the top, but when it came to Yume he was too timid. Maybe love was making him go soft.

"Hey."

"What, you twisted pile of poop?!"

"I think you should put it into words for her."

"Shut up, you antique snotball!"

"You never know what might happen, or when. I think, even without me telling you this, you already sense that, and you're prepared for it."

After a moment's hesitation, Ranta said, "Of course I am."

"This may be the only chance you get, you know?"

"You sound so full of yourself..."

Ranta jabbed Haruhiro in the ribs. Haruhiro had expected a pretty hard punch, but he didn't try to avoid it. Unsurprisingly, it hurt. He kept his cool, a calm expression on his face.

Ranta muttered, "But, well...you could be right..."

At that moment, Itsukushima came to a stop.

"Nyuh?" Yume looked at Itsukushima and cocked her head to the side.

"Just so you're aware..." Itsukushima said, petting Poochie on the head. "Even if I'm no match for this little guy, I have good ears for a human."

Haruhiro hesitantly asked, "Why bring this up now?"

Itsukushima awkwardly cleared his throat. "I heard more or less everything. I suppose you thought you were talking in secret, but..."

"About what?" Yume asked, looking from her master to Haruhiro and the masked man. "What were Haru-kun and Ranta talkin' about? Yume knew they were whisperin' 'bout somethin' but couldn't tell what."

"N-nothing!" Ranta shouted back at her, making Yume purse her lips. However, it's just human nature to get more curious when someone says it's nothing. Yume was going to interrogate Ranta. The moment he saw her coming, he decided to act first to cut things off. "Later! I-I'll tell you later, okay?! J-just not now. We've got, uh, stuff to deal with. So, I-I'll talk to you about it later..."

"Nngh..." Yume nodded reluctantly. "Well, okay. That's fine, then."

Itsukushima gave Yume a caring look. But he quickly lowered his eyes, nodding as if to convince himself of something, then faced back toward the front.

He must have mixed feelings about this, Haruhiro thought, perhaps somewhat presumptuously. Itsukushima loved Yume like a daughter. Eventually the chick would leave the nest and find a mate. But did her partner have to be the masked man, of all people?

Haruhiro would have struggled if he were in Itsukushima's position. Ranta was human, so he did have some good traits. They'd been through their ups and downs, but he trusted the masked man as his comrade. Still, there were some things about Ranta that were just plain bad, or even downright awful.

Setting that aside, the team sent to fetch water kept moving ahead. It was maybe a hundred meters or so to the Iroto now. There were few tall trees, but quite a few plants with jagged leaves—maybe ferns of some sort. The ground was mostly moss-covered rocks. The air felt moist, but it wasn't so much refreshing as unpleasantly cold.

Itsukushima raised his right hand, motioning for the team to stop. He pointed toward the south, and Haruhiro looked where he'd directed.

Something's there.

Ranta let out a very tiny "Whoa..." from behind his mask.

It was quite far away, but he could still make out its general shape, so it had to be a pretty big animal. It wasn't just one, though. There were several of them. Four-legged beasts with tusks. Not just on their heads either—they had protrusions coming out of their backs too.

It's a pod of long-tusked hippos. Are they heading toward the Iroto?

"Wow. Those're them, huh?" Yume was delighted. She'd said she wanted to see them. Haruhiro wished he could think *Good for you,* but, frankly, he was scared of them.

"Are we okay?" Ranta asked quietly.

"At this distance, we're probably safe," Itsukushima answered before starting to walk again.

"Oh, great. 'Probably.'" Ranta sounded less than satisfied. It didn't do much to alleviate Haruhiro's fears either, but he had to trust Itsukushima's decision.

WILD NATURE

The team kept going and finally reached the bank of the Iroto. It had a narrow beach. A few steps over wet rocks and sand would take them to clear water.

"There's a sandbank in the middle of the river," Haruhiro said, pointing to it, but Itsukushima shook his head.

"No, that's no sandbank."

"Huh? But..."

It was hundreds of meters to the opposite bank, possibly even a kilometer, but he could see what looked like a little island in the middle.

"Haru-kun, take a gooood look at it."

At Yume's urging, Haruhiro squinted hard at what he had assumed was a part of the terrain. He didn't get it at first, but gradually he noticed something was off.

"Hmm?"

"Whoa! That thing..." Ranta shifted his mask to his forehead. "Isn't it moving? Downstream? No, the other way?"

Yeah, Ranta's right, Haruhiro thought. The island was moving against the current, albeit slowly.

"Its head is about to come up," Itsukushima said.

It happened not even a moment later. Something actually broke through the surface of the river upstream from the island, which itself seemed to rise a bit at the same time, from what Haruhiro could see. It had to be two, maybe three hundred meters offshore, so he couldn't make out the details, but that thing sticking out of the water had to be its head. The mass Haruhiro had assumed was a sandbank might, in fact, be the body of whatever that thing was.

"It's...a creature, then?" Haruhiro asked.

If it is, it's gotta be over a hundred meters long.

"The Iroto giant tortoise," Itsukushima explained with disinterest. It was impressive how he could remain so aloof when there was something like that right in front of their eyes—or at least within eyeshot, even if it wasn't *right* in front of their eyes.

"Some say they live for centuries," Itsukushima continued. "Look at the size of it. They have no natural predators, and they're incredibly docile. I've even heard of people riding them safely."

"Wooooo..." Yume's eyes widened. "That's amazin'. Yume wants to try ridin' one too."

Itsukushima smiled with wry amusement. "You'd just get gobbled up by the river sharks, black-and-white spotted snakes, or Iroto crocodiles before you could swim over to it."

"Oh, yeah. Guess so, huh? Yume's gonna give up on that for today. Until next time."

Thank goodness she let it go so easily, thought Haruhiro. He hoped she'd get someone else—say, Ranta—to help her realize her dream of riding an Iroto giant tortoise one day.

The team got back to work. They went to the riverside and filled the waterskins they'd brought with them one after another. That was all it took. The labor itself was incredibly simple. Iroto crocodiles and long-toothed otters were big, so if any started getting close, then Itsukushima, Yume, or Poochie would notice and raise the alarm. As for the black-and-white spotted river snakes, their colors were easy for humans to distinguish, making them comparatively easy to detect. The problem was the river sharks. They ranged in size from fifteen centimeters to thirty, maybe forty for particularly large specimens, with muddy brown coloration, making them impossible to spot at first glance unless you had incredibly sharp eyes. On top of that, they were speedy, letting them close the distance to their targets in no time.

Itsukushima and Yume crouched by the water's edge. It might have looked like all they were doing was leisurely filling waterskins, but in truth they were constantly monitoring the water. Meanwhile, Poochie was keeping watch on the area around them.

Haruhiro was nervous, and couldn't help but sigh due to the tense situation.

"Heh, you chicken..." Ranta mocked Haruhiro, but he was clearly intimidated himself, to the point that he was stretching his arms as far as they'd go to dip the waterskin into the river.

To top it off, Yume walked up beside him and thrust her hand into the water with a splash. Haruhiro wondered what was up until she pulled her hand back out, holding a twenty-centimeter river shark. With its eyes bulging, it snapped its sharp teeth and flailed around violently.

"Eek!" Ranta fell on his backside.

"You've gotta be careful, y'know?" Yume said, giving the river shark a toss with an arm that was like a whip. The motion of her shoulders was incredible. The river shark sailed through the air, gnashing and flailing, until it landed in the river with a splash. "You get bit once, and they'll be comin' in droves. Maybe not even Yume'll be able to help you then, okay?"

Haruhiro shoved Ranta's back. "Why don't you thank her? She just saved your hide, after all."

"Y-you saved me..." Ranta looked down and cleared his throat. "Thanks."

Yume beamed. "Think nothin' of it!"

Ranta glanced up at her before mumbling something inaudible. Something along the lines of, "You are my sun."

Haruhiro heard, but pretended he hadn't. He might have thought, *What, you're a poet now?* but he decided to keep his comment to himself.

Love makes poets of us all—or so Haruhiro figured. Irrespective of whether the poems we come up with are any good. It's all a matter of whether you have the sense for it. And Haruhiro, it goes without saying, had none.

"We should quit while we're ahead," Itsukushima said as he put a waterskin into his backpack. "Let's call it here."

If Itsukushima said it was time to call it quits, he was probably right. Ranta could have been bitten by that shark if Yume hadn't saved him. That was one crisis averted, but there was no telling when the next might come along.

The team moved away from the Iroto. It was just a matter of going back the way they'd come now. Or so Haruhiro had convinced himself. Itsukushima chose a different route, though.

Haruhiro casually asked, "This isn't the way we came, is it?"

Itsukushima simply shrugged, declining to explain. He probably wasn't doing this just because he felt like it, so there must have been a reason, right?

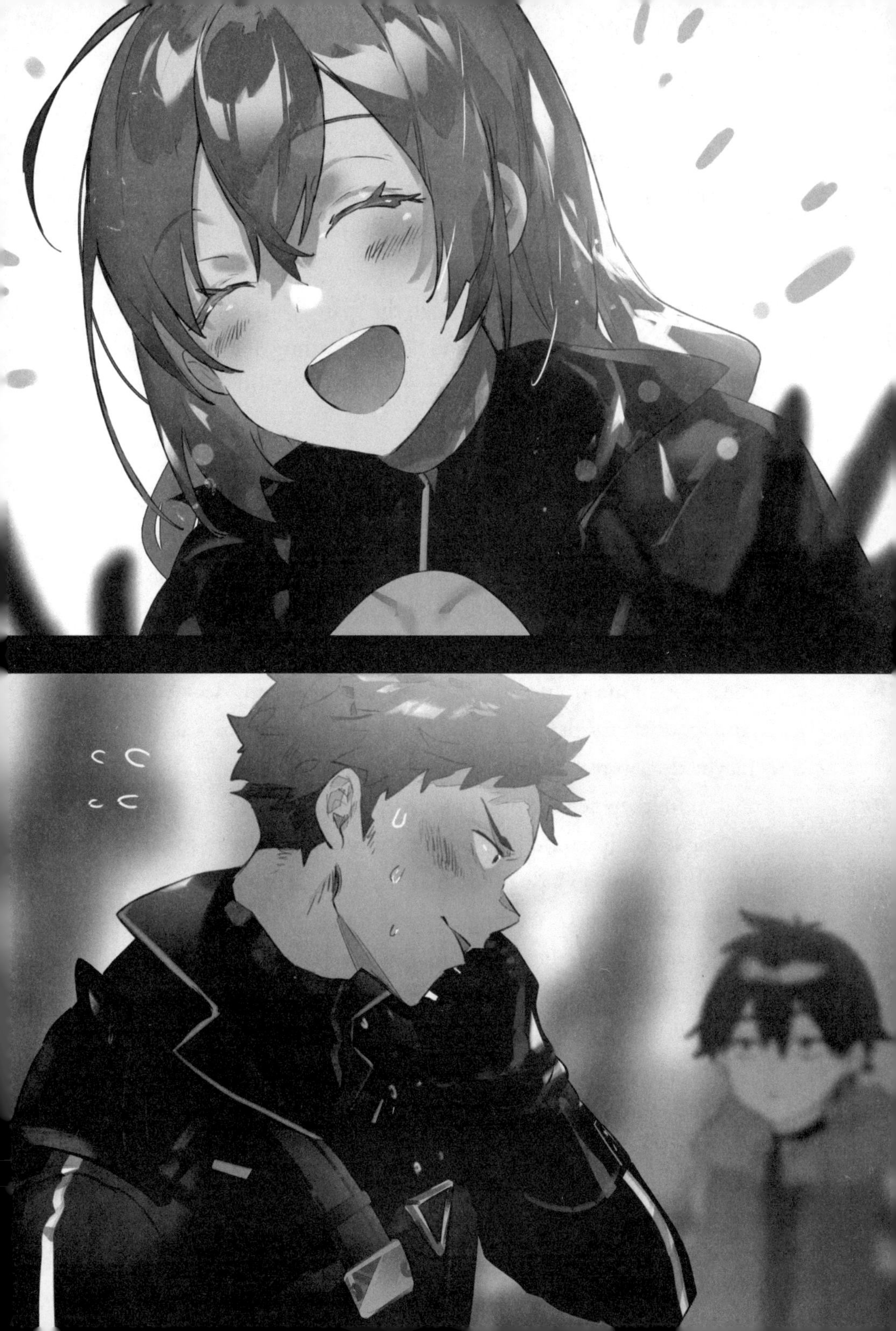

"Nurrrm. Somethin's up..."

Yume was looking around a lot, and making that weird *nurrrm* sound, whatever it meant, so, yeah, something probably was up.

They had been walking through the sparse woods for a while when Poochie came to a stop and began growling. He was facing north. Was there something there? Haruhiro squinted, but he couldn't see anything that stood out.

"Master?" Yume asked.

"Hmm..." Itsukushima thought for some time, then patted Poochie and had him keep going.

There was something fishy going on. Haruhiro grew more alert as he followed behind Poochie, Itsukushima, and Yume. The masked man was quiet. It wasn't that he had no ability to read the mood of the groups he was in, he just occasionally decided to disregard it outright. That was the kind of idiot Ranta was. But maybe they were worried for nothing?

Soon, they saw the other group up ahead. With four horses among them, it would have been hard to mistake them for anyone else. Haruhiro didn't see any of his own party members, but Bikki Sans was there, tending their mounts.

Haruhiro was relieved, and he almost relaxed despite himself. Suddenly, he thought, *Whoops. It's always moments like this. I almost did it again. Can't let my guard down.*

Poochie stopped again. His ears were perked up and he looked around restlessly.

Ranta cocked his head to the side. "Huh?"

Haruhiro put a finger to his lips and shushed him. Ranta nodded.

Itsukushima turned to look back and waved at Haruhiro. The thief crept up next to the hunter who whispered, "Come with me."

Before Haruhiro could even respond, Itsukushima was already making hand signs at Yume. It looked like he wanted her to take Ranta and Poochie and join back up with the others.

Itsukushima started walking. Haruhiro followed. The hunter's ability to creep would have amazed even the most talented thieves. The man was pretty incredible. His abilities were above average in all respects, and he'd likely have made a first-rate thief or warrior, and probably even a mage or priest. It was unlikely he cared, though. The man loved animals, nature, and the people who were important to him, and he could adapt to any situation he found himself in.

Itsukushima stopped in the shadow of a tree. He was pointing north, apparently at some bushes maybe fifty meters away.

Haruhiro held his breath and watched the bushes. Suddenly, they shook. Something stuck its head out. It had scaly green skin. It was…a crocodile? No, not likely. Its head was too high up for that. A lizard, then?

Itsukushima signaled for Haruhiro to read his lips: *"Lizardman."*

Haruhiro had heard of those. Lizardmen. Humanoid lizards. They weren't as intelligent as humans, elves, dwarves, or orcs. But they could make and use crude tools, and they were smart enough to have a society that was more complex than simple packs.

"That's a scout. Can you kill it without being detected?" Itsukushima mouthed, and Haruhiro nodded. He wasn't proud of it, but this was his specialty.

He used Stealth, sinking his mind into the ground. He was able to enter it without trouble. In this state, he didn't need to think about much. It was like he was looking down on himself at an angle. Obviously, he wasn't actually looking down at himself. It only felt that way.

Itsukushima was here. The bushes where the lizardman was hiding were over there. And so, Haruhiro crept toward them. Were there any other lizardmen? In the trees? The other bushes? No. It was only the one.

The lizardman poked its head halfway out of the bushes, looking toward the south. The broad gap between its eyes suggested it had a wider field of vision than humans did. It would be unlikely for Haruhiro to get spotted at this point, barring unforeseen circumstances, but he decided to sneak around behind it just to be safe.

He drew his dagger with his right hand, holding it with a backhanded grip. Closing in as if he were floating, he wrapped his left arm under the lizardman's chin. At the same time, he stabbed with the dagger, slashing its windpipe and veins, then immediately plunged his blade through its right eye and into its brain. How deep did he need to bury the dagger? How much damage did he need to do to kill this creature as fast as possible? It would be too late to act once he'd thought it through. He let his body move on its own.

Haruhiro laid the now-motionless lizardman down in the bushes and headed back to Itsukushima.

"You're good," Itsukushima said in a low voice, sounding a little shocked.

Haruhiro shook his head. "There's more of them, right?"

"Well," Itsukushima said with a scowl, "the lizardmen normally live farther to the north. This is strange... Oh, I see. I should've known..."

"What?"

"It's the Southern Expedition, or whatever they call it. They're widely deployed across the southern side of the Kurogane Mountain Range."

"Which is where the lizardmen were living?"

"Yeah. That must've pushed them out, so they've migrated south." Itsukushima sighed, twisting his neck to one side, and then the other. He took a deep breath. "Not much choice," he finally said. "We're changing course. We'll move away from the Iroto for now and head north. I'm not keen on the idea, but it looks like we'll have to go through the Gray Marsh."

"Is it dangerous?"

"Everywhere is dangerous," Itsukushima said, one cheek tensing. "But the Gray Marsh is cold this time of year. And full of leeches to boot. It'll be especially rough on the horses. And the leeches can jump, just come flying out of the swamp at you, so we humans can't let our guards down either."

"Sounds..." *Awful,* Haruhiro was about to say, but he swallowed the word when Itsukushima slapped him on the shoulder.

Itsukushima was already dashing away. Haruhiro ran after him. He didn't ask what was up, or why Itsukushima was going so fast. There was some sort of emergency. That was the only explanation.

He must have given some orders to Yume when he'd sent her to join up with the others. They had already loaded up the horses and were getting ready to set out.

"Good, you're ready to go! We have to get out of here fast!" Itsukushima shouted, then raced off to the west with Poochie. "Follow me! And don't dawdle! They're going to surround us!"

Ranta shouted, "Who're 'they'?!"

"The lizardmen!"

Haruhiro turned to look back the way they'd come, where he could hear the sounds of rustling leaves and voices. He couldn't see anything, but the lizardmen were coming after them. Definitely. And in no small number.

Bikki Sans jumped onto his horse. "Neal, Yume-kun, Setora-kun! Mount up! Let's go!"

Neal needed no encouragement. He was already halfway into his saddle. Yume meowed in response, while Setora was silent, and both of them got up on their horses.

"Hurry!" Haruhiro shouted at Kuzaku and Merry. Bikki Sans was leading the mounted group away.

"Parupiron and I are the rear guard?! Heh!" Ranta slid his katana out of its sheath. "My partner may not be up to the task, but oh well!"

"You think it's me who isn't up to the task?!" Haruhiro countered, jumping to one side. Two or three slim projectiles had shot out of the trees. Arrows? After dodging them, he looked at the shafts sticking out of the ground. They were unfletched. The heads weren't iron or any other metal—they were stone. They were primitive, but arrows nonetheless.

A handful more flew in. Ranta swatted them away with his katana, not bothering to dodge.

"Hah! Got yourself some projectiles, do you? Real fancy!"

Normal dagger in his right hand, flame dagger in his left, Haruhiro took a quiet but deep breath in, then let it out. His eyes weren't focused on any one point, but they were watching a broad area with their full field of vision. He rallied his hearing and other senses as well.

In a second or so, Haruhiro had detected eleven lizardmen. It went without saying, but this wasn't all of them. There were still many more. These were just the ones rushing in toward him.

Ranta looked ready to pounce on their enemies at any moment. "Do we fight here?!"

"No, we pull back for now!" Haruhiro had already turned to go by the time the words left his mouth. Ranta followed after him, nimble as some sort of jumping bug.

The arrows came in scattershot, but didn't hit. Lizardmen were chasing after Haruhiro and Ranta with stone-tipped spears now, and several even had wooden shields. They wore no clothes, but some had accessories made of bone, fang, or polished stone.

"Ha ha!" Ranta laughed as he ran. "Looks like we're gonna have some fun!"

As the idiot said idiot things because he was an idiot, Haruhiro tried to eyeball the distance between himself and the lizardmen at the front of the pack. These creatures weren't slow by any means. If he ran full-tilt, he could probably shake them, but this wasn't a race, so he needed to avoid that sort of simplistic thinking. He and Ranta were badly outnumbered, and they couldn't afford to underestimate what the lizardman race was capable of. They surely had to be natural hunters. And in that case, they might try to surround or corner their quarry.

The two of them were caught between their enemies and a steep hill up ahead. Before they could retreat that way, they needed to hit the lizardmen and intimidate them first.

"Ranta, we'll do it there!"

"Hah! About time!"

Ranta accelerated. He was aiming to find favorable ground for fighting the lizardmen. Haruhiro looked back. Arrows were flying, but not with the right speed or trajectories to hit him. He ignored them and kept running. Ranta was racing up the hill.

They say smoke and idiots like high places, so that explains that, Haruhiro thought as he steeled himself for what was to come.

He'd kill quickly and efficiently, then pull out.

Time to get to work.

10 | LOVE

THE LIZARDMEN didn't chase the delegation onto the flatlands of the Quickwind Plains. In about half a day, the threat they'd posed was completely gone. Traded in, so to speak, for the return of the gangly giants to the west and southwest. They were also stalked by packs of beasts called jackyles that were somewhere between cats and dogs.

The jackyles looked way smaller than Poochie the wolf-dog, but they actually weren't. They had short legs and long bodies. Although they were low to the ground, they grew to lengths of up to a meter and a half, tail not included. Their fur was brown with black spots all over their bodies. Their heads were close to pitch black, which made it hard to make out their faces. Creepy.

They were definitely carnivorous, according to Itsukushima, though he didn't know much about them. They traveled in packs of anywhere between ten and thirty, and they were pursuit predators, as evidenced by the way they were pursuing the Frontier Army delegation now.

"Unfortunately, I've never seen them hunting before. But..." Itsukushima explained that he had seen them join in opportunistically when another predator attacked a herd of herbivores.

The story freaked Kuzaku out a bit. Ranta started going on about how it was cowardly, and they were such trash, but the jackyles would probably have argued with that interpretation. To them, hunting wasn't a battle for pride. It was something they did so they could survive and leave descendants. They needed to minimize their losses while also maximizing their chances for success. To that end, they were skillfully taking advantage of others in order to acquire food. If anything, it was impressively cunning. That said, now that they had set their sights on the delegation, it wasn't the time to be admiring them.

It was risky to assume the delegation would be safe until another, fiercer beast showed up. There was no guarantee the jackyle pack wouldn't move in for the kill on their own. Even once the sun went down and it was dark out, they were nearby. Haruhiro could sense them moving occasionally, and he heard their distinctive bark, *bogyah*, so he wasn't just imagining it.

The delegation stayed at their highest level of alertness, sleeping in shifts. It was hard to rest properly, given the situation, but even just being able to lie down for a while made a big difference.

When dawn broke, Haruhiro was shocked. There were jackyles sitting around and relaxing a mere twenty meters from the delegation.

"Maybe we should just kill the mutts?" Ranta suggested.

Haruhiro couldn't deny it was tempting.

"Are we gonna go for it?" Kuzaku asked, sounding pretty enthusiastic. "We can take 'em if we give it everything we've got, right? I don't see us losing. Once we kill a few, I bet the rest will probably run off."

"Not a chance," Yume said, vigorously shaking her head with a frown. "No way. No how. These little guys've got serious stamina. We'll end up wearin' ourselves down. Then what? They'll just run away if we attack, right? And if we try chasin' them, they'll run even more."

"We could go after the younger ones..." Itsukushima said, looking at the pack of jackyles with a low grunt. "But outside of the freshly weaned pups, killing them will be a major struggle. We should only fight them if there's no other way."

Whatever the group chose to do, once they got out of the Quickwind Plains and into the Gray Marsh, the jackyles would probably give up. That was Itsukushima and Yume's read on the situation. But getting there would take them another two days, or maybe a day and a half if they hurried.

"Then let's hurry," Bikki Sans decided, and that was that.

Things looked bright afterward, both figuratively and literally, as there wasn't a cloud in the sky. Until afternoon came, that is. Then the sky started becoming cloudy, and the wind picked up.

"This isn't one of those heavy thunderstorms, is it?" Haruhiro asked Yume.

"Nurrrmm..." Up on her horse, Yume screwed up her face in a way that told him she wasn't sure.

"Probably not," Itsukushima said, coming to a stop. Beside him, Poochie was staring at the jackyles.

Something's weird. But what? Haruhiro couldn't tell. He just felt uneasy.

"What's wrong?" Bikki Sans asked from up on horseback. That was when it happened.

The jackyle pack let out a long howl: *bufwooooon!* Or to be more precise, one of them started, and then the others joined in.

"What?!" Neal the scout pulled back on his reins and turned his horse. No, that wasn't quite it. His horse whinnied, then began jumping about wildly. Bikki Sans, Yume, and Setora's horses were doing the same.

"Mwuh?! Whoa, Hendrix III! It's okay! It's okay!" Bikki Sans was smiling and trying to calm his mount. Apparently, when a horse was agitated or excited, it helped to smile. But once a horse started bucking, the rider was bound to be disturbed, so it wasn't easy to fake a smile like that.

"Damn! You! You! Worthless! Jackass!" Neal was yelling at his horse, only making it panic more, and Yume and Setora were struggling to control their mounts too.

Incidentally, Hendrix III was the name Bikki Sans had given his horse at some point. It was a bit too long and awkward to say. But even if Haruhiro thought that, it wasn't his place to object.

"Wh-what? What?! What's happening?!" Kuzaku was panicking and looking all around. Ranta gave him a kick in the butt.

"Hi-yah!"

"Ow! Oh, come on!"

"Haru!" Merry called, pointing north-northwest. Itsukushima was looking in that direction too, which Haruhiro hadn't noticed before Merry had gotten his attention. He turned to face that way. The horizon. Grassy fields. Scattered trees. That was all he saw. Nothing out of the ordinary—no, wait.

Haruhiro turned his gaze upward.

Was it the sky?

There was something in the cloudy sky.

What could it be?

This is stating the obvious, but it was flying. Was it a bird? If so, it was an awfully large one. Could it be a wyvern? But wyverns were supposed to live far away from here, in the Kuaron Mountains.

"Bad luck," Itsukushima said, sighing. "We've got a mangoraf incoming."

Ranta gripped the hilt of his katana. "Huh?! A mandragon?! What's that?!"

"Mangoraf," Merry corrected him. Her expression was tense. Haruhiro couldn't say what made him think so, but—just for a moment—he sensed it. Or maybe it was his imagination.

"Get off your horses!" Itsukushima yelled. "Pull all your luggage off them! Right now!"

"What is this about?!" Bikki Sans shouted back at him.

"The thing about mangorafs is..." Yume responded as she detached the packs from her saddle, "They love eatin' horses!"

"What...did you say...?!" Bikki Sans was speechless.

"Th-this is ridiculous!" Neal the scout jumped down from his horse. Or more like he fell out of the saddle.

Setora was having trouble getting down from her mount. "Urgh...!"

"Setora-san...!" Kuzaku rushed to her side, wrapping his arms tight around the hindquarters of the horse she was riding. "Whoa, he's so freaking strong! Horses're crazy! H-hurry and get down!"

Yume jumped off her horse, slapping it on the butt to get it running. "Meow! Run away!"

The mangoraf, or whatever it was, had gotten pretty close. How close? Haruhiro wasn't sure. Two, three hundred meters away? It didn't seem that fast. The way it flew was kinda ungainly—forced, you could say. It had wings, and it also had four limbs. It looked like someone had stuck a pair of wings on the back of a beast.

Setora unloaded her horse with Kuzaku's help, then got down.

"We're good, now let go!"

"Will do!"

Bikki Sans was still mounted. He was doing everything in his power to try and calm the terrified Hendrix III. "It's okay! I'm with you, Hendrix III! It's going to be okay! I won't leave you alone! It's okay! It's okay...!"

The horses Neal, Yume, and Setora had been riding each ran off in a different direction.

"Hey, Bikki!" Neal got up and shouted. "You're in danger! Lose the damn horse!"

LOVE

The mangoraf dove at one of the horses. The one Neal had been riding.

Thud. The air shook as it landed.

A moment later, the horse was tumbling through the air.

What in the world just happened? The mangoraf struck, biting through the horse's neck, and then threw it into the air in a single moment. That was probably it. It was only the body flying high. Everything from the neck up was gone.

"Gyahhhhh!" Bikki Sans screamed as if he were the one the mangoraf had bitten. "Arsenus! Arsenuuuus!"

Incidentally, Arsenus was the name Bikki Sans had given that horse. Even Neal just called it "you," or "horse," but Bikki Sans had given every one of the horses a proper name. He even had a policy of never using the same name twice. That was probably why they were all weirdly long, and there were a bunch of them that were "the second," or "the third." Not that it mattered.

The mangoraf that had bitten off Arsenus's head raced like a coursing river toward the next horse and sprang. This time, it was Setora's former mount. The mangoraf knocked the horse over and held it down with its front paws, then tore its head and neck clean off with one bite.

Horses from the mainland weren't that big. Still, they had a shoulder height of about 1.3 to 1.4 meters. Horses were never small animals. That said, the difference between them and the mangoraf was like the difference between an adult and a child. No, if the mangoraf was an adult, these horses were babies.

"Ohhh, not Teristarchus too!" Bikki Sans let out a cry of pure anguish. Teristarchus. Right, that was the name of the horse Setora had been riding.

Haruhiro glanced over to see the pack of jackyles swarming around the fallen Arsenus. It was opportunistic, but he had to respect their boldness.

The mangoraf was marvelously fast for its size. With Teristarchus down, it went for Yume's horse next. The massive winged beast ran. No, it leaped. It flapped its wings just once, not taking it very high, and then glided.

Yume's horse ran for its life, but the mangoraf plowed it into the ground. Then, coming to a sudden stop dozens of meters away, the mangoraf turned again and, this time, finally looked toward Haruhiro. Its blood-drenched face—was human.

Human, yes, but what kind? Male? Female? Young? Old? He couldn't say. However, the mangoraf's features were definitely humanlike, and not only vaguely so. A smirking person, covered in the blood of their victims. That was what it looked like.

"Bikki Sans, forget the horse!" Itsukushima yelled at him sharply.

"Hendrix III!" Bikki Sans, however, made no attempt to dismount. He clenched down on the rampaging Hendrix III's sides with both legs and twisted his body around. It was clear Bikki Sans was trying to make his horse run. If he got down from it now, what would the outcome be? Obviously, Itsukushima must have been aware of that when he made his plea. The hunter was probably no more eager than Bikki Sans to sacrifice the animal. But now there was no other option because, like it or not, it was hard to imagine how the horse could get out of this unscathed.

Even so, Bikki Sans was ordering Hendrix III to run. No, not ordering. This is what Bikki Sans was shouting to his horse: "I'm with you," and, "It's okay, I won't leave you alone," and, "Let's run away together." Bikki Sans was entreating the horse with all of his soul.

Did Hendrix III respond to him? Haruhiro didn't understand horses. But Hendrix III started to run. That much he was certain of. And Bikki Sans was still riding, of course. The man and the horse were one. It was a beautiful start. From the moment he began galloping, Hendrix III's head was down. Bikki Sans raised his butt from the saddle, but kept his profile low, as low as he could. Their vigor was a sight to behold.

Go, thought Haruhiro.

Please, go. He couldn't help but pray.

Bikki Sans, Hendrix III. Get out of here.

Let there be a miracle.

"Ahhh..." It wasn't just Haruhiro. Ranta, Kuzaku, and even Yume all let out a similar groan at the same time.

They all knew. Miracles don't happen that often. It's why they're called miracles.

Still, the mangoraf was merciless. It ran after Hendrix III, caught up, and just for a moment ran alongside them. Then, *chomp,* it bit the horse's head off.

"Hen—!"

Bikki Sans's beloved mount was decapitated before his

very eyes. What must the shock of that have been like? The heartbreak? Not being a horse lover himself, Haruhiro couldn't imagine it.

Now headless, Hendrix III tumbled to the earth, Bikki Sans and all.

"You idiot...!" Neal's voice was shrill.

Hendrix III was the last of the four horses that the mangoraf took down. It hadn't cared about anything below the neck on the previous three, but, perhaps satisfied with its work, it absolutely tore into Hendrix III, devouring him messily. The incredible sound of its bite told them it was chomping through meat and bone all at once.

"Argh...! No! Stop...! Augh...!"

"I-I-It's eating the old man...!" Ranta shouted, even though there was no need to. Haruhiro could tell that for himself. Honestly, while he thought, *He's still alive?* it wasn't actually that strange that Bikki Sans was still breathing. Hendrix III had died instantly when the mangoraf bit its head off, but the rider had simply fallen with the horse's body.

"W-we've gotta—" Kuzaku looked at Haruhiro.

"Save him...?"

"Way too late for that..." Neal said, sounding like an empty shell of himself. What had happened had taken all the fight out of him.

It was hard to respond with either "Yeah" or "I dunno." As Haruhiro's eyes wandered, he noticed the jackyle pack on the move. They had been devouring Arsenus a moment ago, but now they were polishing off Teristarchus. *Am I fleeing from reality?* Haruhiro wondered to himself. *Do the jackyles even matter?*

No, wait... Maybe they do?

"Itsukushima-san, Yume...!" Haruhiro called out to the hunters, and incredibly they instantly knew what he wanted from them. It was almost touching how fast they picked up on it. Obviously, this wasn't the time for him to be getting all emotional, though.

The master and pupil who were like a father and daughter readied their bows and nocked arrows.

They fired.

It looked like they'd both aimed at Teristarchus's remains. The arrows hit one of the jackyles devouring the horse. Instantly, the beasts scattered like flies. But only for a moment, because the arrows had simply surprised them. The jackyles began circling Teristarchus again. Some were eyeing Itsukushima and Yume, while several others rushed to sink their teeth into the fallen horse once more.

Their movement drew the mangoraf's attention, and from its perspective, they were stealing its prey.

It let out a throaty roar, "Obahgogahhhhuhgohhh...!" Its voice sounded almost human. Like a ridiculously big old man who was absolutely livid and screaming incoherently.

The jackyles jumped. The moment they flinched, the mangoraf pounced toward Teristarchus's remains.

"Now!" Haruhiro shouted, already running himself. Neal and Merry followed him. Kuzaku was about to chase after them, but Setora stopped him.

"You stay here!"

Ranta was with Itsukushima and Yume, gathering up their stuff and preparing to retreat. Seeing the dread knight already doing what Haruhiro needed from him, the thief couldn't help but think, *Aw, damn it.* Only a little, though.

Haruhiro hurried toward Hendrix III with Neal and Merry. The horse had been brutally torn apart, and sadly, Bikki Sans was no different. He was still just barely identifiable by his upper torso, but his lower half was such a mess of blood, meat, and bone that you couldn't tell where he stopped and his former mount began.

Despite this, Merry still raced to Bikki Sans's side. Unconcerned about getting blood on her, she pressed her fingers to his neck. After just a moment, she looked at Haruhiro and shook her head.

"The letter!" Neal shouted, pushing Merry aside and rifling through Bikki Sans's pockets until he found the rectangular leather envelope that contained the letter. It was covered in blood, but free of tears or holes. "Okay!"

The mangoraf threw Teristarchus's corpse high into the air to catch in its mouth on the way down. The jackyle pack that had been scattered by the mangoraf were running around in a panic, but it seemed they hadn't fully given up on the horses' meat just yet. They weren't fleeing.

Itsukushima was leading the way northeast with Poochie the wolf-dog.

"You damn fool!" Neal spat on the ground before running off. On the ground, not on Bikki Sans's corpse, obviously. "Go and play with your horses in the afterlife!"

"Let's move!" Haruhiro said to Merry, who nodded.
"Okay!"

Grimgar of Fantasy and Ash

11 | Inscrutable Causality

They say fortune and misfortune are intertwined. Disaster and blessings are two sides of a coin. Failure can lead to success, and unexpected good luck can lead to bad luck. Things go well sometimes, and sometimes they don't. It's just how things are.

Maybe the delegation had caught the mangoraf's attention because they were being stalked by jackyles. Perhaps if they hadn't been attacked, Bikki Sans and the horses would have been all right. But whether they could have gotten through the Gray Marsh with horses in tow was far from certain. Besides, thanks to the jackyle pack, they'd been able to divert the mangoraf's attention, allowing the survivors to escape. If not for the sacrifice of Bikki Sans and his four horses, someone else might have ended up as mangoraf or jackyle food.

The seeping chill of the Gray Marsh was punishing, and its multitude of leeches couldn't have been more troublesome.

Nonetheless, after all the difficulties they'd faced on the Quickwind Plains, this was perfectly tolerable in comparison. The delegation crossed the Gray Marsh in three days, and then they finally made it to a sea of trees in the foothills of the Kurogane Mountain Range.

According to Itsukushima, the lizardmen had previously lived here in the forests along the Iroto. It was probably pressure from the Southern Expedition that'd forced them to migrate south. And if they assumed that these woodlands were now Southern Expedition territory, the delegation needed to be even more careful now.

That being the case, the party redoubled their efforts to scout for enemies, practicing an almost excessive degree of caution as they moved through the forest. Though, even if they hadn't, they couldn't have rushed ahead. The forest was made up of trees that were unbelievably tall, with twisted, intertwined roots that seemed to be trying to invade the surface, creating an intense battle for survival between plants. The way that the trunks of the trees and the roots crawling across the ground created ridges and troughs everywhere, leaving almost no flat land to be seen, made it difficult to walk.

"This isn't a place humans belong..." Neal the scout kept muttering to himself.

Incidentally, with the death of Bikki Sans, Neal had taken over the man's responsibilities as chief delegate in an acting capacity. That made him their leader, at least on paper, but nobody treated him any differently from before. Ranta started calling him the "deputy" out of spite, and everyone else followed suit. Neal didn't like it, but they didn't care. Generally, no one responded to Deputy Neal's grumbling.

Still, in the time between when they entered the forest in the morning and when it got dark, they estimated that they had only progressed ten kilometers. The way things were going, they'd move even slower here than they had in the Gray Marsh.

They set up camp for the night, but couldn't start a campfire, so they were all basically just hanging around in the same spot. Hardly any moonlight or starlight breached the forest canopy here. It was impossible to see anything, so they had to stay clumped close enough together that they could sense one another in the darkness.

"Whoops, sorry," Deputy Neal apologized with a laugh.

"Mew?" That was Yume's voice. Ranta flew into a rage.

"Hey, you bastard. You just touched Yume, didn't you?!"

"Huh? Not intentionally. I apologized, didn't I? I can't see any better than you can."

"I don't trust a word out of your mouth."

"You sure do hate me, huh? What'd I ever do to you?"

"Do you need me to go through the entire list?" Setora asked.

"No, please don't."

It was easy to imagine Neal ducking his head. If Setora were to lecture Haruhiro about all the things the thief had done wrong, he'd never recover from it either.

"But y'know..." Kuzaku said, stretching as he did. "The nights here aren't as cold as in the Gray Marsh, and the air has just the right amount of moisture. It feels pretty good. Makes me kinda sleepy."

"How are you so easygoing?!" Ranta retorted.

Haruhiro forced himself to smile. "If you think you can sleep, go for it. We'll wake you if we need to, but you're pretty good at getting up by yourself."

"'Kay. G'night, then..." Kuzaku said with a yawn. He was already lying down. He might have even been asleep already.

"That's certainly a talent, of a sort..." Setora mumbled to herself.

Haruhiro felt the same. He was thinking about how he couldn't sleep the way Kuzaku did, while also feeling very conscious of the way Merry's right arm was touching his left as she sat beside him.

I want to hold her hand, he thought. In this darkness, no one would be able to see. It might have been a weird thought to have, but no matter what he and Merry got up to, as long as they didn't make any noise, no one would notice. That didn't mean they could just do whatever they wanted. Or much of anything at all. He didn't have the guts, you could say. But holding hands? That was fine. Maybe thinking so much about all this made him a creep, but even though Merry's arm moved a little sometimes, she wasn't pulling away from him. Maybe this was that kind of thing. What kind of thing? You know, *that* kind of thing.

Maybe Merry was thinking she'd like to hold Haruhiro's hand too?

Who knew, really? He had no way to find out. He couldn't very well ask her. Like, "Can I hold your hand?" No way. Not an option.

"Hey, Yume," Ranta said, clearing his throat. "You, uh...wanna sleep with me?"

"Way too soon," Itsukushima said, and there was a sound like he'd hit Ranta.

"Ow! The hell, old man?! You just whacked the back of my head like you could see it!"

"I can't see where it is, exactly, but I have a rough idea. Don't take us hunters lightly, dread knight."

"Oh-hoh... So Yume'd be able to tell too, then?"

"Kinda sorta," Yume confirmed.

"Whoa!"

"Your side's here, right?"

"D-don't touch me there! That's a delicate spot..."

"Your sides're ticklish, huh? Cootchie-cootchie-coo!"

"S-s-stop! Stop it! And wait, what's with the cutesy—!"

"Cootchie-cootchie-wootchie-coo, cootchie-wootchie-coo..."

"Eek! Stop it already! Are you trying to kill me?!"

"I'm not sure they'll ever be ready..." Itsukushima mumbled to himself.

Tell me about it, Haruhiro thought, secretly feeling triumphant.

While Ranta and Yume were fooling around, he'd been able to take hold of Merry's hand. Their arms and fingers were firmly intertwined too.

Oh, man. Holding hands like this makes it feel like we're one. Like it's not just our hands, not just our bodies that are connected, but our souls. I'm not just imagining it, right?

No? Maybe I am?

Merry rested her cheek on Haruhiro's left shoulder right when he was starting to hope she would. The top of her head brushed up against the side of his face. He could feel her hair, smell her scent.

This might have been obvious, but the members of the delegation had been unable to bathe all this time. While it wasn't uncommon for them to get wet in the rain or the swamps and marshes, it was surprisingly hard to actually wash themselves. They'd maybe get a chance to wipe their faces once in a while, at best. Honestly, there were times he thought, *Man, I reek.* Pretty often, in fact. He was inured to it, but to be honest, they were all kinda filthy.

However, for some strange reason, beyond their combined body odor, there was a sweet, mellow scent he didn't find all that offensive.

That scent varied from person to person. Considerably. And this might have been Haruhiro's imagination, but he felt there was a difference between the guys' and the girls' too.

Basically, Merry smelled really good to him.

That was incredibly dangerous.

Haruhiro's urges weren't very strong, to the point where he questioned whether it was okay for a young male like him to be this way. But they weren't nonexistent. Zero times anything is always zero, but multiplying even a small number can give you a big one.

You might say Merry's scent was too big a multiplying factor.

Now he was feeling her hand too, on top of that, which added another multiplier.

Haruhiro had never anticipated feeling this sort of powerful urge. He wasn't used to it, and he struggled to put it into words, but basically he was lusting after Merry.

Furthermore—though this might have been a misunderstanding on Haruhiro's part—he suspected Merry might be feeling the same.

It went without saying that, even if she was, they couldn't, uh, do the deed here.

Obviously.

That was painful, but, in some sense, also made things easier for Haruhiro. Even if his desire caused certain bodily changes, and gave him all sorts of inappropriate thoughts, he could keep himself under control. He had no choice, after all. But if this were a situation where he didn't need to hold back? What then? If they were in a situation where they could do it if they wanted to, would he have any choice but to go ahead with it?

Haruhiro had serious doubts whether he could. Like, he wasn't the right type. Maybe it wasn't a matter of type, though. Still, he didn't think he was suited to it.

Anyway, no matter how much he wanted to do it, he couldn't, and that was reassuring. He held Merry's hand tight, felt her warmth, her softness, inhaled her scent, and got all hot and bothered. That was the goal. Nothing more. He could never go any further.

Even if Merry pressed her head against him. Even if as a result his lips brushed her forehead. Even if he could clearly hear her every breath. Even if an emotion that could only be described as

Aughhhhh, I love her so muuuuuch welled up inside him, threatening to escape through every pore in his body, he had to restrain himself.

"I'm going to leave for a bit," Itsukushima said, and Haruhiro sensed him getting up. It sounded like Poochie the wolf-dog, who had either been sitting or lying beside him, got up too. "I don't think there's much danger, but stay alert. And don't get too crazy."

What did that mean? Don't get too crazy? Haruhiro wanted to ask, but it would probably only stir up trouble.

"Okay..." Haruhiro responded simply.

Itsukushima had said he couldn't see. He'd also said he could get a rough idea of things, so maybe he could see just a little after all.

Haruhiro and Merry moved apart, though it wasn't clear who moved first. Not that they weren't still in close contact. They were still holding hands. They hadn't signaled to each other what they wanted to do, specifically, and yet it still felt so right.

This is nice, Haruhiro thought from the bottom of his heart. It wasn't really the time for him to be thinking that, though. He wasn't alert enough. *Yeah. This isn't good. It's no good at all.*

"We can't do this, can we?" Haruhiro mumbled to himself.

"Can't do what?" Merry asked.

"Oh, no... Um...it's not that we can't, just that we shouldn't..." Haruhiro knew he wasn't making any sense.

"Yeah," Merry said, laughing a little. "We need to stay focused."

With that, she squeezed Haruhiro's hand tight. Obviously, Haruhiro returned the favor.

"Yeah..."

INSCRUTABLE CAUSALITY

Kuzaku was snoring. What were Ranta and Yume doing? Neither of them were saying anything. That much he could tell, but nothing more. Setora was silent too. Was it Deputy Neal who'd just sighed?

The night went on. They slept in shifts, and until the moment a faint light began to shine through the canopy, it felt like the darkness was never going to abate.

Itsukushima and Poochie returned at dawn.

"It looks like the situation's changed considerably since I left the Kurogane Mountain Range."

"Ooh. Somethin' happened?" Yume asked while doing what looked like exercises. She sure was full of energy.

"Well, yeah," Itsukushima said with a shrug before looking around at the other members of the delegation. "Okay. Haruhiro, Ranta. You two come with me."

"Huh?" Kuzaku cocked his head to the side. "We're not setting off yet, then?"

"I'll go too," Neal said.

Itsukushima didn't refuse. "Maybe that's better. I'll leave Poochie here. Yume, you're in charge until we get back."

"Mew got it!" Yume winked and Itsukushima winked back. His was an awkward wink, making half his face twitch, but it made Yume grin nonetheless.

Haruhiro, Ranta, and Deputy Neal followed Itsukushima through the deep woods. He was fast.

"Hey, not so fast..." Neal muttered, but Itsukushima didn't slow down in the slightest.

"You're the one who wanted to come."

"What the hell's out here?"

"You'll know it when you see it."

"Explain it to me first, would you?"

"I'm not much of a talker, I'm afraid."

"Except with your cute little apprentice, right?"

"If you bring Yume up again, I'm leaving you behind."

"You can't even take a joke?" Neal shut up after that.

Haruhiro and Ranta never wasted their breath to begin with, instead focusing on keeping up with Itsukushima. The hunter was moving at twice his pace from yesterday. It wasn't pushing them to their limits, but they couldn't slack off either.

Was it two hours they ended up walking?

Itsukushima had been right; they did know it when they saw it.

The forest opened up ahead of them. For a moment, it looked like the end of the sea of trees, but the area hadn't been clear-cut. There was one massive tree there, and its thick, dense roots spread out far and wide across the ground. It was probably the fact that it covered such a large area that had allowed it to grow to that size. However, its height wasn't as impressive as the thickness of its trunk or the reach of its branches, so it was more just broad rather than big. But it wasn't just a stupidly huge tree standing there all alone like a king with no clothes.

"Seriously...?" Ranta murmured.

Itsukushima didn't step into the area covered by the great tree's roots. The group lay low in the shadows of the forest surrounding it. It seemed wise to hide.

INSCRUTABLE CAUSALITY

The trunk and branches had been used to provide a frame and support pillars for roofs and floors. There were rope and wooden ladders here and there, as well as stairs, and they could see shadowy figures climbing up and down. Those figures weren't human, though, but orcs and undead.

There were also watchtowers and fences scattered around in the area covered by the great tree's roots. Near those towers the orcs and undead were sitting in circles, lazing about, swinging weapons around for training or fun, and just generally doing whatever.

"Whoa, whoa, whoa..." Neal ducked down and clutched his head. "Those are all enemies? They've gotta be, right? Our enemies are building something in a place like this? It's practically a fortress! How long have they been here...?"

"I didn't know about it either. I only found them last night," Itsukushima explained dispassionately. "They're building it around the tree, so it might not have taken as much effort as you'd expect. There's no shortage of material to work with here."

Ranta shifted his mask up to his forehead, eagerly observing the great tree fortress. The look in his eyes was awfully serious. Perhaps "grave" would be the right word for it.

"Ranta?"

Ranta replied with a low, "Yeah," never taking his eyes off the great tree fortress.

"What's up?" Haruhiro asked again.

Ranta held up his left hand as if to say, *Hold on.*

Itsukushima looked up to the sky. Haruhiro did too.

It's a bird.

There was a black bird, descending with its wings spread. It was a big one. Its wingspan was easily over two meters. Was it an eagle? A large, black eagle.

"Forgo..." Ranta said.

The great black eagle suddenly lifted off, shooting into the branches of the massive tree.

"Jumbo's here." Ranta sighed, then adjusted his mask. "Forgo is Jumbo's buddy. Which means this fortress is a Forgan base."

While he might, at least in part, have felt he had no other choice, Ranta had once betrayed Haruhiro and the rest of the party to join Forgan. There seemed to be no reason why he couldn't have stayed with them permanently. But Ranta hadn't done that. He'd escaped Forgan and been chased for it.

Haruhiro didn't really know all the details. He didn't plan to dig for them either. But he just sensed that Ranta had been through some stuff. He seemed to have powerful feelings about Forgan—ones he couldn't fully express.

"Let's circle around it once," Itsukushima said and began walking.

The others followed the hunter, observing the great tree fortress.

"There's a thousand of them," Neal said. The man specialized in reconnaissance. "No... More than that. Two, maybe three thousand?"

"That's a lot," the masked man said, groaning. "Forgan only had two or three hundred people. They were a bunch of guys who thought alike, gathered around Jumbo. Like a sort of mock family..."

"You know an awful lot about them, huh?" Neal said, turning a dubious gaze on the masked man, but didn't really try to interrogate him further.

"Jumbo, huh?" Itsukushima got a far-off look in his eyes.

After a moment, Ranta asked, "You know him?"

"It was a long time ago, but I was camping in the mountains while traveling when he suddenly appeared by my fire. All the orc had with him was booze. Something I just so happened to be out of at the time. We shared drinks that night, then went our separate ways. I haven't seen him since, so I don't know if he'd remember it."

"Oh, I'm sure he does. This is Jumbo we're talking about."

"He didn't strike me as the type to be interested in war."

"Sounds like they've got hostages, so he has no choice. But when they've gotta do something, those guys go all out. They can be tolerant and generous too. Maybe the group got this big because they kept taking in misfits..."

Suddenly Ranta stopped and pointed somewhere. Haruhiro squinted in that direction.

"That's huge," Itsukushima said, sounding awed.

The tower was, indeed, bigger than the rest. Were they storing supplies inside it? It was crudely made, but looked like a tall warehouse. However, it clearly wasn't the building that Itsukushima was talking about.

There was an orc sitting in front of the building. Orcs, as a general rule, were larger than humans. Even so, this one was absolutely unbelievable. He was so big that it could mess with your sense of distance. His clothes weren't like the other orcs' either. He wore an outfit that resembled a kimono made of deep blue fabric with silver patterns.

"It's Godo Agaja," Ranta said. Haruhiro recognized the name. He remembered Forgan had an orc who was like an up-sized version of Jumbo. Godo Agaja. In the flesh.

At that moment, a dog or wolf howled in the distance. Not just one. There were several of them howling. Itsukushima's brow furrowed and he murmured, "There's black wolves."

Hunters prayed to the White God Elhit, a massive wolf god. Elhit's older brother was the Black God Rigel, who ate their mother Carmia soon after he was born. That caused a rift between Elhit and Rigel, and their kin, the white and black wolves, hated each other and fought violently.

White wolves made packs consisting of a mated pair and their children, and they mainly hunted bears, panthers, and deer. The black wolves, on the other hand, could form packs of more than a hundred, and they would surround and chase their quarry in large groups. They actively hunted humans, orcs, and livestock. Unlike white wolves and normal wolves of the forest, like gray wolves, black wolves were cruel and ferocious by nature. Haruhiro knew all this trivia because Yume had gone on about it at length before.

"Onsa's wolves, huh?" Ranta said. "Forgan's got this goblin beastmaster. He's good. You can't tame black wolves normally, right?"

Itsukushima shook his head a little. "Wolves aren't dogs. They look alike, and they're close enough that they can have offspring, but they're different animals. Wolves never get used to people. That's why we hunters crossbreed them with hunting dogs to create wolf-dogs. I couldn't tell you if that goblin actually had black wolves obeying him, or something else, but if they *were* wolves, he hasn't tamed them. He must have made them recognize him as the head of their pack."

"Hey, something came out," Neal said, gesturing toward the warehouse-like building with his chin. "What's with them?"

Godo Agaja turned to look at the door of the warehouse-like building. Figures in green coats filed out of it. There were maybe around ten of them. No, not *around*—there were exactly ten.

Haruhiro sensed something amiss. What was it? He thought about it, but couldn't immediately come to an answer.

"Those things they're carrying are..." Itsukushima said, a tone of suspicion in his voice. The green coats were all shouldering long pole-like objects. They didn't seem to be swords, spears, or anything of the like.

Nine of the ten green coats were hooded. Only one wasn't. The one at the rear of the group had taken theirs down. They were far away, so it was hard to make out the person's face. But one thing that could be seen was their cream-colored skin.

"Gumows?" Haruhiro said, then immediately it hit him.

Gumows. They were the offspring of orcs with other races. The inhabitants of Jessie Land had been gumows. Jessie had given a number of them green coats, calling them rangers, and assigned them to hunt and to guard the settlement.

Were these the same rangers? For the moment, all Haruhiro could say was maybe.

One of the rangers, a female gumow called Yanni, had been especially trusted by Jessie. He had a feeling that the unhooded gumow vaguely resembled her. It was too far to tell for sure, so it just remained a hunch for now.

"You don't know them, do you?" Ranta asked in a hushed voice.

"Not sure..." Haruhiro replied, giving the only answer he could.

Ranta clicked his tongue. Had the vague response made him cranky? It didn't seem like that was it.

More people came out of the building.

Two of them this time. One was human, and he had no right arm. A one-armed man. And, while it was impossible to tell from this distance, he probably only had one eye too.

Ranta touched his mask. He probably meant to shift it up or down, but he soon took his hand off of it.

"Old man Takasagi..."

Takasagi. The man had a long pole-like object in his left hand too, and he was carrying it over his shoulder. As was the other person who was with him.

That person wasn't human, nor was he an orc. He probably wasn't undead either. His skin was a yellowy, earthen color, and his face was rugged like a rock. He was short, with an incredibly hunched back, but an impressively well-built upper body.

INSCRUTABLE CAUSALITY

In fact, everything from his shoulders to his chest to his arms was bizarrely well developed. He seemed to be dressed in clothes of the same make as Godo Agaja.

Takasagi twirled the long object around in front of Godo Agaja. It was clear they were talking about something, but of course none of it was audible at this distance.

"Ah..."

Haruhiro finally realized it. Those objects were what had felt so wrong to him. Those long, pole-like things. They weren't swords, and they weren't spears. They were ranged weapons. Why hadn't it come to him immediately? Haruhiro had seen them for himself before too. "They're guns."

"Guns...?" The masked man looked at Haruhiro, then back to Takasagi. Then he looked at Haruhiro again. "Huh?!"

"How do they have guns?" Itsukushima wondered aloud, stroking the face hidden beneath his thick beard. The hunter had been the one to bring word of the dwarves' new weapon to the Frontier Army. Being a hunter, he had good eyes too. He must have realized those were guns a while ago.

"By guns, you mean that new weapon you were talking about, right?" Neal gulped. "What are they doing in enemy hands? The dwarves wouldn't give them away. Does this mean they were stolen? Whatever's going on, it's bad news..."

"Hk!" Suddenly, Ranta moved his head, which had been sticking out, behind cover and pressed his back to a tree.

Haruhiro checked and saw Takasagi looking in their general direction. They hadn't been spotted, had they?

The group hid in the trees, holding their breath.

"Have we been found?" Haruhiro asked, but Ranta shook his head.

"Dunno. The old man's senses are ridiculously good. I think we're safe, but..."

"Let's head back," Itsukushima said without hesitation. No one objected.

It took about two hours for the group to rejoin their comrades. Nobody chased them, so it looked like they hadn't been spotted. Once back, they told the others what they'd seen and heard. Yume and Merry remembered Jessie Land, and agreed that the green coat gumows were probably the rangers.

Still, they hadn't expected Forgan to have guns. It wasn't clear how many the enemy had, but Haruhiro had seen more than ten of them with his own eyes. How much of a threat was that?

"Is it not possible that some of the dwarves switched sides, bringing those guns with them as a gift?" Setora suggested, never hesitating to say things that would be hard to hear. Itsukushima didn't dismiss it out of hand.

"The dwarves aren't a monolith. The Ironblood Kingdom was already divided between a faction led by the minister of the left and another led by the captain of the royal guard."

According to Itsukushima, the minister of the left came from a good family and was a progressive in favor of reconciliation who had pushed for the spread of guns throughout their society.

By contrast, the captain of the guard, who had a very undwarf-like build, was a militarist and a conservative who had initially rejected firearms. Guns were powerful, but as they were ranged weapons, using them was cowardly. They were at odds with the dwarven values of guts, courage, and grit.

The dwarves had this concept of masculinity. To them, being masculine, regardless of the dwarf's sex, was more important than life itself. Men did not fear death. They drank like men, fought like men, and died like men. A dwarf had to be manly. Living and dying as a man, that was the dwarvish way of manhood.

Guns were unmanly. Even now, many dwarves believed that.

However, if you simply pointed a gun and fired it, the bullet would even tear through steel armor, making them just too overwhelming. A fight between a hundred men with guns and a hundred without would frankly be no contest. The dwarves understood this, and so, despite bemoaning the unmanliness of firearms, they had come to use them.

However, while there was a new generation of dwarves who accepted that guns were the future, there were also conservative dwarves who hated guns from the bottom of their hearts for being unmanly.

"The problem is that it's not just the minister of the left's faction using guns now. All of a sudden, the captain of the royal guard's side started deploying with them too," Itsukushima explained, drawing out a simple diagram on the ground.

The Ironblood Kingdom was in the Kurogane Mountain Range. In reality, it was made up of hundreds, maybe even thousands, of vertical and horizontal mine tunnels. These tunnels could largely be divided into the workshop and residential areas, the food and alcohol production and storage areas, the iron king's palace, and finally the mining and refining areas.

There were entrances to the Ironblood Kingdom in two locations. Well, there was a third, actually, but Itsukushima wasn't familiar with it.

One of the two locations he did know was basically a back entrance. It was said that the dwarven hero Walter once fought a great battle there, defending against the forces of the other kings. This gate, named the Walter Gate in his honor, was in the west of the Kurogane Mountain Range. It was disguised with rocks, natural objects, and dwarven engineering, making it difficult to find without knowing it was there.

The other location was the main entrance, called the Great Ironfist Gate, and anyone could find it by traveling up the Iroto.

"Obviously, the Southern Expedition tried to assault the Great Ironfist Gate, but the Ironblood Kingdom was prepared for them."

Itsukushima used a small branch to draw a rough map of the Kurogane Mountain Range and the Iroto, then indicated the location of the main gate. Next, he made five markings around it.

"Fort Ax, Fort Greatsword, Fort Halberd, Fort Warhammer, and Fort Gun. I hear Fort Gun was built from scratch, but the foundations of the other four have been there since long, long ago. The dwarves hardened their defenses at these frontline bases and didn't let the Southern Expedition anywhere near them."

INSCRUTABLE CAUSALITY

Of the five forts, two were held by the minister of the left's units, while the other three were held by units that had been newly organized by the captain of the royal guard. All of these units were composed primarily of dwarven gunners.

"I don't know the details, but I've heard that the units in the captain of the guard's faction aren't as well trained as the minister of the left's. By which I mean they use guns because they have no choice. Deep down, they want to fight like men. The captain of the guard insists that's true of the majority of dwarves."

"So, what do we do now?" Neal asked.

"Aren't *you* supposed to decide that? You're the deputy," Ranta said mockingly, earning him a smirk and a shrug from Neal.

"Cool. In that case, you go charge into the middle of the enemy forces and slash away with reckless abandon. While you're distracting them, we'll walk right up to the Great Ironfist Gate and enter the Ironblood Kingdom."

"Oh, nice idea," Kuzaku said with a laugh. Ranta punched him in the head.

"No, it's not!"

"Ow! You're awfully quick to hit people. Is it really okay for you to act like that? You're gonna make Yume-san hate you."

"Wha?! How does Yume come into this?!"

"Huh? Well, I mean...it's obvious, right?" Kuzaku shot a glance at Yume. She puffed up one cheek and cocked her head to the side.

"Huh? Well, Yume's not fond of people who're quick to hit others."

"I won't hit them anymore, okay?" Ranta said, suddenly changing into a different person. Okay, maybe not so much. "But, listen, it was Kuzaku's fault too, okay? Don't go agreeing with a plan that sacrifices me, even as a joke. You dumbass heap of trash."

"Funny thing is, I wasn't joking."

"If you weren't, that makes it even worse!"

"Nah, I figured you'd be fine, Ranta-kun. Like, you could probably pull it off. I mean, this is you we're talking about, right?"

"Yeah, I guess... It's not like I *couldn't* do it, okay? I could, if I tried. Obviously, right? Who the hell do you think I am? I'm the great Ranta-sama!"

If I leave them be, they'll keep sparring like this forever. They get along surprisingly well, huh? Despite all their bickering, Haruhiro thought before interjecting.

"I'm curious what's happening with the forts."

"Should we get a little closer to the Great Ironfist Gate?" Itsukushima asked. That more or less decided what they'd do next. The delegation moved in that direction with utmost caution. They would investigate enemy movements and the situation with the five forts for themselves.

The Southern Expedition was highly active. There were camps, large and small, spread all around, even if they weren't on the scale of Forgan's great tree fortress. Soldiers came and went, and there was a lot of movement. That said, the enemy wasn't just spread all over the place. They moved together in noticeable clumps, making it easy to stay aware of them.

While it wasn't possible to get a full picture of things, the enemy likely numbered in the tens of thousands. They had set up numerous bases in the forest behind them, and were constantly sending soldiers to the front line near the Great Ironfist Gate, then pulling them back to be replaced over and over again.

The delegation took two days to get close to the Great Ironfist Gate. In that time, there was one enemy base that particularly caught their attention. A large number of individuals belonging to that race with the incredibly hunched backs and overdeveloped upper bodies were stationed there. They could see gumow rangers carrying guns on their shoulders too. Was that Forgan's frontline base? It had fences and a large number of sentries on patrol. Security there was pretty intensive compared to the other enemy positions. It wouldn't be easy to approach.

It was getting dark out, so Haruhiro decided to infiltrate the base on his own. It might have been impossible if the black wolves with their sensitive noses were around, but he was able to make it deep inside without alerting the sentries.

The one-armed, one-eyed Takasagi was there. As were the gumow rangers, led by the one who looked like Yanni. There was also the man from the hunchbacked race with the overdeveloped upper bodies who was wearing clothes like Jumbo's and Godo Agaja's. Takasagi called him Wabo.

Wabo was with the others of his race, naked from the waist up and digging holes. There were orcs and undead helping with the work too.

It didn't look like they were digging graves or pits to throw refuse in. Were they digging wells? No, the holes were too wide for that to be it. They were reinforcing the sides with wood, however. Tunnels, huh? Were they making underground passages? Whatever it was, they were building *something*. It was a major construction project.

Haruhiro spotted some guns too. It wasn't just Wabo or the gumow rangers who had them. While Takasagi wasn't carrying one—they were probably hard to use with just one arm—there were more than ten orcs and undead with guns carried on straps over their shoulders. There might have been dozens of them. Maybe fewer than a hundred, but still, Forgan seemed to be in possession of *dozens* of guns.

Haruhiro headed back to his comrades. When he talked about the construction going on, Itsukushima seemed to figure something out.

"Oh, I get it. Gnoll tunnels, huh?"

There was a diminutive race in the Tenryu Mountains south of Alterna known as the gnomes.

Gnomes were natural miners, no less talented than the dwarves. Some said they were more talented with their hands, able to invent and manufacture all kinds of mechanical contraptions. The problem was that they were extremely xenophobic. They didn't negotiate or trade with other races unless there was a major benefit to them in doing so. Long ago, when the Kingdom of Arabakia had escaped to the south of the Tenryu Mountains, they'd had the gnomes dig a massive tunnel called the Earth Dragon's Aorta. It was said that the price they'd paid for it amounted to more than half the royal treasury.

Gnolls were apparently close relatives of those gnomes.

However, unlike the creative and inventive gnomes, always dedicated to their craft, gnolls were primarily thieves. They made nothing for themselves, instead stealing it all from others. These parasitic gnolls were eventually expelled thanks to the ingenuity of their gnomish host society. After that, the gnolls chose new hosts to parasitize in the Kurogane Mountain Range—the dwarves.

The gnolls dug tunnels throughout the whole mountain range, infiltrating the Ironblood Kingdom through them to steal everything from clothing to weapons to food to alcohol, and even dwarven babies sometimes. After the war with the No-Life King and the Alliance of Kings came to a close, the dwarves' greatest foes were these determined parasites eating away at the Ironblood Kingdom. For better or for worse, the dwarves had no shortage of enemies to keep fighting.

According to one estimate, the total area of the tunnels the gnolls had dug far exceeded that of all the mine tunnels that made up the Ironblood Kingdom. What's more, the gnoll tunnels weren't limited to the Kurogane Mountain Range, but extended out into the Iroto River Basin.

"When gnolls dig holes into the Ironblood Kingdom, the dwarves try to close them up, of course. But where there's one gnoll hole, you have to assume there's a dozen. It's difficult to block all of them."

"So the enemy is attacking the Ironblood Kingdom through these gnollish tunnels, then," Setora stated plainly.

Kuzaku seemed mystified by all the new information being thrown at him. "Isn't this...kinda crazy? I mean, I know you're always this way, but I'm amazed you can stay so calm, Setora-san."

"What point would there be in us losing our heads?"

"Okay, that's fair. But I don't think it's a matter of whether there's a point or not. It's more, I dunno, a matter of how you feel."

"And is there a point to those feelings?"

"When I'm already cornered, you just keep pushing, huh? It's not going to get you anything, going after me like that. Maybe you'll make me cry, but that's it..."

"I see. There's no point in doing that. Enough of this, then."

"Hearing you say that makes me feel a little lonely, though."

"But hold on!" Ranta said, sniffling a lot, something Haruhiro had noticed he tended to do when he was about to say something decent. "That doesn't sound like the kind of strategy you could come up with unless you had someone familiar with what the situation on the inside is like, right?"

"True..." Itsukushima said, pausing to think on that point. Deputy Neal let out a short laugh.

"So there *is* a traitor, after all."

They had no answer to that.

The next day when dawn broke, the delegation went to work, finally moving into a position where they could check the situation at the five forts. Haruhiro, Itsukushima, and Neal split up to go scouting, and it appeared that two of the five forts had been occupied by the Southern Expedition. The Southern Expedition troops guarding those two forts didn't all have guns, but about one in ten did.

"It's looking like we should go in through the Walter Gate," Itsukushima decided. "If we try to go to the Great Ironfist Gate, we'll have to pass by Fort Warhammer and Fort Gun, which have fallen to the enemy. We don't want them spotting us."

"Sounds fine to me." Neal agreed. Since he was the chief delegate, at least in an acting capacity, he made the decision to head for the Walter Gate.

Grimgar of Fantasy and Ash

12. Like No Other

It took another two days to reach the Walter Gate. Along the way, the delegation spotted well-ordered enemy units marching through the forest. Half were orcs, half undead, and there were maybe a thousand of them altogether. Most of the orcs had bleached their body hair white and wielded one-handed swords with jagged, sawlike blades. Judging from their distinctive appearance, these were probably the orcs that had been encamped at Mount Grief. They were trying to join up with the main Southern Expedition force besieging the Ironblood Kingdom.

The Walter Gate was halfway up the western slopes of the Kurogane Mountain Range. The way to the gate went through a canyon, up a valley, and between the gaps in broken hunks of rock. Itsukushima and Yume found footprints made by something that wasn't four-legged and took note of them, but a thief like Haruhiro wouldn't have noticed. Without someone to lead him here, he wouldn't even have been able to wander into this place by accident.

The entrance to the Walter Gate was indistinguishable from a natural cave. However, Haruhiro and Neal were able to spot the multiple watch stations in the area around the entrance. There were little rock huts in all directions with the bearded faces of dwarves peering out of them—some of them with guns held at the ready.

A dwarf came out of one of the huts carrying a gun. The greatsword that was hanging diagonally over his back was more impressive for its girth than its length. He had a face that kinda looked like it had been twisted by anger and hatred—an evil countenance, the mask of a villain. He was a pretty scary-looking dwarf.

Ranta's hand twitched toward the hilt of his katana. Haruhiro gulped too. He could understand how the dread knight felt.

"Whoa! Scary..." Kuzaku murmured, which was a questionable choice. Haruhiro nudged him in the side with his elbow. "Oops, sorry."

"Really now..." Setora looked at Kuzaku coldly.

"Willich."

When Itsukushima called out to him, the sinister-looking dwarf raised his right fist.

"Itsukushima. Glad you're back," he replied with a voice that was as grim as his face.

"Looks like you're in trouble."

"We sure are."

After that short reply, the dwarf, who was apparently called Willich, started walking toward the cave-like entrance to the Walter Gate. Did he want them to follow him?

Itsukushima patted Poochie on the head.

"You wait here, boy."

Poochie looked up at Itsukushima, blinking as if to say, *Got it.* He rubbed up against Yume a bit, then quickly darted off down the slope.

"See ya later, Poochie," Yume called after him, causing Poochie to stop and give a short bark in response. He didn't turn back after that.

The group followed Willich. Around fifty meters inside the limestone cave, there was an iron gate with a number of dwarves stationed at it. Willich gestured at the guards to let the group through, and it took all those burly dwarves working together to pull the gate open. It was more than half a meter thick.

Beyond the iron gate, things changed completely. There was a flat stone-tiled floor. The walls and ceiling had been neatly carved too, and reinforced with iron. There was even lighting—lanterns embedded in the wall that seemed to rely on something other than fire to provide illumination. How did they work? Haruhiro wondered about it, but he didn't feel at liberty to ask. Their guide, Willich, didn't say a word, so the group followed him in silence.

"Heh... Hic... Heck... Achoo...!" Unable to bear the silence any longer, Ranta let out a strange sneeze. It got no response from Willich.

"Hey, hey," Yume said, hopping up and down as she stepped forward to walk beside Willich.

Ranta tried to stop her with a "Hey," but it was too late.

"Are you and Master friends, Willup?"

"Who's that?"

"Oh, your name wasn't Willup, huh?"

"It's Willich, Yume..."

Even with Itsukushima kindly providing her with the right name, though, things didn't work out.

"Mew. Oh, that's right. It's Willie. Sorry 'bout that. Yume's always gettin' stuff wrong."

"I'm not really Itsukushima's friend... More of a friend of a friend."

"Ohhh. That right? Well, a friend of a friend's a friend, y'know. Yume thinks you oughta be friends too."

"I don't follow, but fine, we're friends, then."

"Oh, you are? Well then, since Yume's Master's apprentice, and Master's like Yume's dad, that makes you like Yume's uncle, huh, Willie?"

"However you like it..."

"Okay, you're Yume's uncle now. Nice to meet you."

"Nice to meet you..."

"Fistbump!" Yume declared, thrusting out her fist. Willich lightly knocked his fist against hers.

"Wow..." Merry murmured. Haruhiro knew how she felt. He'd just been thinking the same thing.

"I know, right? Yume's got some freaky mad skills at communicating..." Kuzaku said, but his choice of words was pretty weird itself.

The tunnel bent in places, going through iron doors and up and down stairs as it continued for a long way.

Suddenly, Itsukushima asked Willich, "Have you ever been to the hethrang dens?"

"No," Willich responded immediately, spitting the word out with distaste. "Don't even say that name. They're filthy."

"So there *are* hethrang dens. They *do* exist, huh?"

When Itsukushima pushed him on the issue, Willich let out a powerful snort. It probably meant something like, *You're being annoying, drop it.*

Yume leaned close to Itsukushima and whispered, "What're hefferuns, Master?"

"I only know a little, myself. The dwarves don't like to talk about them," Itsukushima said, avoiding explaining further. "And it's hethrang, not hefferung."

"Nuh? Well, what're hethrangs, then?"

"Later," Itsukushima said with a sheepish smile before ending the conversation.

The fourth iron door brought them into what appeared to be a warehouse. It was packed full of red armor and helmets with silver trim, shields, and weapons like halberds, axes, spears, and swords. Some of them were on display in glass cases. There were even machines with lots of complex parts. The lamps hanging from the ceiling, casting a faint light across the room, seemed pretty intricate in design.

"The Walter Gate connects to the private residence of the eminent House of Bratsod," Itsukushima explained in place of the taciturn Willich. "The current minister of the left, Axbeld, is of the House of Bratsod. I hear their house has been around for five or six centuries, since before the Ironblood Kingdom was founded."

Willich snorted again, earning a shrug and a smile from Itsukushima. It seemed the dwarf was not fond of the House of Bratsod.

Willich knocked on the door leading out of the warehouse and a dwarf wearing red armor and a helmet opened it. The residence of the House of Bratsod was spacious, and there were more dwarves in red armor standing around the place. They all even had red beards, though it took a moment for Haruhiro to notice that. It looked like they had dyed them.

Exiting the private residence, they came out onto a street lined with blacksmiths' workshops. It was really loud and super hot. Dwarves with hammers in hand, clanging away. Shouting back and forth. The smell of sweat steaming on hot iron was mixed with the scent of the alcohol the smiths sometimes knocked back. It filled the place with a stench that was like nothing else.

Willich stopped in front of one workshop. A dwarf with flowing orange hair, his long beard cast over his shoulder as he hammered, caught Haruhiro's eye. Dwarves were, as a general rule, shorter than humans, but this dwarf was a marvelous mass of muscle that was incredible to behold.

"Gottheld!" Itsukushima called out to him, and the muscular dwarf stopped hammering. He turned his eyes—which were green, surprisingly—toward the hunter.

"Itsukushima?"

The dwarf, whose name was presumably Gottheld, set his hammer gently down on the floor before walking over. As might be expected, he wasn't even as tall as Yume. Even so, he gave Haruhiro the impression that he was a big guy.

He's probably stubborn, thought Haruhiro. *Strong-willed, but forbearing. He's got that in common with Itsukushima.*

Gottheld grabbed Itsukushima's arm with a hand that looked as hard as metal and smiled. "Glad you made it back," he said before glancing at Yume. His eyes had a fatherly affection in them. "And this must be your darling apprentice. You were able to meet up with her, huh? I'm happy for you."

"Yeah..." Itsukushima said with an embarrassed smile. "The force that retook Alterna was the Frontier Army, made up primarily of reinforcements from the mainland. I've returned bearing a letter from their commander."

"Did you come in through the Walter Gate?"

"Yeah. Going through the Great Ironfist Gate seemed impossible."

"You'll be seeing the king, then."

"That's the plan."

"I'll go with you. Hold on a moment."

Gottheld headed back into his workshop. He was wearing work clothes, so maybe he meant to get changed.

"This workshop..." Ranta said, looking around. "Does he make guns here, maybe?"

"That's right," Itsukushima said with a nod. "My friend Gottheld is the best gunsmith in the Ironblood Kingdom. The concept of a gun had been around for a while, but there's no question that he was the one to make them practical. Thanks to that, they call him the father of firearms."

When Gottheld returned neatly dressed, Willich took off somewhere, probably figuring his job was done. The delegation then headed to the Iron Palace with Gottheld.

Along the way, Itsukushima asked Gottheld about the hethrangs that he'd mentioned before. "Willich wouldn't hear me out, but could you tell me about the hethrangs?"

After a moment, Gottheld scowled and asked, "Why do you want to know?" Was it that sore a subject?

"There's something that concerns me," Itsukushima said, his expression grim. "There was a group I didn't recognize among the enemy."

"You're not suggesting they were hethrangs, are you?"

"Dunno. All I know is that the Ironblood Kingdom has people who the rumors say are descended from orcs, and you use them for heavy labor like digging mines and mining ore."

"The hell?" Ranta turned bright red with anger. "I know humans, elves, dwarves, and orcs can have kids together. Most orcs call those kids gumows, and they won't even treat them as their own kind. Are you telling me dwarves do the same asinine crap?"

"Hey..." Itsukushima was about to warn Ranta to tone it down.

However, Gottheld said, "It's fine," turning toward Ranta to give him a firm nod. "You've got it right. For a long time now, we've kept the hethrangs shut up in their dens in the mining and refining district where we treat them like slaves. Hethrangs aren't seen as dwarves. We give them the bare necessities, not letting them really live, but not killing them either—no, we do work them to death. We don't just treat them *like* slaves. They *are* slaves. If you go to the most dangerous reaches of the mine tunnels, all you'll find are hethrangs, or their corpses. This is something every dwarf who isn't a child knows. But we don't talk about the hethrangs. Because we all know. They are the shame of dwarvenkind."

"*They* bring shame on *you*?!" Ranta ground his teeth loudly, glaring at Gottheld. "You oughta be ashamed of *yourselves*. If you know what you're doing, then set them free and let them live normal lives. Have some goddamn decency!"

"Ranta-kun, you're getting too worked up about this..." Kuzaku said hesitantly. Ranta wasted no time rounding on him.

"You shut up, moron! I'm getting worked up because this shit pisses me off. What's wrong with that?!"

"Hethrangs..." Haruhiro murmured, thinking of the man he'd seen, Wabo. "Do they have yellowish-brown skin and disproportionately big upper bodies?"

Gottheld's eyes widened. After a moment's pause he said, "I'm told some hethrangs try to escape. We execute all the ones we catch. Are there some who got away? I couldn't tell you. Honestly...I've never wanted to find out. But..."

"It wouldn't be surprising if there were," Setora said in her usual disinterested tone. "I think we can more or less see what's going on now. The hethrangs have been oppressed by the dwarves, forced to do heavy labor. Some escaped and are now collaborating with the Southern Expedition..."

Maybe the hethrangs had used the gnoll tunnels in their escape. If so, they might use them to get into the Ironblood Kingdom too.

"Heh. What goes around comes around," Ranta said with obvious contempt. Then, sighing, he shook his head. "If we weren't here ourselves, I'd just say the dwarves are getting what's coming to them, and that'd be the end of it."

"Let's hurry," Itsukushima said, pushing Gottheld's back to urge him onward.

Soon the group came to a major road ten meters across with a downward slope, with a ceiling ten meters high. There were stalls on either side of it, and dwarves going about their business. There were some rather petite human women around too—or so Haruhiro thought, but it turned out they weren't human at all. When Gottheld explained they were all dwarf women, Kuzaku was shocked.

"Huh?! Are all dwarf women little girls?!"

It surprised Haruhiro too, but he liked to think he had better manners than Kuzaku. "They can't all be little girls, that'd be crazy. And you're being kinda rude..."

"Oh! Yeah, I guess I was, huh? Urgh. Still, it's pretty shocking. I mean, look how different they are from the men."

"Did you think dwarf women had beards too?" Ranta asked, his tone mocking.

"Well...I considered the possibility. My image of dwarves was that they're hairy, beardy, and drink a lot."

Gottheld gave that a strained smile. "If you limit it to just dwarf men, you're not far off the mark."

The massive black door that towered over them at the end of the road was the entrance to the Iron Palace. It was called the Great Iron King Gate. There was a group of black-bearded dwarves standing on a sort of battlement above the gate. It wasn't just their beards that were black. Their armor and shields had been stained black too. The black-bearded dwarves all carried halberds.

"The royal guard," Itsukushima explained. "They're dwarf traditionalists. As you can see, the elites who guard the Iron Palace don't carry guns. They're not fans of Gottheld, and they hate outsiders to boot. I don't expect them to openly do anything to us, but stay alert."

Gottheld asked to enter, and the black-bearded dwarves silently opened the Great Iron King Gate. There was no word of acknowledgment from them, not even so much as a nod, but Gottheld didn't seem to mind. He probably got treated like this all the time.

They didn't call it the Iron Palace for nothing. There were steel plates covering the floors, walls, and ceilings—all of them polished to a mirror-like finish.

"It's shiny-shiny, huh?" Yume said as she looked at the floor. "If this were a skirt, people might see Yume's panties."

"Good point..." Merry quickly brought a hand down to her hemline in front.

"Oh...?" Kuzaku tried to look directly under Merry, but Haruhiro whacked him on the back of the head.

"Don't do that."

"Ow! Sorry, couldn't help myself..."

"It's not as though you lose anything from him seeing them," Setora said, impassive.

"Huh? So you don't mind if I look, then?" Kuzaku asked, earning him a faint smile from Setora.

"If you want to look, look. It costs me nothing. I simply find it unpleasant."

Deputy Neal, who had been looking at Setora's feet, subtly turned his head to face forward. Who knew what she'd do to him later if he upset her? She was probably saying anyone who was prepared to find out was welcome to.

After walking down the steel hallways a while, a group of black-bearded dwarves approached them from the other direction. The lead dwarf was so tall he didn't look like a dwarf at all. He might not have been as tall as Kuzaku, but he was probably taller than Haruhiro.

Gottheld, who was leading the way, came to a stop.

"Why, if it isn't Sir Rowen, captain of the royal guard."

The tall dwarf he'd referred to as Rowen didn't open his mouth until he was standing right in front of Gottheld. "Master Gunsmith. What business have you here in the Iron Palace?"

"Itsukushima made it back from Alterna."

Gottheld had no choice but to look up at Rowen. The height difference made it unavoidable, but if there were a little more distance between them he wouldn't have had to turn his face up quite so much. Basically, Rowen was forcing him to look up. What an ass.

"I've come to request an audience. Could you see us in?"

"You would ask me to guide you?"

"I believe I just did, yes."

"You bring in this gaggle of humans I've never seen before, and expect to be brought before the royal personage."

"Gaggle of humans, he says," Ranta muttered, clicking his tongue with distaste.

Haruhiro lightly elbowed Deputy Neal in the side. "You should introduce yourself."

Neal scowled, but reluctantly stepped forward. "Uh, I'm, er, I mean, I am Neal, an envoy...is that the word? Yeah, an envoy sent by His Excellency Jin Mogis, Commander of the Frontier Army."

"The Frontier Army, you say?" The captain of the royal guard glared at Neal, making him back away half a step.

"Th-that's what I said, yeah?"

"Do you mean you are an envoy from Margrave Garlan Vedoy? Who is Jin Mogis?"

"Uh, no, the Margrave died, er, I mean, passed away, and our reinforcements from the mainland of the Kingdom of Arabakia retook Alterna. General Jin Mogis was the leader of those reinforcements, and he has now become the new commander of the Frontier Army." Neal puffed his chest up as if to say, *Aw, yeah.*

Did you see that? I said it good and proper. Though maybe he was just trying to puff himself up so he didn't give in to the pressure he was feeling from Rowen.

"And you brought this envoy of theirs all this way, Sir Itsukushima." Rowen glanced at Itsukushima, then laughed. "I am sure it was not easy. But who can say if this representative of the reinforcements, or the Frontier Army, or whatever they call themselves, is of any value to us..."

Itsukushima gazed up at the ceiling, a look of exhaustion on his face. He'd probably been harassed by this captain of the royal guard many times before, and was thinking, *Not this again.*

Ranta was looking at Haruhiro, mouthing something: *"Do we kill him?"* That was what it looked like.

"You're an idiot," Haruhiro mouthed back at him.

"I get it," Gottheld said with a shrug. "I'd hate to trouble our commander of the royal guard. I'll ask the minister of the left to see us in instead."

Anger flashed in Rowen's eyes. It seemed he was pretty emotional. "We of the royal guard are the ones charged with protecting the Iron Palace and the iron king. Would you dare slight me, their captain?!"

The dwarf could be decently scary when he got angry. He hadn't just reached for the greatsword on his back—he was full-on gripping the handle, and he gave off the impression that if he drew it, this wouldn't end with just threats. Maybe it was an act. But he could have also been serious. Which was it? Honestly, Haruhiro couldn't decide one way or the other.

At some point, Neal had hid himself behind Haruhiro and the others. *Screw you, man.* Haruhiro wanted to shout at him, but had no time to curse out the useless deputy. *I'd really like to end this peacefully. But how do I do it?*

"Would you give it a rest?" Merry's tone was so cold it could freeze eardrums. "Your enemies are at the gates. Is this the time for infighting? Enough already."

He'd forgotten. Merry wasn't just kind, pretty, serious, and the most considerate of her comrades out of any of them. She was also awfully scary when she got mad. And she wasn't afraid to speak her mind when she wanted to.

Rowen's black beard was shaking. Was he thinking about what he'd like to do to this uppity human wench? He seemed so surprised he didn't know how to react.

"Meow!" Yume suddenly jumped up.

"You're a cat now?!" Ranta quipped.

"Mweh? Nfuh!" Yume cocked her head to the side, making more weird noises, then finally approached Rowen and started pounding on his armor.

"We're in a hurry, okay? The enemy's got hetsuns with 'em. They're gonna go round-n-round the tunnels, and then maybe they'll be comin' out in the Hotblood Kingdom."

"She's gotten a lot of things wrong there..." Setora said with a sigh. "There are people in the Ironblood Kingdom called hethrangs, yes? It seems they've turned against you. A unit of enemies carrying guns they stole from you may be planning to attack through the gnoll tunnels. That is the information we want to pass along to the iron king. I would think it should be a pressing issue for you."

"Hethrangs, you say? Through the gnoll tunnels…"

Rowen growled like a beast. While the dwarf was arrogant and prone to fits, he also seemed to have considerable confidence in his strength. He was quick on the uptake too. Despite having been so blatantly hostile before, he buried the hatchet in a second, and even smiled slightly as he nodded.

"That would indeed seem to be a pressing issue. Sir Envoy, I will see you and your entourage in to meet the iron king. Follow me."

Once he had taken on the task, the black-bearded captain of the royal guard moved things along quickly. He sent his subordinates to go contact the appropriate people and had the delegation wait in another room for about five minutes. Rowen then led them through the steel halls himself, where they boarded an impressive elevator that was majestic to the point it seemed pretentious.

"This elevator, which will take us to the audience chamber, was designed by the great inventor Duregge for the iron king of the time, and is powered using a mechanism known as a steam engine," Rowen explained eloquently despite no one asking. He was like an entirely different person from before. It was kinda creepy.

"Our Ironblood Kingdom has had many successive generations of wise and brave kings, but the current iron king is a great ruler of a kind rarely seen. Sir Envoy, you can expect your words to be received kindly. However, as a retainer, I ask you not indulge in my liege's benevolence overmuch. Under normal circumstances, none but those who have sworn loyalty to the royal personage would be allowed in the audience chamber."

That said, the way he spoke suggested any politeness was only superficial, and he held nothing but contempt for them.

The elevator finally came to a stop. Stepping out of it, they emerged into a spacious hall. This was only the antechamber. The black-bearded dwarves of the royal guard were protecting a set of steel doors. They weren't large compared to the size of the hall, and were lacking in ostentation, even feeling a little rough and boorish.

Rowen nodded at the black-bearded dwarves and they opened the way. The double sliding doors parted smoothly.

The steel audience chamber was rather long. The far side was raised a number of steps, and there was a blind concealing part of the platform at the top.

The audience chamber wasn't lined only by black-bearded dwarves. There was also a red-bearded dwarf in red armor, as well as two elves. One looked to be a middle-aged man, but it was hard to tell an elf's real age. As for the other elf, Haruhiro wasn't even sure what gender they were. The elf's features were so perfectly symmetrical that, while he could tell they were beautiful, the elf didn't even feel like a living creature anymore.

"That's the elven elder, the honorable Harumerial Fearnotu, and the head of the Seven Sword House of Mercurian, the honorable Eltalihi Mercurian," Itsukushima explained quietly. The middle-aged elf was probably Mercurian, while the elf of unclear gender was the elder.

"Sir Red Beard," Gottheld said, nodding to a red-bearded dwarf.

"He's Axbeld, the minister of the left," Itsukushima said, glancing at Rowen before adding, "The captain of the royal guard's competitor."

Rowen approached the platform and knelt. Gottheld did likewise. The minister of the left, Axbeld, and the middle-aged elf struck the same pose. The elven elder turned toward the platform, face angled downward slightly. The black-bearded guards didn't budge an inch.

Neal cleared his throat, then took a knee. Haruhiro, Ranta, and the rest nodded and knelt too.

Complete silence without the slightest noise fell over the room.

"Itsukushima, it's good to have you back," said a woman's voice from beyond the blind.

"Ohhh..." someone moaned. Gottheld, maybe? Rowen and Axbeld both lowered their heads even further.

"Huh...?" Kuzaku mumbled. "Hold on, it's a queen?"

"What insolence..." Rowen said, his voice filled with annoyance.

"Are you stupid?" Ranta asked, clicking his tongue in distaste. "She might just be the royal speaker or something."

"Oh, yeah," Kuzaku replied with a laugh.

Itsukushima sighed. "No, it's her."

"This is the problem with you humans..." Rowen said, noticeably irritated. Haruhiro was wishing his comrades would keep quiet, but it wasn't out of any sense of reverence. No matter how great the iron king was, she wasn't their monarch.

"I've heard the gist of it."

However, when he sensed the owner of that voice stand up on the other side of the blind, Haruhiro felt a little tense for some reason. He looked with upturned eyes, his face still pointed toward the ground, and saw the blind rising.

"Y-Your Majesty..."

Rowen was clearly shaken. That probably meant the iron king didn't show herself often. It could be that she didn't speak with her own voice often either. Ranta had brought up the idea of a royal speaker before. There was a throne that looked like a mass of iron up on the platform, and a single woman standing in front of it. Behind the throne and off to one side, there was another black-haired girl. Could that girl be a court lady who normally spoke on behalf of the king?

That's a king?

The dwarven king.

The iron king.

They say the name of a thing represents its form...

Uh, how?

The elven elder had an unearthly appearance, but the dwarves' queen was in a whole other dimension. The words "fair skin" could have been invented just to describe hers. Her sparkling silver hair was a work of the most sublime art, and her blue eyes were unique jewels that no one else could ever have had. Haruhiro had seen dwarven women outside the Iron Palace. He'd seen the

215

court lady behind her too. The court lady, well, she was slender, and her appearance put her a league ahead of the ordinary dwarf women, but the queen went even beyond that.

She's like no other, thought Haruhiro. *Surely there isn't a woman like her in all of Grimgar. Her build, the structure of her face, it's all so special. Is she really a queen? It'd be more believable if they told me that she's actually a goddess. Isn't she a goddess?*

Haruhiro was overcome with emotion. To put it in simple terms, he was thinking, *Wow, I'm glad I got to see that.* This was the kind of thing you'd lay eyes on once in a lifetime, if that. Many wouldn't even have a single such opportunity. That was how incredible the queen of the dwarves was. If, just theoretically, that queen were to say, *You there, swear loyalty to me and give me your heart,* would he be able to refuse? Haruhiro wasn't sure. As for Ranta and Kuzaku, they'd instantly reply "With pleasure," wouldn't they?

"I wish not just to hear from you directly, but to listen to your opinions. I think we must hold a council. At once."

The iron king's eyes narrowed slightly. That was all she did, but it was enough to convey that she was thinking deeply about the future, and was also concerned for the well-being of the members of the delegation, exhausted as they were from their long journey.

"Gottheld, Itsukushima, and the members of the Frontier Army's delegation. Could I ask you to attend?"

Haruhiro almost said "With pleasure" despite himself, but he swallowed the words and bowed his head.

"'Kay."

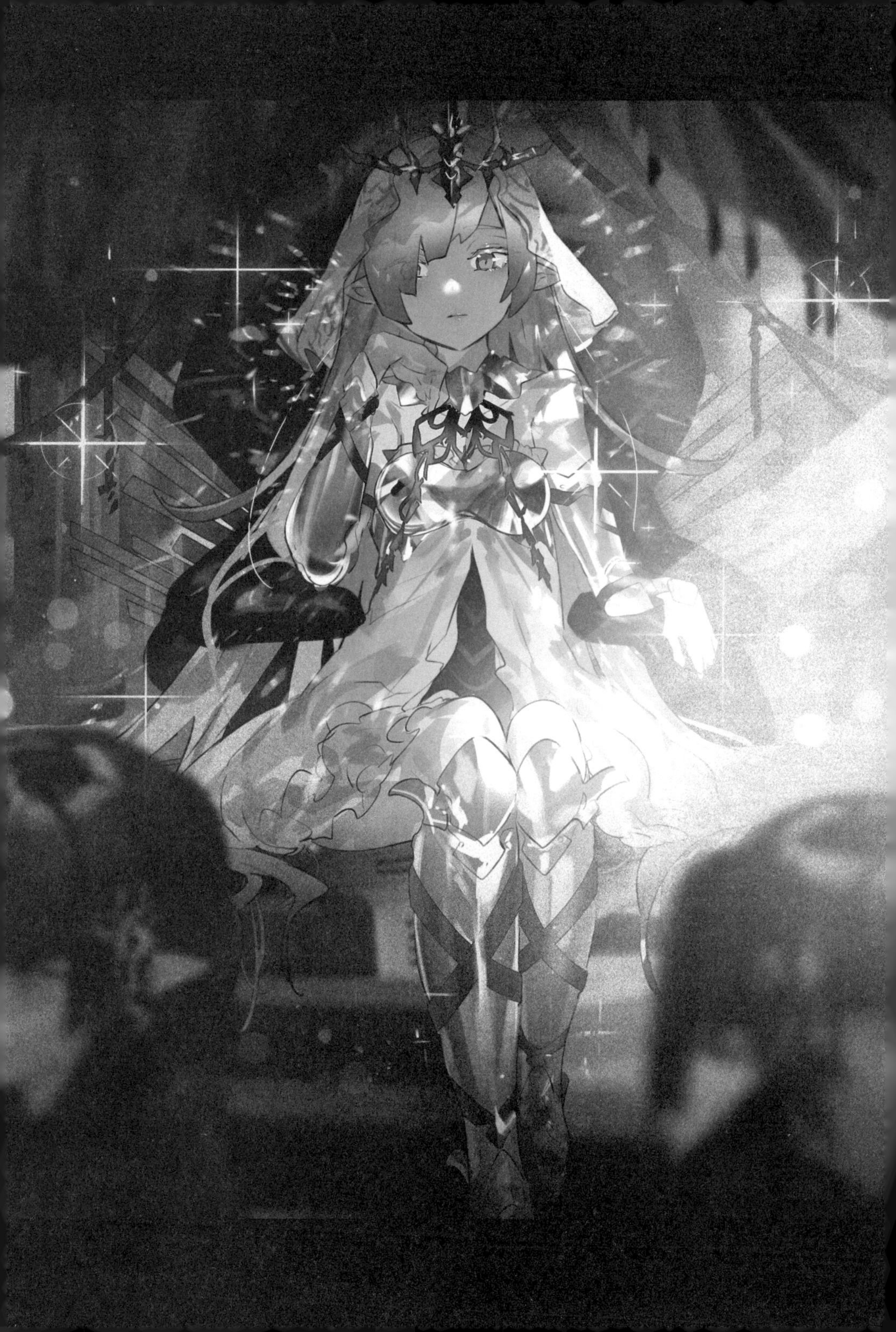

He ended up sounding like Kuzaku instead. Maybe he should have gone for "With pleasure" after all.

13. A Legend

There was a room next to the audience chamber, and that was where they held council. In attendance were the iron king, Minister of the Left Axbeld, Captain of the Royal Guard Rowen, Gottheld, Elder Harumerial Fearnotu of the elves, Eltalihi of the House of Mercurian, and Itsukushima. The delegation was represented by Deputy Neal, together with Haruhiro and Setora.

The conference room was iron from ceiling to floor, with a large oblong table that was also made of iron, and the chairs were iron too. Okay, the table made sense, but the chairs? Really? Or so you would think, but they were surprisingly not that uncomfortable. The seat and backrest were both made of thin, interwoven iron bars, allowing them to fit to the body of whoever sat in the chair. It was a testament to dwarven technical prowess.

As one might guess from the fact Haruhiro felt the need to admire an iron chair to take his mind off things, the atmosphere in the conference room was oppressive. It was, perhaps, to be expected that the hethrang problem would weigh heavily on the dwarves of the Ironblood Kingdom. The iron king in particular seemed deeply pained by it.

"If the hethrangs are lending aid to our enemies, I have much to regret. However, repent as I might..." The queen trailed off into silence.

What could he say to her? Well, it would have probably been rude for Haruhiro to say anything, and she was too beautiful for him to muster up the courage to speak anyway. Ranta had wanted to attend this council. Haruhiro should've left it to him. Still, Haruhiro was their leader, even if he wasn't much of one. As leader, there were things he could do and things he couldn't. In fact, even setting aside all this leader stuff, there was a whole lot of stuff that Haruhiro couldn't do.

Haruhiro looked at Setora, who was sitting next to him. He was about to ask what she thought their next move should be, but she opened her mouth first.

"This is a waste of time," she said, unconcerned with the way her comments made the room freeze over. Haruhiro broke out in a cold sweat.

"You wretch...!" Captain of the Royal Guard Rowen shouted as he slammed his hands down on the table, incandescent with rage.

"She's right," the iron king agreed. If not for her intercession, Rowen might have flown at Setora. "There are things we must do before I can wallow in regret."

A LEGEND

"I suppose the first thing we must do is confirm the facts," Minister of the Left Axbeld said, stroking his red beard. "We know that the enemy is digging holes, but is that enough to say for certain that they mean to invade us through the gnoll tunnels? The gnolls have been relatively quiet recently, but we've also discovered multiple new gnoll holes. Also, they operate on the principle of 'what's mine is mine, and what's yours is mine too.' Would they let outsiders use their tunnels uncontested? And is it beyond doubt that the ones you saw with the enemy were really hethrangs?"

"We can't say it's beyond a doubt," Itsukushima answered. "I've never seen them before, after all. If they're out there in the mine shafts somewhere, could you let us meet them? We'll be able to tell then."

"Their dens are no place to take guests. However..." The minister of the left furrowed his brow. "It would seem wise to have you make the trip, yes. I will arrange for it. Now, I would like to ask Honored Elder Harumerial, do you have any intel that can back up what Sir Itsukushima's group has told us about the enemy's movements?"

"No," the elven elder said with a voice like a wind instrument made of glass. There was something transcendent about the elf's tone and facial expression, which carried a hint of sorrow but were also aloof from the world. "The elves we have sent outside your country have not as yet reported any large-scale digging of tunnels. Regarding the hethrangs, I was aware of them, but very few elves should have much knowledge of them. Obviously, our scouts have not made one report of hethrangs, or those who appear to be hethrangs."

"Hmm," the minister of the left hummed, nodding. "For now, I've ordered my men to search for and check gnoll holes. If we are to seal all of them off, our defenders have their hands full at the moment, so we would have to mobilize other people."

"The problem is the hethrangs," the captain of the royal guard interjected, full of anger. "If those ingrates have escaped after all we've done for them, and even provided aid to our enemies, this is a rebellion, ma'am. It's dangerous to let them keep living inside the kingdom. Shouldn't we execute them all, without exception?"

"I'm not so sure about that, Captain," the red-bearded minister of the left said with an exaggerated frown and a shrug of his shoulders. "You might not be aware of this, but the hethrang population has grown to be as large as half of our own. Even if you were to volunteer to go around executing them personally with that greatsword you're ever so proud of, it would be more than a day's work. And that aside, if we do kill the hethrangs, what will happen to the expansion of the mine shafts and mining operations that are the lifeblood of our kingdom?"

"Do you mean to say we should suffer these traitors to live, Minister?!"

"Calm yourself, Captain. It's not as though all of the hethrangs have escaped. Many of them are still working hard down in the mines for the Ironblood Kingdom and all dwarvenkind."

"When the time comes, they may all bare their fangs at us."

A LEGEND

"No, no. The hethrangs inside the kingdom are no threat to us, at least. We don't let them carry anything more dangerous than a pickax."

"Pickaxes are for digging through hard bedrock! I could easily put a hole in your skull with one, Minister! Would you like a demonstration, perhaps?!"

"The hethrangs aren't as strong as you, Captain."

The minister of the left and the captain of the royal guard opposed each other. Haruhiro had heard that. He hadn't suspected it was so bad that they would openly squabble in front of their king like this, however. The minister of the left appeared to be trying to calm the captain of the royal guard down and let the issue rest, but that only served to irritate his counterpart more. Honestly, it was a wonder that the captain was holding back from punching him. Maybe he was showing some self-restraint after all.

"I do not wish to execute the hethrangs."

It was probably thanks to the iron king. One word from her made the hot-headed captain of the guard and the slippery minister of the left shut their mouths tight.

"Rowen. Red Beard. I understand both of you serve me and the kingdom with all your hearts."

"Yes, ma'am!"

"You are too kind."

The captain of the royal guard and the minister of the left bowed their heads. The iron king nodded, then, after a moment, continued.

"Let us consider what to do with the hethrangs later. For now, we must prepare for the enemy. My concern is whether we would be able to defend against the enemy invasion, assuming we were to block all of the gnoll tunnels we've currently located."

"If I may?" Setora raised her hand. The iron king quietly pointed to her, granting Setora permission to speak. "Am I correct in my understanding that 'gnoll holes' refers to places in which the gnolls' tunnels have penetrated the Ironblood Kingdom?"

The red-bearded minister of the left nodded. "You are."

"In that case, simply sealing the gnoll holes won't be sufficient. Unless you make the tunnels themselves impassable, they'll just open new gnoll holes. I assume that's what has your king concerned."

"You are to address her as 'Her Majesty'!" the black-bearded captain of the royal guard shouted in anger, but Setora was unflappable. Haruhiro felt both impressed and exasperated with her. How could she be so indifferent?

"You say that, but she is not *my* king."

"The iron king is the sovereign of the Ironblood Kingdom, the ruler of the dwarves! Have you no manners, you human swine!"

"I might ask you the same. I cannot imagine a man who shouts at others to intimidate them whenever he pleases has any right to speak about manners."

"What was that?!" The captain of the royal guard made as if to rise from his seat.

Setora laughed coldly at him. "See, you did it again. If you wish to cut me down, do it, but I would like to see some acknowledgment that you have not been minding your own manners."

Haruhiro was caught between thinking, *Yeah, you tell him!* and, *This is bad for my heart. Please, just stop.*

A LEGEND

"Stand down, Rowen," the iron king interceded, appearing unamused. Seeing even the slightest discomfort on her face made something stir in Haruhiro's heart, like he had to do something about it.

"Setora, was it? My concerns are exactly as you laid out."

"Well, how about it?" Setora asked, looking at the other attendees.

Rowen crossed his arms and looked away. "We've gone in to kill gnolls on several occasions, but that was a long time ago."

"I went in a few years ago, when the gnolls were getting out of hand." The minister of the left smiled slightly. It didn't seem like he was mocking the captain of the royal guard. Maybe it was a fun memory for him? "I was with the humans renowned in our kingdom as the great heroes, along with Gottheld."

"Kisaragi, huh?" The iron king had a far-off look in her eyes. The corners of her lips turned up.

"Wait, isn't Kisaragi..." Haruhiro mumbled without meaning to. The far-too-beautiful iron king shot a piercing glance in his direction, leaving him too tense to be grateful for the honor of her gaze.

"You know Kisaragi?"

"Yeah... You, uh, could say that. We were taken in under his umbrella, sort of. He runs the K&K Pirate Company, right? In the Emerald Archipelago. Come to think of it, I think I ended up becoming a K&K employee..."

"I've heard that he saved Vele, and then effectively became the leader of an organization that manages pirates."

It was pretty crazy when the iron king's eyes sparkled. *Wait, I never knew eyes could shine,* Haruhiro thought to himself. They must have been reflecting light, but it was uncanny the way they glittered. Her fair skin flushed a little red.

"I see. Your name was Haruhiro, yes? Are you a friend of Kisaragi's?"

"A friend of his...? I dunno about that. One of my comrades was with K&K for a while, so maybe she is."

"Is that person familiar with Kisaragi?"

"To be completely honest, I don't know much about what went on there, so I can't speak for her, but I'd think so?"

"I see." The iron king placed a hand over her chest and closed her eyes. Even Haruhiro, who knew he was dense about these things, could be pretty sure of what was going on here.

She's in love, isn't she? The iron king. With Kisaragi of K&K. And, wait, the dwarves know him as a great hero? What in the world did he do?

The iron king opened her eyes when Minister of the Left Axbeld cleared his throat. She didn't act awkward about it, but she was clearly despondent. Haruhiro didn't really understand the niceties of the heart. In fact, he barely understood them at all. But he knew the iron king was deeply in love with Kisaragi.

"Erm, I don't know what to tell you. Her name's Yume, and she's in our party. Maybe she'll be able to tell you some stories about Kisaragi? I'll check with her later. Anyway, what I'm gathering is that it's not realistic to collapse the gnoll tunnels and make them impassable that way, right?"

A LEGEND

"Correct," the minister of the left said, nodding. "It would be better to come right out and say it's impossible. If we could, we'd have done it a long time ago. We've been fighting the gnolls here in the Kurogane Mountain Range for over two centuries now, you see."

"Hey..." Deputy Neal whispered. When Haruhiro looked at him, he started mouthing words. *"This country's in some deep trouble. Maybe we should just give them the letter and then get out of here."*

While Haruhiro thought his reasoning was a little questionable, this was coming from Neal, so he wasn't particularly surprised by it at this point. The deputy did have a good nose for these things. If Neal were the only one here, the situation was probably bad enough that he'd be right to scram in a hurry.

The head of the House of Mercurian was whispering something in the elven elder's ear. The elder nodded before addressing the council.

"For now, I will order our elves to redouble their surveillance of the enemy. Our swordsmen, archers, and shamans have been defending the Great Iron Fist Gate, but if you request it, they can be moved at once."

Minister of the Left Axbeld shook his head and snorted. "Now that it has come to this, the loss of Fort Warhammer and Fort Gun—and consequently the seizure of our firearms—hurts even more..."

"Are you saying that out of spite for the men under my command?" Captain of the Royal Guard Rowen ground his teeth. It was likely his men who had been defending the two forts that were taken. The minister of the left arched his eyebrows and spread his arms.

"Captain, I've said nothing of the sort. It could just as easily have been Fort Ax or Fort Halberd, held by my own Red Beards, that were attacked instead. It was also a failure on the part of the other three forts that reinforcements didn't arrive at Fort Warhammer and Fort Gun in time. While it *is* important that we make clear where responsibility lies for such failures, wouldn't you agree that it's a little pointless for you and I to quarrel about every little thing at this point?"

"To begin with, Minister, you are a political advisor, and your decision to involve yourself in military matters, including the positioning of troops, is causing confusion. Weren't the Red Beards supposed to be no more than your personal forces?"

"Oh, very well. Then I'll entrust command of the Red Beards to you. I'll not involve myself in the war beyond defending Her Majesty with my own body. Does that satisfy you?"

"You're only saying that because you know the Red Beards won't go to their deaths at my command. I'm sick of your conniving ways, you old fox!"

"And I am sick and tired of putting up with all of your tantrums, Captain."

"This wouldn't be happening if you weren't so needlessly ambitious, Minister."

"I support Her Iron Majesty, and I have no ambition other than to serve the Ironblood Kingdom. They say a scoundrel sees bad actors everywhere when he thinks all men are as unscrupulous as himself. Oh, but it's too much to call you a scoundrel. Well, I was just sharing a bit of common wisdom. Allow me to apologize."

"I see you're better with your words than your hands, as always!"

"I do believe you're every bit as talkative as I am."

"As I can't afford to rust my greatsword lopping off that bearded face of yours, I'm left with no other choice."

"We both have beards, you realize. Our guests can scarcely tell us dwarven men apart other than by the color and length of our facial hair."

"Oh, is that right? I see one dwarf here whose face looks noticeably more conniving than the rest of ours, wouldn't you say?"

"Hmm. And you're so much larger than the rest of us, they can tell you apart at a glance. Honestly, it's hard to believe you're a dwarf at all."

"What's that supposed to mean?!"

"I'm not insinuating anything. No one doubts you're a pure-blooded dwarf, I'm sure."

"Of course not! No matter how far back you trace my lineage, it's nothing but proud dwarves all the way!"

It felt like this fight was getting pretty serious, but maybe this was just business as usual for the two of them? Only Haruhiro and Neal were worried. Setora pinched her chin, as if she was thinking about something. As for the rest of the people here, perhaps they were used to it?

"What if we were to travel through the gnoll tunnels ourselves to attack the enemy?" Setora suddenly suggested. The minister of the left groaned, a consternated expression on his face.

"The gnoll's tunnels are interconnected in complex and incomprehensible ways. They're not just labyrinthine, they're an actual maze. We've made attempts to grasp their full extent in the past, but new connections are constantly being added, while others collapse and are lost. They change so frequently that our efforts have never panned out."

"Why don't we try entering them ourselves?" Setora asked, looking at Haruhiro.

Deputy Neal was flapping his gums. *"Why would we need to go so far?"*

It wasn't like Haruhiro didn't get where he was coming from, but the Ironblood Kingdom might be their lifeline. If the stronghold of the dwarves and the elven survivors was wiped out, the Frontier Army would lose a promising ally. It was questionable how far they could trust the goblins of Damuro, so they needed to remember that they might be betrayed at any time in favor of the Southern Expedition. He wanted to avoid a situation where the Frontier Army and Volunteer Soldier Corps found themselves isolated.

"It's a thought..."

They would work with the Ironblood Kingdom to the best of their ability and drive off the Southern Expedition, or at least hold them back. That had to be the best move available to them.

Setora was thinking the same thing. That was why she was being so proactive here.

"We're used to exploring unfamiliar places. But could you give us a guide? Someone as familiar with the gnoll tunnels as possible. I think that would increase our chances of success somewhat."

"Red Beard." The iron king looked at the minister of the left. He nodded.

"We have those who joined Kisaragi's gnoll hunt. I am sure they will be of assistance."

"Kisaragi..."

The iron king's blue eyes sparkled again. And not just her eyes. Her silver hair and fair skin seemed to shine too. Haruhiro couldn't help but stare. She was incredible.

"Here is an idea," the king said. "Why not issue an official notice that the great hero Kisaragi's friend will be exploring the gnoll tunnels and is looking for volunteers to join him?"

"Ohhh. That would be excellent. I am sure many of the smiths would set their work aside to join him. And Kisaragi is popular with the ladies too, so I expect it will be highly effective."

"My own little girl's head over heels for him, after all," Gottheld said, his smile a little strained.

"Your little girl? She's a dwarf, right?" Haruhiro asked, and Gottheld nodded, as if to say, *Of course she is.*

"She went off pirating with Kisaragi. I hope she can be his head wife, but he's got a lot of good women around him. Who can say what will happen?"

Haruhiro glanced at the iron king, curious how she'd react. Like he expected, her eyes were downcast, filled with sadness and loneliness. Just seeing her like that made Haruhiro miserable too.

"To tell you the truth, I've already sent a messenger to the K&K Pirate Company," the red-bearded minister of the left revealed. "The Emerald Archipelago is a long way away, so there's been no response yet, but Kisaragi is a man who lives by the motto that knowing what is right and not doing it is a mark of cowardice. He may even be able to get the Free City of Vele—which stayed neutral in the battle against the No-Life King and his Alliance of Kings—to move on our behalf."

"That's enough indulging in ridiculous dreams, Minister!" The black-bearded captain of the royal guard slammed his hands on the table. "You think a human has that kind of power?! Rather than rely on outsiders, we dwarves should smash the enemy with our own strength! We're critically lacking in that kind of mettle! Dwarves have lost their manhood! We must take our pride as men back now!"

"Red Beard, Rowen." The iron king looked at the minister of the left and the captain of the royal guard, then around to the rest of them. Her eyes were no longer sparkling, and she sat with a commanding posture. "Elder Harumerial, Honored Eltalihi, Gottheld, Itsukushima, Sir Neal, Haruhiro, Setora. I will do what little I can to help too. Please, lend us your strength. If the worst should come to pass and the Ironblood Kingdom falls, Grimgar will be trod underfoot by the orcs and undead. They say the orc leading the Southern Expedition, the high king Dif Gogun, took

A LEGEND

control of all the orcish clans, or enslaved them, and put pressure on the undead, earning him the awe of the other races. He is a dangerous man who hopes to eradicate us, the hated enemies of the orcs, in order to solidify his hegemony. We cannot submit to him. There is no path to peace. We absolutely must win."

The minister of the left, the captain of the royal guard, and Gottheld all responded with a firm "By your will." The elves elegantly touched a hand to their shoulders and bowed to her, while the members of the delegation each responded in their own way.

The iron king rose from her seat. The council was adjourned.

High King Dif Gogun. It was a name Haruhiro hadn't heard before. There were probably a lot of things he and his party still didn't know. They needed to learn as much as they could, and not just about the gnoll tunnels—about everything else too. He was going to quickly gather information while preparing for the exploration mission. With that decided, it felt like his options had opened up a little.

"Ahhh!" Neal shot up out of his seat in a hurry. He was fishing around in his pockets. "I still haven't given her the commander's letter."

The minister of the left, the captain of the royal guard, and the iron king, who had been about to leave the room, stopped and turned to look at him. That was when the door opened.

A black-bearded dwarf from the royal guard rushed into the room, out of breath. He must have been shocked to see the iron king because he leaped backward and threw himself on the floor, groveling before her.

"Y-Your Majesty...! I-It is an honor above my station to behold your royal countenance..."

"What is happening?!" the captain of the royal guard bellowed at him, and the black-bearded dwarf raised his head.

"Sir! The enemy suddenly appeared inside the kingdom, and the battle has been joined! The people took up arms to repel them, but they have already suffered heavy casualties!"

"What..." The captain of the royal guard's voice failed him, and Minister of the Left Axbeld slapped his own forehead with his right hand.

For a moment, the iron king gazed up at the ceiling. But only for a moment. She recovered immediately, faster than any of the others.

"Rowen, you take command of defenses inside the kingdom. I will come up with a plan. Red Beard, you help me."

"By your will!" The captain of the royal guard, large enough to seem like he wasn't a dwarf at all, raced out of the room so fast he threatened to smash through the door. Though Axbeld's red-bearded face was twisted with anguish, he allowed himself what was likely a deliberate smile.

"Well, it seems they've beaten us to the punch. Now we'll just have to fight like men. They've called me a stain on the proud beards of the House of Bratsod, but even I've got the dwarven blood in me. This may be the last thing I ever do for you, but my old bones are eager for the task, ma'am."

"I would be in serious trouble without your continued service. I haven't your skill with words."

The iron king turned to look at the others. Her expression was stern, not grim. She wasn't shaken at all by this. Or perhaps she was trying to keep up that appearance. If so, her acting was flawless.

"This is the Ironblood Kingdom, the country of the dwarves. If I were to let elves and humans die under my care, it would be a black mark on our name. I swear we will carve a swath of blood to evacuate you all to safety."

The elven elder, Harumerial, disagreed. "Your kindness touches us all, ma'am. But whatever fate awaits the dwarves, we elves will share it with you. That is what we, the elves of the Shadow Forest, have collectively decided."

Neal grabbed Haruhiro by the arm. He was mouthing words at him: *"What do we do?"*

Haruhiro looked at Setora. *You decide,* her eyes demanded. It wasn't that Setora was trying to pass the responsibility off to him. If he made the decision, she would follow it, and she believed in him enough to trust he wouldn't screw up too badly.

Haruhiro took a deep breath. This wasn't the time for him to get wildly overeager, or to look for a way to flee, or to run around in confusion. Now that he had his memories back, Haruhiro more or less knew what kind of guy he was. So long as he stayed true to himself, his comrades would probably stake their lives on his decisions. Some of his comrades would even set him straight if he started acting too crazy. That meant he shouldn't waver.

"We'll do what we can too. For now, let's hang tough."

Grimgar
of
Fantasy and Ash

14. All in One

Haruhiro, Setora, Itsukushima, and their tagalong, Deputy Neal, met up with the rest of their comrades, who had been waiting for them in the elevator hall outside the room. The others had already been filled in on what was happening.

"Damn, they move fast. But that's Forgan for you," Ranta said with a smile, licking his lips. He looked pretty excited. "The enemy probably ought to be launching a total offensive matched to the timing of their infiltration. If they get past the forts and break the Great Ironfist Gate, we're screwed, no matter how things go here."

"Wait, what're you so happy about? Are you crazy, Ranta-kun...?" Kuzaku asked.

"You nitwit! Every crisis is a golden opportunity!"

"Uh, I dunno about that. I think a crisis is a crisis."

Yume nodded in agreement. "Crises are crises because they're always crisesin.'"

What's that even supposed to mean? Haruhiro thought, but he decided not to poke fun at her. Yume was just being Yume, like always. And that was fine.

As for Kuzaku, despite sounding negative, he was calm. He had a certain resiliency that let him bounce back when he was feeling cowed. There was nothing to worry about with him, other than his lack of consideration for his own well-being.

When Merry and Haruhiro's eyes met, she exhaled, then nodded. Though stiffly, the corners of her mouth turned up. It was beautiful. Seriously beautiful. Well, her face was always beautiful, no matter what expression she made. Sure, he might have found the iron king bizarrely attractive, but Merry was special. It was possible this was only true in Haruhiro's eyes, but if so, he was fine with that. He might even prefer it that way.

Don't get distracted, Haruhiro warned himself. Uh, not that he was. He was just reminding himself of how special Merry was. Every second of every minute. No matter how many times he thought about it, he kept discovering new feelings for her.

No. I can't do this. I'm gonna get caught in a loop, Haruhiro thought, slapping his cheeks and stopping himself.

"I'd like to see us set some goals," Setora said plainly.

Goals. Yeah. Setora was usually right about these things. Haruhiro would have liked to say she was *always* right, but she was too stringent to accept that. *Everyone makes mistakes, so it's not possible for me to always be right.* That was what she'd probably say.

"Itsukushima. Sir Haruhiro," the red-bearded minister of the left addressed them. He approached the team, beckoning the two of them to meet him halfway. "I have a favor to ask of you, but I need you to be discreet about what I am about to say."

Haruhiro and Itsukushima glanced at one another and shared a nod.

Axbeld lowered his voice, speaking to them through his red beard. "In addition to the Great Ironfist Gate and the Walter Gate, our kingdom has another entrance—the Duregge Gate. Or rather, it *had* another. The great inventor Duregge made a path that leads from the king's bedchambers to the east of the Kurogane Mountain Range through a series of elevators and moving walkways. Only a select few know this secret..."

The minister of the left explained that there had been no one like Duregge before or after him. The great inventor did have apprentices, but none of them had lived up to their master's reputation.

The Duregge Gate had functioned flawlessly for fifty years after its inventor passed away. However, after that, it began to break down frequently before finally becoming completely irreparable. Even so, they were able to make the contraptions man-operable, allowing it to continue serving as an emergency escape route for the king until a decade ago.

"But now even just getting to the other side is incredibly difficult. It has almost no practical use whatsoever."

The Iron Palace was divided into the lower levels, where the iron king resided, and the upper levels, which were connected to the city. If the elevator that connected the two sections were destroyed, there would only be narrow tunnels left between them.

If they caved those in, they could seal off the lower levels. And even if the enemy made it to the lower levels, they could still shut themselves in the audience chamber and hold out there.

Even in the worst-case scenario, they could still defend the iron king. However, in the event that they did shut themselves inside the audience chamber, it would be little different from being buried alive. The ventilation ducts were well hidden, and there were stores of food and running water, so they could survive for quite some time. But without support, eventually starvation would get them, or the enemy would destroy enough of the ventilation ducts to suffocate them.

"Which means..." Itsukushima said, "if it comes down to it, rather than have her take shelter in the lower levels of the Iron Palace, you'd prefer for Her Iron Majesty to flee somehow. Do I have that correct, Minister?"

"Precisely." Axbeld's eyes had this glassy, fixed stare. No, he wasn't drunk, and he wasn't angry, so maybe it just showed how determined he was? "Her Majesty is not yet aware, but I will do my utmost to persuade her. It would be meaningless for her and her retinue to survive alone in the bowels of the Iron Palace, and if she were to fall into enemy hands or be slain, we dwarves would fight until every last one of us was dead. I am sure many dwarves would like nothing more than to die fighting. However, as one of our elders, I cannot allow the dwarven race to end here. To ensure that doesn't happen, Her Majesty's survival is essential. So long as we have her, no matter how great a blow my people take, we will be able to rise again."

Axbeld's passion was so fierce it threatened to burn them. The dwarf was driven by an intense sense of duty. His reasons and motives weren't hard to understand.

That said, for a human like Haruhiro, being exposed to that kind of passion didn't make him want to take risks to help the dwarf; it just weirded him out a bit. Still, he wasn't so heartless that he could brush away the hand of someone desperately grasping at straws.

Haruhiro was a mediocre guy like that.

"What do you want us to do?" he asked.

"I'd like to ask you to guard Her Majesty," Axbeld responded instantly. "Depending on the circumstances, if there is no other way, I would like Her Majesty and the elven leaders to escape. In the event that no other choice remains, I will stay here and send Rowen with you."

"Shouldn't it be the other way around?" Itsukushima said bluntly "Maybe it's not my place to say this, but tough guys like him are replaceable. A dwarf like you? You're one of a kind."

"I'm happy to hear you say that," Axbeld said, smiling behind his thick beard. "However, while you humans likely can't tell, there are enough years between Rowen and me that he could be my son. No matter how much time goes by, he'll always be a snot-nosed brat to me. Because of his unusual size, he was always rumored to be a cursed child or the son of an orc. He cried about it all the time. From a young age, whenever he threw a tantrum, no one could stop him. He still has a short temper now, and he likes to boss people around, but his men respect him. He needs to be given the chance to grow up. This stays between us, but I am hoping he will marry Her Majesty. That will, of course, be up to her, however..."

"Okay, enough already. We get it, old man," Ranta said, clapping him on the shoulder. "We wouldn't be real men if we said no when you're asking like this. Leave your king to us." Grinning, he gave Axbeld a thumbs-up.

"You have my thanks," the minister of the left said, bowing his head to Ranta.

Kuzaku grumbled, "What's Ranta-kun making the decision for?"

"Are you stupid? That's just the way things are going! Instead of Haruhiro taking forever with his wishy-washy responses, it's better if I just come right out and say we'll do it. Obviously."

"Understandable," Setora said, shocking Haruhiro with her immediate agreement. Okay, yeah, he kinda agreed. He was well aware he could be a little wishy-washy.

"Uh, don't just ignore me..." Neal grumbled, but no one cared.

The party quickly hashed out the details with the minister of the left.

Rowen, the captain of the royal guard, had already left the Iron Palace to command troops in the battle for the city. The iron king, her guards from the lower levels of the Iron Palace, the minister of the left, and Haruhiro's group were going to relocate to the upper levels. If the battle went well, then good. However, if things looked bad, they would immediately escort the iron king to the House of Bratsod's residence. Elder Harumerial and the other prominent elves would join them if possible. Then, when the time came, they would recall Rowen and organize an escape party, which would flee the Ironblood Kingdom through the Walter Gate.

As the minister of the left had already declared, he would remain in the Ironblood Kingdom and fight to the end. Nothing would break his resolve. He was a dwarf as hard as nails, after all. Red-bearded Axbeld had two sons, three daughters, and six grandchildren. Even if the iron king left the Kurogane Mountain Range, dwarves of the House of Bratsod would continue to serve her.

It seemed Axbeld, always a shrewd operator, had planned out what would happen after such an escape in advance.

Before the dwarves put down roots in the Kurogane Mountain Range, they'd had mine shaft cities in other mountains here and there. All of these had since been invaded, destroyed, or otherwise abandoned. But some small number of these mine shaft cities, though only a very few, were intact enough they could be made livable again with some work.

Axbeld had his eye on a former mine shaft city about a hundred miles to the east, in Mount Spear. He'd also located another, a further two hundred kilometers north, in the Kuaron Mountains. He'd invested the House of Bratsod's own money in the mine shaft city in Mount Spear, sending his family members to prepare it for a group of anywhere from a few dozen to maybe a hundred to live there long-term.

Their guide would be an old dwarf, Utefan, who was celebrating his hundred-and-thirty-fifth birthday this year. He was a direct descendant of the House of Bratsod—Axbeld's uncle, as a matter of fact—but had been disowned in his youth for his prodigal and free-spirited ways. He had taken this as an opportunity to travel the world, and he was known as far as the Red Continent, if one believed the stories he told.

The party rode the elevator to the upper levels of the Iron Palace with Itsukushima, Neal, and Gottheld. The palace was abuzz with activity. The Great Iron King Gate was especially hectic, having been turned into a frontline base.

A barricade had been erected in front of the open gate, and black-bearded dwarves from the royal guard were manning it with guns. There were more gunners on the battlement above the gate too.

There was a constant stream of black-beards or red-beards coming out in squads of five to ten dwarves and deploying onto the main street through the Great Iron King Gate.

The air in the Ironblood Kingdom was never that clean to begin with, but it was extra smoky now. Because of the gunpowder? There was this uniquely metallic, powdery smell. Was it gun smoke? No one seemed to be firing near the Great Iron King Gate, but gunshots rang out almost ceaselessly. The sound echoed through the Ironblood Kingdom, which had no sky, hurting their ears.

The party approached the barricade. Merry cast a support spell with Haruhiro, Ranta, Kuzaku, Yume, Setora, and Itsukushima as the targets. The priest's light magic spells that strengthened or defended people were built around the six points of Lumiaris's symbol, the hexagram, so they had a limit of six targets.

"What about me?" Neal looked dissatisfied.

"I'm sorry," Merry quickly apologized. Neal shrugged and said no more.

Ranta asked one of the black-bearded dwarves manning the barricade, "How do things look?!"

"How should I know?!" the black-bearded dwarf shouted, pointing his gun toward Ranta, who panicked.

"Whoa, man! That's dangerous! What if that thing goes off?!"

"Then there'll be another dead human! That's all!"

"Wow, dwarf humor sucks!"

"Was he joking, though?" Kuzaku said under his breath. The dwarf must have heard him because he smiled. Maybe it had been a joke, of a sort.

Six red-bearded dwarves were running out past the barricade, and there were another twenty or so near the Great Iron King Gate, preparing to head out.

"It's Captain Rowen!" one of the dwarves up on the battlement shouted.

"Rowen!"

"Rowen!"

"Rowen!"

"Rowen!"

The black-bearded dwarves were all calling his name. The black-clad dwarf leading a squad as they rushed back up the main street toward the gate was clearly larger than the rest. No one could mistake him for anyone but Captain Rowen. He was carrying something over each shoulder. Whatever they were, they didn't look like weapons.

"Support the captain!" the black-bearded dwarf who'd just been joking about Ranta shouted. The black-bearded dwarves manning the barricade readied their guns. If any enemies were pursuing Rowen's squad, they were going to shower them with suppressive fire.

It was hard to see through all the smoke, but the enemy didn't seem to be chasing them. Rowen circled around the side of the barricade.

"Where's the enemy?!" Haruhiro asked, and Rowen gave him a death glare. His armor and helmet were pitch black, so Haruhiro hadn't noticed until now, but the dwarf was covered in blood. He was carrying a black-bearded dwarf on each shoulder.

"They need healing!" Merry said, about to rush over, but Rowen shook his head. He set the two dwarves down, laying them on the ground.

"No need. They're already dead."

It wasn't just Rowen. The other black-beards who had returned with him were also carrying the remains of their comrades. It wasn't just royal guards, though. There were red-beards too. They'd all been shot by the enemy. Haruhiro watched as they laid eight corpses in front of him.

"The entire city is in chaos. We can't contact the Great Ironfist Gate," Rowen said, letting out a powerful snort. His eyes were bloodshot. "Our first order of business has to be securing lines of communication with the Great Ironfist Gate. Does the enemy have only one point of ingress, or several? How large is the force that's entered the city? There's much to do! If you want to survive, you people had better help!"

"You don't have to tell us that..."

Honestly, Haruhiro's head was already full thinking about how to get the iron king out through the Walter Gate. The Ironblood Kingdom would never be able to survive. The captain of the royal guard had rushed off to take command, and now he'd turned back after getting a bunch of his men killed. It was best to cut their losses early. Or rather, Haruhiro had already given the city up for lost.

At the same time, he could understand how Rowen felt. This mine shaft city was the dwarves' home—their motherland. It wasn't easy for them to accept that they probably couldn't defend it and they should cast it aside.

"You just need to know what's going on at the Great Ironfist Gate, right?"

As soon as the words left Haruhiro's mouth, Ranta tried to stop him.

"Whoa, Haruhiro, you're not gonna—"

"I'm going to head there alone. It'll be easier that way. We need someone to check if the Great Ironfist Gate has been breached either way."

"You're talking sense," Neal said, nodding sagely. "Okay. Haruhiro and I will both take separate routes to go check out the Great Ironfist Gate. We want to be sure about things, after all. I'll leave this with you, for safety's sake."

Neal produced something from his pocket, which he handed to Setora. It was the letter from Jin Mogis. *He's planning to run,* Haruhiro thought. That was just how Neal lived his life. Haruhiro couldn't blame him, and it really wasn't his place to.

"If you don't come back, we won't be waiting for you," Setora told Neal, her tone cold.

Neal smirked and shrugged his shoulders. "Wasn't expecting you to."

"This guy..." Kuzaku said with a sigh.

"Haru-kun!" Yume showed him a clenched fist, like she was saying, *Do your best.* Merry looked him in the eye and nodded.

"Make sure you come back alive," Rowen said, grabbing Haruhiro and Neal's shoulders. Maybe he thought he was just placing his hands on them lightly, but it kind of hurt. His hands and fingers were unusually thick and incredibly powerful.

"Be back soon," Haruhiro said, shaking free of Rowen's grip and turning to go. He jogged around the side of the barricade, then off down the main street. Neal was still following him.

The farther they got from the Great Iron King Gate, the thicker the smoke and the louder the gunshots. He could hear screaming dwarves. Haruhiro leaped over a dwarven corpse. It wasn't one of the royal guards or a red-beard. It was a man, naked from the waist up. Had he been working a forge when the attack came and taken up arms to defend the city, only to be shot? Maybe he had tried to flee then, making it this far before succumbing to his wounds. There were others like him lying all around, and not only bearded dwarven men. There were the bodies of dwarven women, built like particularly sturdy young human girls too. From the look of things, it wasn't half and half, but maybe a third of the fallen were women.

They'd be at the first major four-way intersection soon. Neal still hadn't separated from Haruhiro.

There was intense gunfire down the street on the right, and the gun smoke blew against him from that direction like a sudden gust of wind. It came mixed with the sound of shouts and cries of anguish.

"The enemy's already penetrated this far in?!" Neal said, but not to Haruhiro. He'd probably said it without meaning to.

Haruhiro turned down a side road. He let his consciousness sink. Stealth.

The shooting down the road to the right soon stopped.

There they were. The enemy. Yellowish-brown skin. Hunched backs and overdeveloped upper bodies.

Hethrangs.

They had guns. Were there ten of them? Twenty? No, more. Some had halberds instead, and their armor varied. Some wore chainmail, others bronze plate. He saw some hethrangs that were half-naked, with only helmets. They gathered in the middle of the intersection, seemingly trying to get into formation.

One hethrang stood out. His clothing was of the same design as Jumbo or Godo Agaja's. He swung his gun around and spoke with a deep, throaty voice.

It's Wabo, thought Haruhiro. He must have been the leader of the hethrangs. They were all shouting his name.

"Wabo!"

"Wabo!"

"Wabo!"

"Wabo!"

The Ironblood Kingdom had been using hethrangs as slave labor. They must have hated the dwarves and the iron king pretty badly. The unit of escaped hethrangs pushed up the main road, looking ready to launch an attack on the Iron Palace.

Neal was trying to slip between two buildings facing onto the main street. Haruhiro moved closer to the scout and grabbed his sleeve.

"The hell are you doing? Let go." Neal moved his lips, glaring at Haruhiro.

Haruhiro indicated the escaped hethrangs with his eyes, then looked back at the Iron Palace. *"Go back and tell the others about them. I'll check out the Great Ironfist Gate."*

"Why should I?"

"Just do it."

Haruhiro gave a strong tug on Neal's sleeve. The scout was surprisingly pliable. In the end, Neal turned back toward the Iron Palace, albeit reluctantly.

The ranks of the escaped hethrangs had swollen to about a hundred. It didn't look like any more were coming. Wabo fired his gun upward.

"We! Not hethrang! Clay dwarf!"

The hethrangs shouted in unison. "We! Clay dwarf!"

It sounded to Haruhiro like they were saying they weren't hethrangs, they were clay dwarves.

"Go, go, gooooo!"

The escaped hethrangs moved forward on Wabo's command. They were all basically running. What incredible momentum.

They probably couldn't break through the Great Iron King Gate. That said, both sides had guns. It would be a pretty intense battle, wouldn't it?

Haruhiro felt uneasy. He was worried for his comrades. But right now, even if he turned back, there wasn't much he could do.

Haruhiro turned right at the intersection. The gunshots never stopped ringing out from somewhere in the city. Haruhiro occasionally spotted dwarf men and women running around confused, carrying axes or swords. Many of them had already been shot. The enemy picked these dwarves off from a distance. He saw some go down—shot in the chest, back, or head—while other times the shots missed. Even when they were momentarily spared, though, if they stood around looking for the enemy who'd shot at them, another shot would come.

Some dwarves fled into buildings. When they did, the green-coated gumow rangers, orcs, or undead would rush inside after them. The royal guard and red-beards were having a pretty hard time locating the enemy, apparently. If the enemy shot at them, they returned fire. But by then, the enemy had scattered. Haruhiro watched one black-bearded dwarf go down to a hail of bolts and arrows. The enemy had archers and crossbowmen. It looked like there was close-quarters combat going on too. One orc, his head split half open and his entire body grievously wounded, was crawling along, soon to breathe his last.

There was a barricade in front of the large tunnel leading to the Great Ironfist Gate too. Dwarven and orcish corpses lay scattered around it, but there was no sign of an active battle there.

Haruhiro maintained his Stealth as he crept toward the barricade.

Someone poked their head out over the top.

An elf. Female? He'd had the impression that elves were fair-skinned. Not her, though. Her skin was tan—a light brown or golden color.

"Huh?" Haruhiro was flabbergasted. He'd been found. Somehow, the elf had noticed him. Haruhiro had thought his Stealth was in full effect, so it'd never occurred to him that someone might discover him. The elf looked him right in the eye.

"A human?!" the elf cried, instantly nocking an arrow. Haruhiro was scared to death, of course, but didn't lose his head. So long as he could see the archer, he might be able to dodge her arrows. But something was strange. The elven archer, she'd been quick to ready her bow, but not eager. Did she not want to shoot? That was the sense Haruhiro got.

It turned out he was right.

"Don't move," said a voice right beside him. It came from his left.

Haruhiro held his breath, moving just his eyes to look in that direction.

When did he get there? I didn't sense him at all.

Another elf had his knife pointed at Haruhiro. The edge of its blade touched Haruhiro's throat—only a little, but it still broke the skin.

This elf's skin was darker than the archer woman's. Gray. Could he be one of those gray elves? Haruhiro was confused. The gray elves, unlike the elves of the Shadow Forest who had sided with the humans and dwarves, had been on the No-Life King's side. They were enemies.

"Who are you?" the gray elf asked.

Haruhiro couldn't help but think, *I could ask you the same.*

"If I said I was with the Volunteer Soldier Corps...no, the Frontier Army...would you understand?"

If the elf wanted to, he could cut Haruhiro's throat in an instant. Haruhiro couldn't be too bold. Not that he was a particularly bold person to begin with.

"Erm, I think we're on the same side, sort of. Probably. Captain Rowen sent me to check how things looked at the Great Ironfist Gate, see. Uh, my name's Haruhiro, by the way."

"Tiebach," the archer woman called out to the gray elf, Tiebach presumably being his name. "You don't need to kill him. It sounds like he's on our side, more or less."

"Yes, Lady Rumeia," Tiebach said, withdrawing his knife. His yellowish eyes never left Haruhiro, though.

"Come, Haruhiro," the female elf whom Tiebach had called Rumeia beckoned Haruhiro.

Haruhiro did as instructed, walking around to the other side of the barricade. Tiebach did likewise. He stayed close to Haruhiro's back, making it readily apparent he was ready to kill the thief at a moment's notice. He probably wasn't even trying to hide that fact. Tiebach had a bow and quiver on his back, and also a thin sword on his hip, in addition to the knife in his hands. He seemed highly capable. Haruhiro likely wouldn't have stood a chance in a straight-up fight.

On the other side of the barricade, there were just ten red-bearded dwarves and about fifteen elven archers.

"I'm Rumeia of Arularolon," Rumeia said with a surprisingly friendly smile, offering her right hand. Her ears were long and pointy, and she was one of several elven archers here. She was an elf, but she wasn't very elf-y. And besides that, the way she was dressed, with just a thin cloth covering her breasts and another hanging around her hips, was indecent.

"Lady Rumeia is one of the Five Bows—the head of the House of Arularolon," Tiebach whispered.

Haruhiro took Rumeia's hand. She shook his hand firmly before letting go and giving him a friendly swat on the arm with her palm.

"I'm technically something like the captain of this unit of elven archers. Though Tiebach's the one who does all the stuff. Tiebach's amazing, you know? He's better at drawing a bow than me, and he can really shoot. Not many archers—even elven ones—can hit a bee in midair."

"Well, I'm not a pure-blooded elf," Tiebach said with a sigh. Rumeia winked.

"Maybe that's for the best, you know? I'd be good with it either way, though. An archer's just gotta be good with a bow, and besides, everyone's already accepted you for who you are, Tie. Or maybe I should say you made them accept you."

"Would you stop, Lady Rumeia?"

"It's nothing to get all bashful about."

"No, that's not the issue..." Tiebach looked at Haruhiro with upturned eyes.

"Oh, I see." Rumeia smiled. "We don't have time to shoot the breeze like this. What was it that you said, again? Rowen sent you to come look? Things are pretty bad in there, huh?"

"Well, yes, they are, but..."

Your lack of seriousness and generally casual attitude are pretty bad too. Haruhiro wanted to say that, but he held back. If he didn't stay on task, he was going to get caught in her groove.

"How is the situation at the Great Ironfist Gate?"

"Fort Halberd fell."

That seemed like a pretty serious development, but Rumeia sounded indifferent about it.

"We have two forts left. Fort Ax was always the toughest, and it's not gonna budge, but I dunno about Fort Greatsword. If they take that one, I'd say we're in big trouble. We elves have our swordsmen and shamans at Fort Greatsword too, so for that one I can't say it's not our problem, you know?"

You sure talk like it's not your problem. Haruhiro suppressed his urge to take a comedic jab at her for that.

"It would seem the enemy has launched a total offensive, like we thought," Tiebach commented.

"Oh, yes, they have. Yes, indeedy," Rumeia said, looking toward the large tunnel. She narrowed her eyes a little. Tiebach's long ears twitched too. "Tie," Rumeia said, addressing Tiebach.

"Yes," he responded briefly.

Rumeia slapped Haruhiro lightly on the upper arm and took off running. That probably meant *Follow me*. Did he have to? Well, the way things were going, it seemed like the only option.

Haruhiro chased after Rumeia. Footsteps echoed loudly in the large tunnel, which had watch fires here and there throughout. It wasn't just Haruhiro and Rumeia's steps either. There were dwarves shouting something. He could hear the high voices of women too.

Soon, the crisis at hand was made apparent. The Great Ironfist Gate was at the end of the tunnel, and there was a large crowd of dwarves amassed right in front of it. Some of them were cowering, and others had fallen. The smell of sweat and blood filled the air.

"What happened?!" Rumeia shouted.

"Fort Ax has fallen!" a dwarf responded angrily. "We need to take it back right away or we're in trouble!"

"Yikes." Rumeia came to a stop. Sighing, she bonked herself on the head repeatedly with her left hand. "That one, huh? My guess was off. They're the ones who fell first, huh? Well, that's not good."

"Harden our defenses in front of the gate!"

Was that a frontline commander? Someone was barking orders. There was shouting all over. The dwarves' morale hadn't broken yet, though. Having seen the way they were, Haruhiro figured they could probably fight a losing battle without getting dispirited. But even if they remained undefeated in their hearts, they'd still die if they got shot. Indomitable spirit could only make up for so much.

"Fire!" the frontline commander barked. A volley of gunshots sounded out. They must have come from the dwarves defending the Great Ironfist Gate. Which meant the enemy had to be attacking. Was that a proper read of the situation?

"Fire! Fire!"

The shots rang out one after another, practically without interruption. It was a deafening, earsplitting noise.

Rumeia pulled Haruhiro close to her to whisper in his ear. "I doubt we'll be able to hold them back! Hurry and let Rowen-san know!"

"What about you, Rumeia-san?!"

"Uh, I dunno, but I can't leave them, so I'll have to do what I can!"

The elves had evacuated to the Ironblood Kingdom after losing Arnotu in the Shadow Forest. They'd been taken in by the dwarves, whom you couldn't say they had ever gotten along with very well. They must have felt indebted, and unable to turn tail just because the tide of battle was going against them.

"Any message for Tiebach-san?!"

"I feel like he'll come this way on his own, so not really!"

"Got it! Take care!"

"You too! Until we meet again!" Rumeia smiled and waved.

Haruhiro started running down the large tunnel, back to where they'd come from. Along the way, he passed Tiebach and the elven archers. They didn't even spare a glance in his direction. Haruhiro decided not to distract them by calling out.

As he came out of the large tunnel, the dwarven gunners noticed Haruhiro and shouted, "How was it?!"

What was he supposed to say? Should he ignore them? Or should he lie? Should he try to gloss it over? Haruhiro couldn't do any of those things.

"Fort Ax has fallen! The enemy is attacking the Great Ironfist Gate!"

One dwarf slammed his gun against the barricade with a wail of despair. Haruhiro kind of wanted to apologize to the guy. Obviously, that wouldn't do anything to help, though.

Haruhiro went around the barricade and headed for the city. He came close to breaking into a full run, but that wouldn't do him any good. *Don't rush it,* he told himself. Sinking his consciousness, he went into Stealth once more.

He encountered the enemy as soon as he turned the first corner. But Haruhiro was in Stealth, creeping along the edge of the road, so they didn't seem to have noticed him. There were undead, orcs, and gray elves too. The undead standing at the front, his entire body wrapped in blackish leather or cloth, didn't have just one pair of arms. He had two. He was a four-armed undead—a double arm.

Haruhiro recalled there was an awfully skilled double arm in Forgan. *What was his name again? Oh, right.*

Arnold.

Undead were pretty hard to tell apart, and it had been quite some time since they'd met. Haruhiro didn't remember him clearly, but that double arm wielding four katanas looked familiar to him. Was it really Arnold?

The double arm that seemed to be Arnold was leading a unit of around thirty enemies. There was one orc at the very rear of their formation who was larger than the rest. That build. The deep-blue kimono with silver flowers. And the massive katana he carried over his shoulder with ease. There could be no doubt. It was Godo Agaja.

Arnold and Godo Agaja. Jumbo, Takasagi, and the goblin beastmaster Onsa didn't seem to be there, but this had to be an elite unit from Forgan. There was a hethrang with them too, right behind Arnold. Was he their guide?

Where was Arnold's unit heading? Haruhiro didn't have to ponder that one for long.

The Great Ironfist Gate.

They were going to attack the gate from behind. That was what Arnold and his team were aiming for.

There was a barricade in front of the large tunnel leading to the Great Ironfist Gate, and dwarven gunners manning it. But more than a dozen of Arnold's men had guns, so who knew if they could defend it.

It seemed kind of iffy. Haruhiro had a feeling they couldn't.

If Arnold and his unit got past the barricade, defending the Great Ironfist Gate would become awfully difficult. In the worst-case scenario, the dwarven forces might completely collapse in no time flat. If enemy forces were able to flood in all at once, the resulting chaos would make evacuating the iron king impossible.

Obviously, that was only the worst possible outcome. Maybe the dwarven gunners would be able to hold out. If they could call for reinforcements, Rumeia and the elven archers might come to their aid. Maybe then they'd be able to hold out for at least a little while.

Arnold's unit turned the corner one after another, heading toward the barricade. The enemy hadn't noticed Haruhiro yet. He could likely wait for them to pass him by. Was that okay? He needed to go back to the Iron Palace and tell Captain Rowen and his comrades about the situation. Someone else, not Haruhiro, would decide how to act on that information.

What if Haruhiro needed to make a decision right now?

Arnold and his unit were likely going to wipe out the dwarven gunners. That would put the Great Ironfist Gate under attack from both inside and out. However valiant their resistance might be, the dwarves and Rumeia's elves would fall one after another. No dwarf would surrender. No elf either, most likely. That was their decision. He couldn't do anything about it. It wasn't Haruhiro's problem.

Godo Agaja was about to round the corner. Haruhiro hid by the side of the road, holding his breath as he watched the massive orc go.

"Damn it..." he muttered.

Godo Agaja stopped.

Haruhiro regretted it, but it was too late. To be fair, he would have ended up regretting his decision no matter what he'd done. Whether he let Arnold and his men go or not.

Godo Agaja turned and instantly spotted Haruhiro.

"Agajjahh!"

That was Orcish. What had he said? Haruhiro had no clue, but Godo Agaja came at him brandishing his massive katana. The orc was awfully light on his feet, given his size. It was probably time for the thief to throw away any preconceptions he had about the limitations of that massive body.

Haruhiro started running. Godo Agaja's massive katana tore into the ground where he had been just a moment before. The sound it made was insane. It was like the carved stone floor had exploded. He had to flee.

Godo Agaja chased after Haruhiro. Would Arnold's unit fire at him? They shouldn't have been able to, with the giant orc in the way. Haruhiro was able to surmise that much, but that was about all the thinking he could manage at the moment.

He's fast.

Faster than I imagined.

No, unimaginably fast.

Godo Agaja's legs are incredibly powerful.

Haruhiro turned at every corner he could. Every time he went right or left, he pulled away a little more. But the straightaways were trouble. He wasn't getting away on those. The gap was actually closing.

Godo Agaja didn't waste his breath speaking. The way he didn't swing his massive katana around any more than absolutely necessary was worrying too. This orc knew his reach precisely. If he swung the katana and missed, that would delay his next chance to strike. That was why he was watching like a hawk for any opportunity. He meant to end this with the next stroke, guaranteed.

It was possible that Haruhiro had taken this too lightly.

Let the orc chase him for a while, then escape at the right moment. That was all Haruhiro had been thinking. He should have thought harder. He had to admit that to himself. Had he known the Ironblood Kingdom like the back of his hand, he might have been able to come up with something he could still do, but he only had a rough idea of what the area was like. The enemy was probably just as unfamiliar, but Godo Agaja wasn't his only pursuer.

"Cowahrd, nawyousrunyaway!"

He heard a voice to his left. Not Godo Agaja's. It was probably an undead.

Most of the dwarven workshops facing onto the street which doubled as homes were row-houses. An undead was dashing across their rooftops. The double arm with four katanas. Arnold. He was running essentially parallel to Haruhiro.

Haruhiro wished he could just let his eyes roll into the back of his head and pass out. He couldn't, though. Obviously. He knew that.

But this is just hopeless.

I'm screwed, aren't I?

What am I supposed to do in this situation?

Unfortunately, rack his brains though he might, no idea was coming. He didn't have the composure left for thinking. But perhaps he might or might not have had the vague notion that he should do the most unexpected thing possible and catch his pursuers off guard.

Haruhiro came to a sudden stop, then somersaulted backward—in the direction of Godo Agaja, obviously.

He wouldn't get cut. Probably. But he might get kicked away. Eating a kick from that orc wouldn't be something he could just shrug off. It was dangerous. But there were no safe choices to be had here anyway. Whatever he did, there was going to be some risk. It was a gamble. He wasn't fond of gambling, but he didn't have much choice now.

"Duowah?!" Godo Agaja exclaimed in surprise. Haruhiro didn't get kicked. The orc, perhaps instinctively, jumped over Haruhiro as he suddenly came rolling at him.

Haruhiro couldn't say this was "just as planned."

He'd gotten lucky. That was it, really.

Haruhiro got back on his feet, turned right, and took off. There were orcs, undead, gray elves, and hethrangs from Arnold's unit in that direction, all looking just as surprised as Godo Agaja. They had no idea what had just happened and had been thrown into confusion. Even so, charging would be suicide. He wouldn't do that. Obviously, he'd never do something so foolish.

Dwarves were shorter than humans, so the ceilings and roofs of their buildings were generally on the low side, perhaps even more so in a mine city like this. The roofs of the workshop houses on his left were especially low, maybe two meters high, if that. Haruhiro jumped and grabbed the edge of one, quickly pulling himself up. There were pipes sticking out of the roofs here and there that served as chimneys of a sort. They snaked around every which way, crawling across the roofs, connecting to other chimneys, or forking off in different directions as they ultimately headed toward the ceiling of the mine city.

Haruhiro weaved between the complex system of pipes as he ran. He leaped from roof to roof, dashing as fast as he could.

Five or six pursuers—a mix of orcs, undead, and gray elves—climbed up onto the roofs after him. Godo Agaja tried to do the same, but at his height his head would end up scraping the ceiling of the mine tunnel, so he gave up on that. It didn't stop him from running after Haruhiro along the road, though. Godo Agaja's head was higher than the roofs, so Haruhiro could easily see where he was. The orc wouldn't give up easily. But Haruhiro figured that now he could find a way to shake him somehow, along with the guys who'd climbed up top in pursuit of the thief.

The problem's Arnold. That double arm's bad news.

Arnold was behind Haruhiro, to his left. But only a little behind. They were almost neck-and-neck. Only about three meters separated them. That didn't feel like anything at all.

Arnold had two of his four katanas sheathed. He was still dual wielding, though. Who knew when he'd strike. Haruhiro was running with pretty much all his might, but Arnold looked like he still had strength in reserve.

He's coming.

Any moment now. I'm sure of it.

I'm screwed.

If Arnold struck first, he probably wouldn't be able to dodge.

"Ngh!" Haruhiro grunted as he drew his normal and flame daggers, then jumped from the roof.

Arnold followed without missing a beat. Haruhiro landed, and then he must have deflected Arnold's katanas with the flame dagger in his right hand and the other in his left. Or so he assumed. He didn't actually see it happen, though. Honestly, Haruhiro didn't even know how Arnold had swung, or from what position. He ran past him, fleeing.

"KYYYYYYYYYYYYYYYYYYYYYYYYYYYYYYYY," Arnold vented with a strange noise, still giving chase. Haruhiro wanted to flee into one of the workshops facing onto the street, but he didn't know anything about how they were designed. If there was no back door, he'd be like a rat in a trap.

He couldn't help but blame himself. It had been so obvious this would happen, so why couldn't he have just left well enough alone? Was he stupid? *Yeah, I must be,* he had to conclude. But not only was he stupid, he kept on getting dumber.

Haruhiro was just running around, turning corners at random, at this point. He wasn't headed anywhere. He simply did whatever seemed like it would work. When he got back up on the roof again, it was only because it felt like the thing to do at the time. He'd just gotten the vague feeling, *If I don't get up on the roof now, I'm gonna get slashed.* The chimney pipes spread out in front of him like spiderwebs, and it didn't seem like he could get through. That he managed to force his way between them to the other side without getting stuck was a complete fluke.

Arnold must have decided he couldn't squeeze through, and he took a short detour around. That bought Haruhiro some distance, but, yeah, it was pure luck. Wasn't there anything he could do now that he had some room to work with? It wasn't like he hadn't thought about that. But it was impossible. His only option was to run for his life. Nothing else.

I mean, I don't even know where I am.

At the very least, he was *trying* to head toward the Iron Palace. Was that a good idea, or a bad one? It probably wasn't all that great. He'd be bringing the enemy—Arnold, Godo Agaja, and their men—to the Iron Palace, after all.

The thought, *Maybe I should just let him cut me down*, went through his head.

No, why would I do that?

If I get cut down, I'll die.

I don't wanna die. Or rather, I can't afford to. I can't die without my comrades around. I wanna see Merry. I don't wanna make her sad. But it's not just about Merry. I've got so many reasons I can't die.

Still, it was impressive he hadn't run out of breath. Wait, he hadn't? Seriously? Was Haruhiro really still breathing? Maybe he'd already stopped.

He couldn't see well through his sweat. If he was sweating, did that mean he was alive?

It had to. Yeah, of course it did. Haruhiro's body was still moving. How was his body moving? That was a mystery at this point.

Haruhiro had reached the limit of his ability to run while dodging chimney pipes. He rolled and got down off the roof as if he were falling. When he landed on the carved stone floor, his knees and ankles must have failed to absorb the impact or something because he ended up pitching forward. Haruhiro couldn't catch himself. He tried, but failed. As he was falling, he realized Arnold was closing in on him. He didn't so much see the double arm as sense him, though. However he knew, it was right at the edge of his perception.

I'm gonna get slashed, he thought.

Haruhiro wanted to use his momentum to roll and get back on his feet so he could flee. But would he be able to run? He wasn't confident of that.

"Hahhhhhhhh!"

So he should've gotten slashed.

Yet, despite that, Haruhiro heard Ranta's voice.

Ranta? Why Ranta?

"Huh?"

Haruhiro would have loved to jump to his feet, but he was still lying where he'd fallen. He wanted to take a breath first. Or did he need to exhale? He didn't know how to breathe anymore. That, or maybe his respiratory system was busted.

It hurt, of course.

It had been hurting so much all this time, and yet, strangely, now it didn't hurt quite so much.

He felt sleepy. No, this was something else. Maybe he was losing consciousness? He wouldn't have minded passing out, really. He almost felt like he wanted to.

"Rueahhh! Keyahhh! Surahhh! Fiyahhh! Tsohhh!"

But Ranta was too noisy.

What was with those shouts?

Was he fighting?

Yeah.

Ranta was trading blows with Arnold.

Why would Ranta be doing that?

Haruhiro didn't know.

Was he hallucinating?

Even if he'd wanted to check, he couldn't. His vision was blurry. What was going on?

"Ahhh!"

Haruhiro rubbed his cheeks with both hands.

I can't breathe? Yeah, right. Breathe in, then out. Breathe out, then in. Then breathe out again. Just repeat that, over and over. I can do it. It just hurts, that's all.

As he endured the pain, breathing became easier. He got ahold of his slipping consciousness and pulled it back to him. Haruhiro forced himself to sit up.

Ranta.

Ranta was leaping to and fro around Arnold. He was using the style particular to dread knights, or to Ranta at least, where he moved like a small woodland creature, or perhaps a grasshopper, trying to get behind Arnold. Arnold was using his four katanas to keep Ranta in check and prevent that. However, Ranta would dodge at the last possible second, or turn Arnold's katanas aside using his own, as he doggedly aimed for the double arm's back. That was why it looked like Ranta was jumping around near Arnold.

A double arm's extra pair of limbs weren't just decorative.

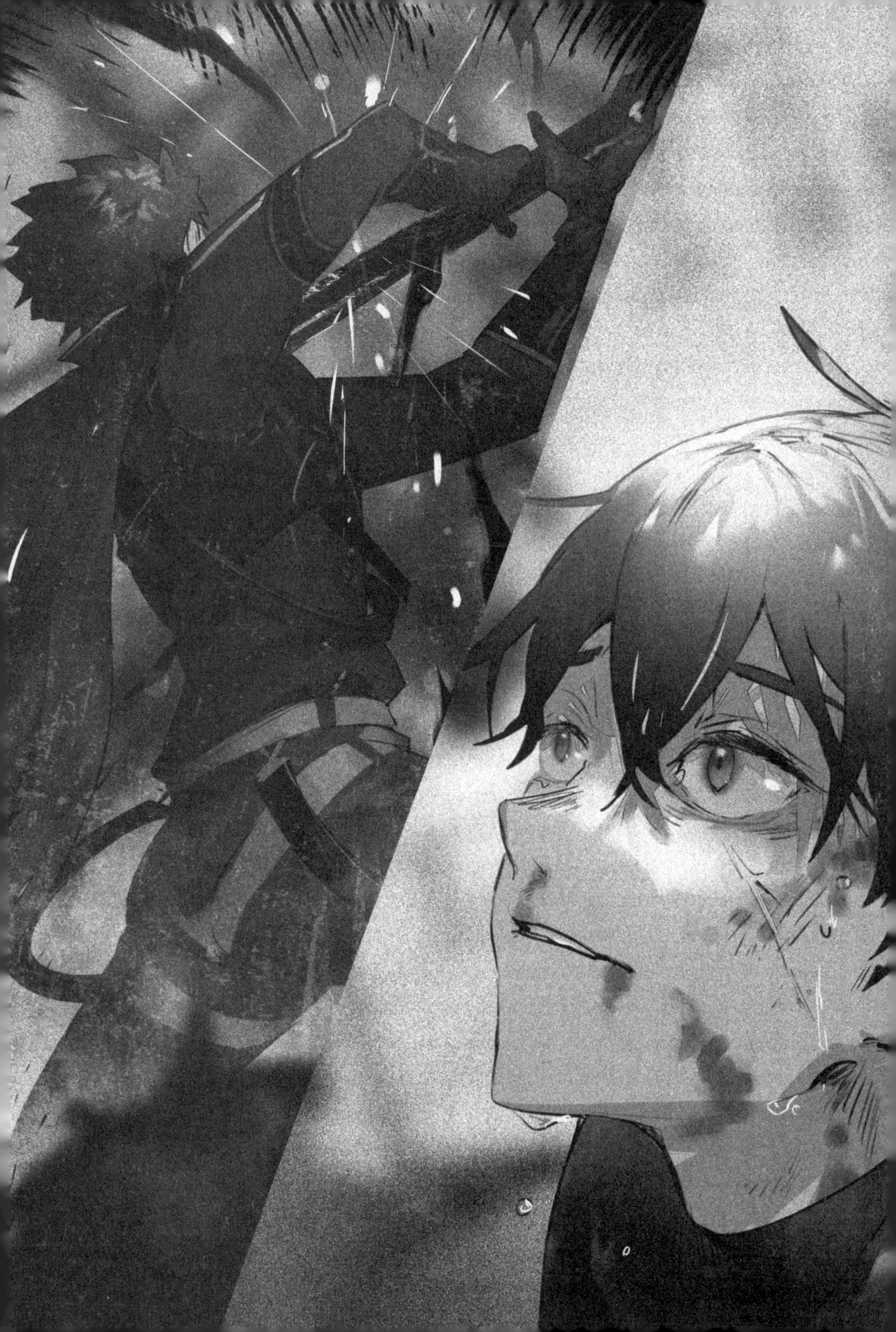

The only place that Arnold's katanas couldn't reach was a very narrow area behind him. Ranta knew that, and was solely seeking to attack that weak point.

Arnold had to be aware of his weaknesses too. He was focused entirely on fending off Ranta's attacks now.

"Ranta..."

Go for it.

All Haruhiro could do now was cheer him on. His body still wasn't moving properly, so if he carelessly tried to get involved he might just get in Ranta's way.

Ranta was focused. His moves toward Arnold's back constantly got faster and sharper. More specifically, every time Ranta stepped in, it was with larger strides that took him deeper.

Arnold, on the other hand, was barely moving. No, he couldn't move. Ranta was slowly closing the net around him. All Arnold could do was turn and swing now. Ranta had the double arm on the ropes. That was how it looked.

But they're just getting started.

Haruhiro had seen Arnold fight. The double arm got stronger when he was pushed into a corner.

"Careful, Ranta!"

Ranta didn't need Haruhiro to tell him that. But the thief couldn't help himself.

Ranta darted in like a flash of light. Arnold moved, deliberately no doubt, to stand right in front of him. He caught the dread knight's katana with two of his own, then struck back with the other two. It was a move only a double arm could execute.

"Personal Skill!" Ranta's katana arched upward from the bottom right. "Flying Lightning God!"

No, that's not it.

For an instant, Ranta's katana seemed to vanish. The next thing Haruhiro knew, the dread knight was holding his weapon in two hands. For a thrust?

That's the stance for a thrust.

"Hk!"

Arnold tried to back away. Ranta's blade thrust after him, driven by both the dread knight's hands. And not just once. Arnold was twisting, deflecting with his katanas, and doing whatever else he could to evade Ranta's flurry of attacks. The double arm had managed to avoid any direct hits, but the black leather, or cloth, or whatever it was Arnold had wrapped around him was getting torn up as bits and pieces were cut off. Black lacerations were carved into the ashen skin underneath.

Ranta was pushing him back.

Please, keep pushing. Haruhiro would have been lying if he'd said he didn't wish that. He hoped for it, but he didn't think Ranta had won yet. Their enemy wasn't that weak.

"Whuh?!"

Ranta's katana was knocked back. It was like Arnold had suddenly turned into a whirlwind as he jumped while spinning.

Had Ranta seen it coming? He instantly did a backflip diagonally to his rear. He then followed it up with a rapid series of steps, taking him farther away from Arnold.

"AAAAAAAAAAAAAAHHHHHHHHHHHHHH,"

Arnold bellowed, rearing back. His four arms and their four katanas reached out, stretching as far as they could—way too far, in fact. It gave Haruhiro goosebumps.

"You're *finally* getting serious, huh?!"

Ranta laughed. It was amazing he still could, even if it was just a bluff. The man had incredible guts. Not that Haruhiro would try to learn from his example. He couldn't have imitated that if he'd tried.

"O Darkness, O Lord of Vice, Demon Call!"

Even Ranta, stout-hearted as he was, must have been feeling intimidated. Something like a blackish-purple cloud appeared and formed a vortex. The maelstrom rapidly solidified into the demon Zodie.

Thanks to all the vice Ranta had accrued, the demon's appearance was now different from how it used to be long ago, though the similarities were there. Zodie wore a suit of armor that seemed to have been made by scraping together dark purple bones, and they carried a long-handled scythe in both hands. Haruhiro was shocked. Zodiac-kun had been kind of cute, but now the demon was something else entirely. If the Dark God Skullhell led his forces into battle, the soldiers would probably look like Zodie.

"Sic 'im, Zodie!" Ranta sent his demon after the enemy.

"Eh heh heh heh heh heh heh heh heh heh heh heh heh heh heh heh heh heh heh heh heh heh heh!" Zodie the demon raced at Arnold, scythe held back, ready to swing.

It was two on one now. When things got tough, dread knights always had this trick up their sleeve.

"KOOOOOOOOOOOHHHHHHHHHHHHHHH."

Arnold unleashed his full power as a double arm, as if to say, *So what?* He was like an arrow loosed from a bow drawn back as far as it could go. Four katanas swung at Zodie from four different directions. But it didn't look like that to Haruhiro. No, to him it seemed the four blades had become one surging wave that engulfed the demon.

Whatever had happened, Zodie got hit with all four blades. But the demon didn't dissipate immediately. Zodie was like a wooden training dummy. They didn't move, and you could ram as many swords through them as you liked, but cutting them in two wasn't easy.

Arnold probably had the strength to do it, though. Zodie was going to get sliced and diced soon. It was just a demon, after all. It didn't have the skill to fight someone as experienced as Arnold.

"Eh... Heh heh..."

"NNNNNNG?!"

Arnold, however, didn't mince Zodie. Instead he froze, stock-still.

"Personal Skill!"

It was Ranta.

What had he been doing since sending in his demon? Haruhiro had been so distracted by Zodie, he hadn't noticed. But that was exactly what Ranta had been aiming for.

He'd used Demon Call, turning it into a two-on-one fight. His next move would be to execute a skillful series of combo attacks with Zodie and overcome their powerful opponent.

No.

That wasn't Ranta's plan at all.

"Deviously Evil! All-in-One Slaaaash!"

Ranta slammed into Zodie's back. But obviously, that wasn't all. *His katana.* His katana was stabbing through Zodie. He'd impaled the demon. Ranta's katana went through Zodie to Arnold on the other side. Ranta held the hilt at waist height, thrusting upward diagonally. The tip of the blade was under Arnold's jaw.

"But that's not really a slash, is it?" Haruhiro couldn't help but quip.

"Shaddup!"

With that, Ranta pulled his katana out, and it disappeared in a flash, moving faster than Haruhiro's eyes could follow.

Zodie crumbled to pieces.

Ranta raced past Arnold's side, falling to one knee.

He'd cut the undead—or had he?

It seemed so.

Arnold's severed head fell, spinning slowly as it did.

His now-headless body didn't go down, though. In fact, it looked more like it might turn and keep attacking.

It was a strange, disgusting sight, and a horrifying moment. Multiple competing feelings and thoughts left Haruhiro a bit confused. It seemed Ranta had saved him. But Arnold wasn't just a simple enemy to Ranta, was he? Besides, he was an undead. Was that enough to kill him?

Haruhiro saw Arnold's severed head opening and closing its mouth. It had no voice, but it was moving.

"That's the thing about the undead..." Ranta said as he stood up.

He walked toward Arnold's body, which was still standing. Using his left hand, the one not holding his katana, Ranta gave the body a push. Not a violent one. Just a nudge. Arnold's body finally keeled over.

"So long as you leave their head intact, they can recover."

Ranta rested the flat side of his katana's blade on his right shoulder and cocked his head.

Arnold's severed head looked up at Ranta.

"Ranta..."

Haruhiro tried calling out to him. But what was he supposed to say? Honestly, he had no idea. Or rather, he ought to leave this to Ranta. Whatever the dread knight chose to do, Haruhiro had no right to decide if it was right or not.

"This is war. I'm sure you understand, right, Arnold?"

Ranta narrowed his left eye and raised the right side of his lips to form an expression Haruhiro couldn't have made if he'd tried.

"The Friendly Fire Slash. That's the killer move I've secretly been working on to use against old man Takasagi. I used you to practice it. Looks like I win this one."

Arnold's severed head opened its mouth. It moved its jaw. Was it trying to smile?

"So long."

Ranta switched his katana to a backhand grip and stabbed it into Arnold's forehead.

What was death like for the undead? Haruhiro didn't know. But if the undead had life in them, then this one's had just been extinguished. Ranta had just rendered Arnold inanimate with his own hands.

Ranta took the mask he'd been wearing on the back of his head and laid it on top of Arnold's.

"You're okay with this?"

That was a really vague question, Haruhiro thought after asking it.

"Yeah." Ranta nodded. Then, suddenly remembering something, he turned to look behind him. Haruhiro looked in the same direction. There was a rumble that threatened to drown out the gunshots echoing from around the city, and it was coming straight toward them.

"Godo Agaja?!" Ranta grabbed Haruhiro by the arm. "Let's go! I may be a badass, but that guy's way too dangerous! I can't even imagine how I'd kill him!"

"Wait, what are you even doing here?!" Haruhiro asked as they ran. Ranta was racing so fast he was threatening to leave Haruhiro behind.

"They've already left the Iron Palace! You were being slow and not coming back! So I came looking for you! You better be grateful!"

"Where is everyone?!"

"They went on ahead to the Bratsod mansion!"

"So they're okay, then?!"

"You're the one who wasn't okay, dumbass!"

"Yeah, sure, but...!"

Haruhiro suppressed the urge to argue and started pumping his legs. His stamina hadn't recovered yet, so he was sure to get winded in no time. Following Ranta was all he could manage. This was going to be hell. He didn't even want to think about what would come next. He had to, though.

Merry. She must be worried about me. I need to hurry and reassure her.

Anyway, he was going to be able to see his comrades again. All he could do now was draw on that motivation and run.

Grimgar of Fantasy and Ash

15. HATE THE WORLD

Yume, Merry, Setora, Kuzaku, and even Itsukushima and Neal were waiting for them in front of the Bratsod residence.

"Haruhiro!" Kuzaku shouted, hugging him.

"Uhhh..." It was a bit annoying, but Haruhiro wouldn't have felt right pushing the guy away. "Yeah..." He patted Kuzaku's way-too-broad back and put up with the embrace for a little while.

In all honesty, if he was going to share a hug with someone to celebrate his survival, he really would have preferred Merry. Obviously, he couldn't do that in front of everyone. But did she feel the same way? Based on the look she was giving Haruhiro, she probably did.

"Thought you'd be okay, but still, thank goodness." Yume put a hand over her chest and sighed.

Ranta rubbed his nose with his thumb, trying to act cool. "Heh. And he's got me to thank for it!"

"Mew. Y'think so?"

Much as it galled him to admit it, it was the truth. Haruhiro was going to have to accept it. "Well, yeah..."

"Pah! I deserve more than a 'well, yeah,' Crapu-piro! It oughta be, 'Thank you so very much, I swear I'll be grateful until the day I die, oh great and mighty Ranta,' and you know it!"

"It's because you act like this..."

"'Cause I act like what?!"

Axbeld, the red-bearded minister of the left, had managed with great difficulty to persuade Rowen, the black-bearded captain of the royal guard, to let him take the Red Beards from the Iron Palace to the Great Ironfist Gate.

The minister of the left planned to absorb any surviving dwarven units and townsfolk they encountered along the way, and then defend the gate to the death. The hope was that they might even be able to strike out from the Great Ironfist Gate, break through the enemy encirclement, and escape.

Haruhiro could only pray the gate hadn't fallen. It was kind of why he'd drawn Arnold and his unit into that chase. If Axbeld and his dwarves could make it to the Great Ironfist Gate, maybe Haruhiro could convince himself that all that running for his life had been worth it.

The group headed to the warehouse where the iron king and her retinue, Captain of the Royal Guard Rowen, old Utefan the guide, the members of the House of Bratsod, Elder Harumerial of the elves, and Eltalihi of the House of Mercurian had already gathered.

"You're late!" Rowen roared at Haruhiro the moment he saw the thief. The dwarf was really agitated. Or it might have been that he was dissatisfied with being the one who defended the iron king during her flight while the minister of the left remained in the Ironblood Kingdom.

"Rowen." The iron king was clad in armor, a helmet, and a cloak, hiding her face. However, the voice that rebuked the captain of the royal guard was unquestionably that of the king. The way her silver hair sparkled as it spilled out of her helmet was unreal. "Now, let us be on our way."

Once the iron king said that, the members of the House of Bratsod began opening the iron door. They and old Utefan led the way, with Rowen, the iron king and her retinue, Harumerial the elven elder, Eltalihi Mercurian, and Haruhiro's group following behind them in that order as they proceeded along the passageway toward the Walter Gate.

"What about Gottheld-san?" Haruhiro asked, but Itsukushima shook his head.

"He went with the minister of the left."

"Oh... Well, it's impressive that you managed to at least persuade the king. I had a feeling she'd be pretty reluctant to do this."

"She must've decided she doesn't want to die," Neal said with a cynical smile. Kuzaku scowled at him.

"I dunno that you should be lumping her together with someone like you..."

"We *are* the same, though, aren't we? What's so different?"

"Lots. Obviously."

"Whether it's me or the dwarven queen, once we bite it, that's the end. No difference between us. Yeah, I know you people wouldn't give a crap if I died. But this is the only life I've got."

"Well, I guess you should take good care of it, then, huh?"

"That's what I'm doing. Don't need you to tell me to."

"Yeah, go figure."

"Mark my words. I'm gonna survive, even if every last one of you dies."

"That's the kind of line a guy who's gonna die says, you know?" Ranta smirked.

Neal laughed it off. "Here's a tip; speaking from experience here. It doesn't matter what I say. It's what I do that'll decide whether or not I survive."

Setora nodded with no particular expression on her face. "An opinion worth heeding."

"I know, right?" Neal smirked. Then, lowering his eyes, he let out a sigh. "What *do* I do, though? That's the one thing I have to think about. If I hadn't kept trying too hard at my job under Mogis, I'd never've ended up in this jam. I should've slacked off a bit. But it was all I could do at the time. I'm not making a mistake. I've been doing well. Yeah. That's why I haven't ended up like Bikki. Screw dying. At least until I can say I was glad to be alive…"

He was mumbling something to himself. It seemed Neal was feeling pushed into a corner.

The delegation's original mission had been to deliver Jin Mogis's letter to the iron king, negotiate with her, and then return with the results. It was always going to be a long road, even if all they did was go and come back. There was always the possibility that negotiations would break down and it would be all for nothing too. Haruhiro had been prepared for that sort of difficulty. But maybe his read on the situation had been too naive? He'd never imagined the journey would be so harsh.

The group walked along the stone corridor reinforced with iron. There were lanterns in alcoves carved into the walls, so they had no need to carry lights of their own.

"Mungh..." Yume groaned.

"What's up?" Ranta asked her.

"Hmm? What's up? Somethin' is..."

Yume kept twisting her head in different directions. Was something bothering her?

There were iron doors here and there along the passageway. The group would open one, pass through, and then close them again before moving onward.

Were they missing something? Haruhiro lacked Yume's perception, but he was getting a weird feeling too. Given how bad things had gotten, they'd probably made tons of mistakes. Were any of those faults or failures ones that he ought to be thinking about now, while he had the chance?

Merry was walking beside Haruhiro. He looked at her face in profile and noticed her eyes were wide and focused up ahead of them.

Haruhiro tried to call out to her. But for whatever reason, he couldn't do it.

Old Utefan pounded on the last iron door. The old white-bearded dwarf looked ancient and walked with a staff, although for some reason, his staff seemed unusually heavy. It was made of metal, and its head bulged out like a hammer. He was rapping hard on the metal door with the end of it now, making an incredible racket.

The iron door began to open. That was presumably the work of the dwarven guards on the other side.

As they were passing through, Captain Rowen asked the guard, "Anything amiss?"

"Nothing."

"I see. Keep up the good work." Rowen clapped the guard dwarf on the shoulder, causing the man to stumble a little.

The group passed through a limestone cave and exited through the Walter Gate. Haruhiro looked up to see what was going on in the watch stations, picking out dwarves who were poking their heads out of the rock huts. One of them came down from his post. It was Willich, the dwarf with the evil countenance.

"Your Majesty..."

Willich was about to kneel down before the iron king, but the king stopped him.

"That will not be necessary."

"Yes, ma'am," Willich responded, not dropping to one knee but still lowering his head. "We will seal the Walter Gate at once. Please, hasten away from here."

"You are to follow us once you finish sealing the gate. We need as many people with us as possible."

"Yes, ma'am."

Willich waved to the others, and dwarves began coming out of the rock huts one after another. They headed to the Walter Gate and were presumably going to make sure it would never open again.

"We'll want to buy as much of a lead as possible by sunset," Setora murmured. Being underground for so long had messed with their sense of time a little, but there were probably still a couple hours before the sundown.

The former mine city on Mount Spear was supposed to be about a hundred kilometers east of the Kurogane Mountain Range. That was strictly as the crow flew, however. Besides, the Walter Gate was on the west side of the Kuroganes. That was going to add several dozen kilometers to the actual distance they'd be traveling. The forests in the foothills of the Kurogane Range were Southern Expedition territory, so their route would probably have to take them through the mountains too.

"This is gonna be rough..." Neal grumbled with a sigh.

Honestly, Haruhiro felt the same, but in for a penny, in for a pound. Once they had escorted the iron king to the former mine city on Mount Spear, then they could either head back to Alterna or visit the free city of Vele. If he remembered correctly, Mount Spear was maybe seventy or eighty kilometers from Vele. The free city was supposedly neutral, but they had ties to the K&K Pirate Company. The party could rest there awhile. Depending on how things went, they might be safer not returning to Alterna and staying in Vele instead. No, that wasn't an option. They needed to do something about Shihoru, and Haruhiro was still worried about the Volunteer Soldier Corps.

Anyway, for now, we have to get to Mount Spear.

The group was marching single file through the gaps in the massive rocks. Haruhiro and the party went along with them.

As they were descending along a mountain stream, Haruhiro noticed Itsukushima was looking around an awful lot. Yume was frowning too, or rather puffing up her cheeks one at a time as she looked this way and that.

"Poochie?" Merry furrowed her brow as she said the wolf-dog's name.

"Yeah." Yume nodded. "Poochie's supposed to be around here, waitin' for Yume and Master. He oughta notice us and be comin' along any moment now, though."

"Well, I'm sure he'll find us in good time," Itsukushima said, but it sounded more like he was trying to reassure himself. It wasn't like him.

Haruhiro turned to look back. The broken rocks that had, in a way, served as a landmark for the Walter Gate were no longer visible from here.

Though these were wetlands, there were rocky areas along the river, and two people could walk across them side by side. As long as they didn't spread out, they could avoid having to step into the running water, which was preferable even if it was shallow.

The area on the left side of the mountain stream was relatively flat, while on the right was a sheer cliff.

"Haruhiro?" Kuzaku called his name.

"Yeah," Haruhiro responded vaguely.

The group was still descending along the mountain stream. Haruhiro was the only one not moving.

"Is something bothering you?" Setora asked, stopping as well and looking up at the sheer cliff on the right. Merry, Kuzaku, Ranta, Yume, Itsukushima, and even Neal stopped too.

"Hey, wait up!" Ranta yelled after the rest of the group. The iron king turned back, and the rest of them stopped too.

"What is it?!" Captain Rowen demanded.

Haruhiro quickly exchanged glances with each of his comrades. They more or less understood him without having to talk it over. "I'm going up top to have a look, just to be safe," he told Rowen, pointing to the cliff on the right.

"Be quick about it," the dwarf said. Then, turning to his men, he instructed them, "Everyone, remain alert!"

Rowen was an impatient man, but he was no fool. Itsukushima joined Haruhiro as he headed toward the cliff.

"I'll go too," he offered.

"That'd help."

Itsukushima probably sensed something too, and feared the worst. The two of them wouldn't have to go back up the stream. They could clamber up the side of the cliff directly. Itsukushima reached the rock face first. Haruhiro took a deep breath, then looked up to the top. That was when it happened.

"Osh!" "Osh!" "Osh!" "Osh!" "Osh!"

"Orcs?!"

Haruhiro saw someone jump off the cliff.

"Ooooooooooshhhhhhhhhhh!"

White hair streaming behind him and a sword held in each hand. He knew that orc. There had been a unit holding Mount Grief with a mixed force of orcs, undead, and kobolds. He was their commander—Zan Dogran.

"Damn!"

When he heard Kuzaku cursing, Haruhiro got the chills. Even Renji had struggled against Zan Dogran, despite having the relic Aragarfald. They were in trouble now, weren't they?

"Kuza—"

"Ngohhh!"

Kuzaku instinctively drew his large katana and went to intercept Zan Dogran. Was he trying to slash the orc as he fell?

"Zweagh?!"

Then, for some reason, though Haruhiro couldn't be sure what because his eyes hadn't been able to catch it, Kuzaku got sent flying by the orc. He collapsed into the river.

"Personal Skill!"

Not missing a beat, Ranta took a swing at Zan Dogran—or made it look like he was going to before suddenly coming to a stop right in front of the orc and quickly lowering his stance. Lower than a crouch. It must have made it look like Ranta had up and disappeared. This was particularly effective against a large orc like Zan Dogran. Or it should have been, but no dice. It wasn't going to work, huh?

Zan Dogran swung the one-edged sword in his left hand. He was clearly aiming at Ranta.

"Tch!"

Ranta did a frog-like jump to the side to get out of the way, but Zan Dogran's right-hand sword was swinging at where the dread knight was trying to escape to.

"Whoa!"

He got him.

It was like Ranta was cut in half, then hastily stuck back together. No, obviously that wasn't what happened. It had only *looked* like the dread knight had been cut. Ranta had actually managed to avoid it somehow.

"Osh!" "Osh!"

"Osh!" "Osh!" "Osh!"

"Osh!" "Osh!" "Osh!" "Osh!"

"Osh!" "Osh!" "Osh!" "Osh!" "Osh!"

The orcs, with their hair bleached white and carrying one-handed swords with single serrated edges, raced down the cliff one after another. Some of them were sliding down. And it wasn't just orcs. The undead who had likely followed Zan Dogran here from Mount Grief were with them too.

"Master!" Yume shouted.

Itsukushima beat a hasty retreat, and Haruhiro backed away too. If they didn't hurry, they'd be swallowed up in the oncoming wave of orcs and undead.

"Dwarves!" Captain Rowen drew his greatsword and came

at Zan Dogran swinging. "We'll hold them back! Please escape, Your Majesty!"

Of the members of the House of Bratsod, maybe half were armed with guns, axes, and polearms. Ten or so dwarves pointed their guns at the top of the cliff, while the remaining ten were bunching up around old Utefan, the iron king, and the elves as they tried to continue down the mountain stream.

"Hurrrrgh!" Rowen swung his greatsword down diagonally. Zan Dogran backed away, stumbling. The captain of the royal guard's sword tore into the ground, sending stones and water flying in a wide radius. Zan Dogran disregarded that and tried to close in on the dwarf, but, incredibly, Rowen went and headbutted the orc.

"Nugh?!"

Zan staggered back after taking Rowen's headbutt to the chest. Rowen did a nearly vertical spin with his body as he followed up with a swing of his greatsword. Not able to take it, Zan Dogran jumped and rolled, managing to get away from the horrifying slash somehow.

No, there was no escape. Rowen kept after Zan Dogran, swinging again and again.

It would have been hyperbole to say that Captain Rowen's greatsword was as long as he was tall, but if you included the hilt in your measurement, it was pretty close. Even Kuzaku—and possibly even some of the orcs, who were larger than humans—might have struggled to wield such a blade. Rowen swung that monster blade around with both hands, and sometimes just his right hand, as if it were light. Despite being fully clad in glossy black armor, the dwarf remained nimble and even flexible. His sword reached out like it was alive, pressing its incessant attack against Zan Dogran.

"Urff! Orgh!"

Zan Dogran had been forced entirely on the defensive. Rowen was overwhelming him.

The orcs and undead hadn't seen this coming, had they? Zan Dogran's feats of martial prowess had stood out during the battle of the old castle on Mount Grief. Surely his men worshiped him as some sort of god of battle. Now he was being pushed back by a dwarf. That had clearly unnerved his soldiers.

"Fire!"

At that moment, the House of Bratsod's dwarven gunners fired a volley. The sound of even just ten guns was nothing to make light of. Furthermore, this enemy unit, having come here from Mount Grief, wasn't yet used to the sound of gunfire. Only three or four of them, possibly even just one or two, had actually been hit, and yet it was clear to see they were ready to run away.

"Haruhirooo!"

"Yeah!"

Haruhiro didn't need Ranta to signal him. The party followed the fleeing iron king. Setora had already helped Kuzaku up, so he was fine. Neal was nowhere to be seen, but Itsukushima and Yume were next to them. Merry was in front of Yume. Or rather, Yume had probably let Merry go ahead of her.

"Diiiiiiiiieeeeeeeiiiiii!"

Something changed about Zan Dogran. His hair stood on end, and his whole body crackled with something like static electricity. He'd been like that when trading blows with Renji too. His twin swords were pretty hefty, but he would swing them around like sticks when in this state.

"Gah! Urgh?!"

In no time, it was Rowen who was on the defensive. Though, defend as he might, was there any way to fend off Zan Dogran's twin swords when they swung down on him this fast and full of fury, too quick for the eye to follow? There was no time to worry about the captain of the guard, though. Once Zan Dogran turned the tables, the enemy quickly regained their vigor. Ranta jumped out and cut down one of the white-haired orcs who had been ignoring the House of Bratsod's gunners to chase after them.

"Aw, yeah!"

There was another one coming. A different white-haired orc. Haruhiro immediately planted a kick on its knee, struck its chin with the palm of his left hand, and almost simultaneously stabbed his right-hand dagger, which he was holding with a backhand grip, through the orc's heart. Once he pushed the orc away and tore his weapon free, an undead sprang at him. Dodging, he got behind it, then used Spider. He grappled the undead, slitting its throat with a twist of his dagger.

"Ranta!"

"Yeah, I know!"

He didn't want to get bogged down and cut off from their comrades. Much as he hated to leave them, Rowen and the

Bratsods were going to have to stand their ground on their own. But they were up against Zan Dogran. Could they hold out? He didn't know. Zan Dogran's unit was supposed to have anywhere from several hundred to a thousand guys. The dwarves were beyond outnumbered. Even if the dwarves had guns, it wasn't going to make much difference. They needed to run. It was the only option.

They'd been found out. The Southern Expedition had known where the Walter Gate was. Come to think of it, Itsukushima and Yume had been worried about some tracks that weren't from a four-legged creature, which must have been left by the enemy. The Southern Expedition had probably deployed Zan Dogran and his unit at the Walter Gate once he joined up with the main force, then launched a general offensive. In short, their escape had already been cut off from the start. They were like rats in a trap.

They continued down the mountain stream. The footing here was awful, the rocks often shifting or crumbling under their feet. Merry nearly tripped, but Yume caught her.

"Sorry!"

"Meow!"

The iron king was out of sight. It seemed she'd made it all the way down the mountain stream and into the forest on the right. Kuzaku, Setora, Itsukushima, Yume, and Merry followed. Neal was gone. Where to? Had he run off? When? And how? That man's ability to run away, to just outright disappear, was the one genuine thing about him.

Haruhiro and Ranta entered the forest. This wasn't a path they'd taken on the way here. Was it a path at all? Maybe the iron king's group had deliberately chosen to chart a new course for their flight.

Either way, all the party could do was follow along. Haruhiro honestly didn't know which way was which at this point. He kept turning to look behind him, checking for enemies. Unfortunately, they hadn't managed to shake their pursuers. He sensed danger not just to the rear, but on the left and right too. Were there enemies scattered all around them now? He spotted orcs and undead here and there, only to lose track of them again.

The forest. This wasn't just a forest. It was a sea of trees. Trunks and roots twisted and intertwined, creating swells and depressions. In some places there seemed to be deep fissures too. Still, this wasn't a problem only for the people fleeing. It had to be just as difficult for the ones hunting them. This wasn't like running across flat ground. It forced them to duck and weave, climbing sometimes, jumping over things at others, using a variety of postures and moves.

It was especially hard on the short dwarves. The iron king, who had her face hidden behind a helmet, was silently jumping from root to root, grabbing on to and clambering up tree trunks, but you couldn't have called her moves graceful, not even if you were trying to be nice.

Yume gazed upward. Was she looking at the sky through the branches?

"Is something up there?" Itsukushima asked Yume.

Yume shook her head. "Mmm, just now, it felt like there was a big bird flyin' by."

"A bird..." Ranta mumbled, looking around.

"Personal Skill..."

Whose voice was that? Above. It came from above.

It's coming down. What? From up in the treetops?

"Ran—"

That was as much as Haruhiro managed to get out. It looked like whatever it was, it was falling toward Ranta. By the time Haruhiro figured that out, it was already attacking the dread knight. Ranta noticed too, but he didn't dodge. He drew his katana and tried to strike it out of the air.

"Great Foul Waterfall! Right?!"

Was Ranta's quick draw and strike too late?

No, probably not.

There was the sound of katana colliding with katana. That thing, or man rather, swept Ranta's katana aside with his own—then slashed. He cut Ranta, landed, and then almost seemed to float as he jumped away. When the one-eyed, one-armed man settled on a root, he had an expression on his face that looked refreshed, as if he'd just gotten out of the bath, but also slightly languid at the same time.

"You've still got a long way to go, Ranta."

"Gwogh..."

The wound Ranta had taken wasn't shallow. Was it his shoulder? No, his neck. It was spurting blood. Had it struck an artery?

The carotid artery? Not even Ranta could try to act tough with a wound like that. It looked bad.

"Ah!"

Merry raced over. She was already making the sign of the hexagram, preparing her spell. She planned to cast Sacrament. If she didn't, it'd be too late. That had to be her thinking.

What did Haruhiro and the others need to be doing? Not letting the enemy disrupt Merry. Escorting her. They might not be able to defeat that man, Takasagi, but they could keep him in check. Yume was already nocking an arrow.

"Mew!"

"I guess instead of holding back I'll show off a bit," Takasagi said, wobbling the katana he held in his left hand. "Secret Technique, Autumnal Illusion."

I don't get it. What is that?

Takasagi was just standing there, shaking his blade. Was that all it was? Takasagi's body moved as if it was swaying too.

Yume loosed her arrow. She followed up with a second, then a third in quick succession. Itsukushima was shooting too.

But they didn't hit.

The two hunters weren't at a range where they'd normally have missed. They were less than ten meters away. Why hadn't they been able to hit him? Was Takasagi dodging? But the one-armed man just seemed to be standing around. It was almost as if Yume and Itsukushima had just barely missed him on purpose. Was that Takasagi's secret technique?

It makes no sense. What the heck is that?

Don't lose your head. Cut yourself off from your emotions, Haruhiro told himself, submerging his consciousness. His mind went to a low place while his vision rose up high. He was looking down on everything at an angle.

Merry would reach Ranta soon. Setora had her spear ready, and was trying to cover the two of them. Kuzaku was swinging his large katana at Takasagi. Wasn't it reckless, just charging in like that? Kuzaku was generally a pretty straightforward guy, but he was playing it way too straight there.

Old Utefan and the other dwarves were focused on guarding the iron king, her retinue, and the two elves. They were all looking at Takasagi, but none of them tried to attack him. Maybe a few of the dwarves were hesitating over whether or not to point their guns at him, but that was about it.

Haruhiro went to circle around behind Takasagi.

"O Light, may Lumiaris's divine protection be upon you..." Merry's hand touched Ranta's shoulder.

"Hahhhh!" Kuzaku sprang at Takasagi. He had his large katana over his head and was about to swing it down. No matter how you sliced it, Kuzaku shouldn't have been so stupid and careless as to try such a straightforward attack. It was like he'd been baited into it. Was there some secret hidden in the irregular and unstable way that Takasagi was moving?

"Sacrament!"

Merry triggered her spell. There was a flood of brilliant light, and Ranta's wounds began to heal.

Kuzaku's overhead swing failed to hit Takasagi, as expected.

Takasagi turned to the side and Kuzaku's blade flew by in front of his nose. At the same time, Takasagi was slicing Kuzaku's flank with his katana.

"Oh, you're a tough one."

"Gwagh?!"

Kuzaku instinctively jumped to the side and rolled. It looked like he'd taken a pretty deep cut, but he hadn't been completely bisected, at least. The question was if he could get back up.

Haruhiro focused his eyes on Takasagi's back from about three meters away. He'd gotten behind his target. From here, he could sense Takasagi's breathing. It was completely steady, even though this man had just sliced Kuzaku.

Takasagi looked like he was just standing there. And yet, that wasn't quite true. He was constantly moving, his center of gravity always changing. It wasn't clear where in his body he was tensing, and where he was relaxing. If Haruhiro tried to stand like that, he'd definitely collapse. It would be hard enough just walking, and using a katana would be out of the question. Takasagi might not have looked like it at a glance, but he was doing something frighteningly advanced here. However he was moving, it probably worked differently from normal human movement.

"Drahhhhhh!"

Ranta's wounds had healed. He exploded into motion, no doubt meaning to get back at Takasagi. Merry moved to try to heal Kuzaku. Setora went with her.

Haruhiro was closing in on Takasagi in Stealth. No one, not even his allies, noticed Haruhiro's existence now. It got to the point where Haruhiro himself had only the faintest sense that he was here.

He didn't think, *I can do this.* He wasn't thinking, *I'm gonna do it.*

His mind was almost empty.

Haruhiro would plunge his dagger into Takasagi's back. In this position, at this angle, it would pierce his kidney. That would promptly render him unconscious, followed shortly by death. It was a lethal blow.

"Whoopsie..."

He felt the dagger tear through Takasagi's clothes and pierce his skin, but then Haruhiro found himself being lifted over the man's shoulder.

What had happened?

He didn't understand the trick, or where the strength to execute it had come from.

Was there a technique that made it possible?

"And down you go..."

Takasagi tossed Haruhiro with a shoulder throw. How had he done it when he had only his left arm, and was holding a katana with it?

"Urgh!" Haruhiro wasn't able to break his fall properly.

He tilted his head forward on the spur of the moment, managing to protect the back of his head, but the impact as his back struck the hard roots made it hard to breathe.

"Y'see, I've got an eye in the back of my head." Takasagi looked down at Haruhiro. "So even after losing one, I've still got two."

He winked with his right eye. The man was calm and composed, bouncing the flat of his blade on his shoulder as he spoke.

"Personal Skill!" Ranta swooped in like a flying squirrel, or something similar, as he slashed at Takasagi.

"Oh, shut up with your personal skills."

Takasagi bent his wrists and elbows, twisting his katana like a snake. It caught Ranta's katana.

"Ah?!"

Did Ranta have no choice but to let go of his weapon? Or did he do it without meaning to? Either way, the blade spun out of Ranta's hands and embedded itself in a tree some distance away.

"Always looking for little tricks. That's the problem with you." Takasagi pressed the point of his katana to Ranta's throat. "When it comes to ordinary guys like us, the absolute minimum we need to do is break ourselves down into little pieces, and then rebuild ourselves from scratch. Basically, if you stop working hard, you're finished. With the way you rely on instinct and flashes of inspiration, in the end, you're just a spoiled, snot-nosed brat."

Ranta tried to argue back. But he just let out a pathetic sigh, grinding his teeth in frustration.

What're you letting him break your spirit for?

Haruhiro tried to jump to his feet, but Takasagi just stepped on his throat without even looking down. The thief then felt a katana go through his right wrist.

"Agh! Guh..."

"Don't move. I'm giving a lecture here. This might be my last chance to, after all."

Takasagi smiled. Just now, the man could have easily snuffed Haruhiro out. He could still kill Ranta too. Did he not want to? He didn't mean to kill them. *That's gotta be it,* thought Haruhiro. It had to be.

"Stop!" Merry shouted. It seemed she'd finished healing Kuzaku. The paladin was getting up.

Takasagi shrugged. "We may not be doing this because we want to, but our motto is that if you're gonna do something, you go all the way. If you don't take things seriously, then it's no fun at all, even when you're just playing. That's a bit of adult wisdom for you."

"Surrender."

That wasn't Takasagi. It was a different voice.

"Jumbo..." Ranta turned to look behind him. Haruhiro looked in that direction too.

Yume had said a bird was flying by. Was it that one? Jumbo's friend, the great black eagle?

A lone orc walked toward them. He was unmistakably an orc, yet he gave off a very different impression from others of his kind. Was it because of his glossy, flowing black hair, his green skin with a slight ashen hue, his beautifully vibrant orange eyes, and his handsome face? He wore a deep blue kimono with a silver flower pattern, and he carried a katana at his side. He was small enough, at least for an orc, that the size of the big black eagle using his shoulder as a perch stood out. Unlike, say, Zan Dogran, he didn't look like a man who dominated others. And yet, there was something about him that demanded attention.

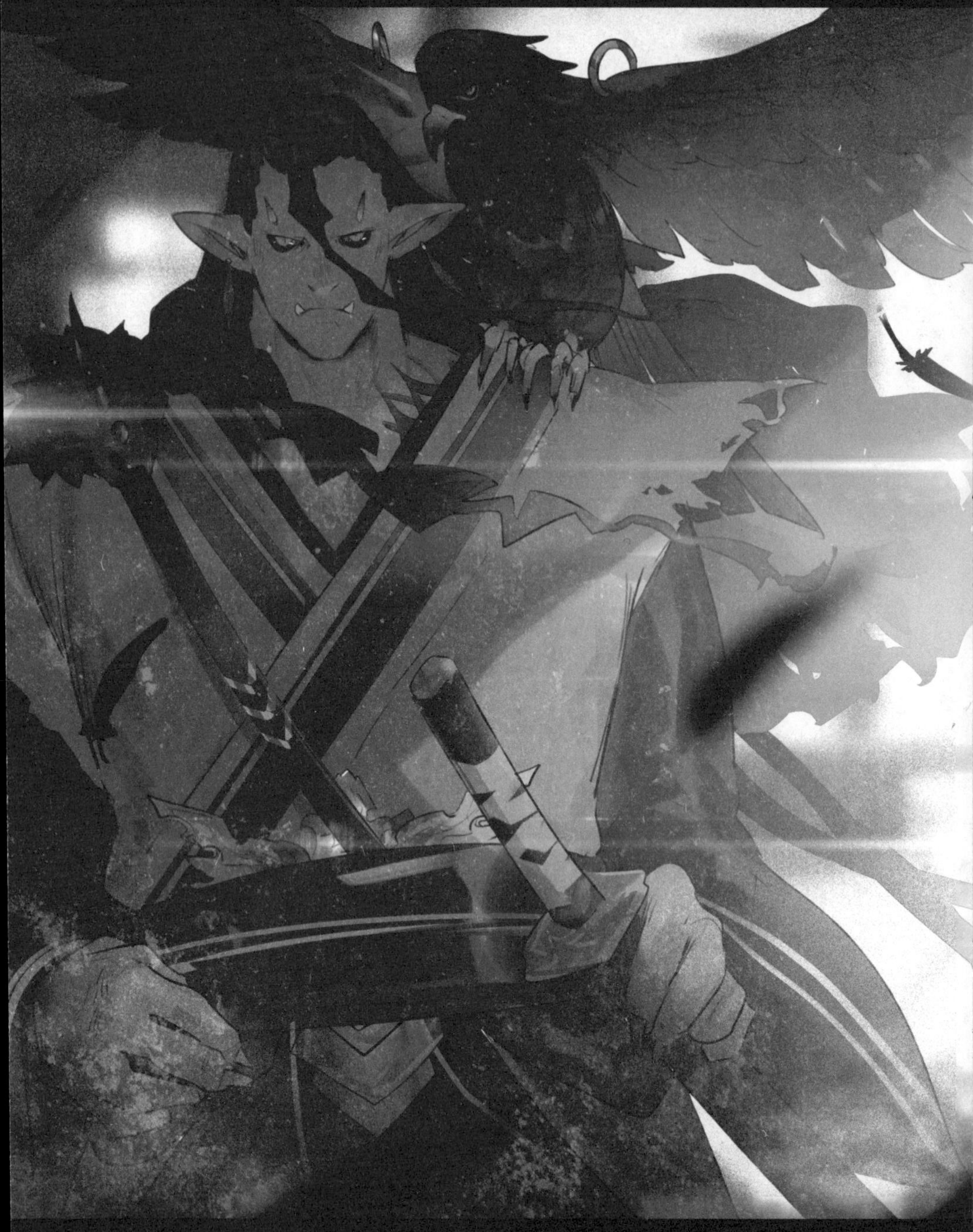

"You people are left with not even a shred of hope. Surrender at once. If you refuse, I will be forced to kill you all."

"Surrender...is not an option," the iron king said. "I cannot possibly bend the knee to the forces of evil who so mercilessly slaughtered my people just to save my own life."

The dwarven queen stood proud with her head held high. Her tone of voice had an incredible purity to it—resolute, without so much as a shred of doubt.

Oh, screw you.

Haruhiro was pissed. He got so mad he thought he was going to lose it.

At the same time, he could understand. Initially, the Ironblood Kingdom had kept their enemies away with guns. Now the guns had been stolen, and not only had the tables turned, but they were on the verge of annihilation. The only options left to them were to fight to the death in the name of pride, or for the surviving dwarves to gather around the iron king and eke out what meager existence they could.

It had been a hard choice for the iron king to flee the Ironblood Kingdom. However, if she had rejected Minister Axbeld's plan, it would have meant the dwarves would be exterminated to the very last person. She likely hadn't made her escape for fear of her own life. It might even have been easier for her to take up the sword herself and fall beside the rest of her kind. She'd decided to head for Mount Spear for the sake of her race, for the sake of dwarvenkind. If Haruhiro were in her position, could he have done the same? He might have given in to desperation and chosen to share the same fate as his fellows. To fight bravely, then die. If the kingdom was to fall, and the entire race to die out, then it wasn't so scary as long as they were all together.

It was harder to be a survivor, and yet the iron king had chosen that.

Obviously, she hadn't taken this course just to surrender now. There was no guarantee the enemy would let them live. She might face unbearable humiliation. But more than that, the shame of being taken alive by the enemy was too much for the iron king to bear. Even if some dwarves had made it out of the Ironblood Kingdom alive, they would learn what had happened to her later. That their queen had abandoned her people, then surrendered to the enemy.

Surrender wasn't an option. Haruhiro got that. But he also knew what would happen if the iron king said those words right now.

"I see." Jumbo nodded.

The great black eagle took off from his shoulder.

Old Utefan immediately raised his hammer-like staff. Maybe he was trying to give an order to the dwarves of the House of Bratsod. *Fight, shoot Jumbo.* A number of them did turn their guns on the orc. But they never managed to fire.

Jumbo dashed. The first step was relaxed, but every step after that was like a sudden gust of wind. Dwarves were sent flying through the air, including the iron king's retinue. One after another, or rather all at once, they each slammed into the ground with a heavy thud.

What had Jumbo done? That wasn't clear. He hadn't drawn his katana. Was he barehanded? Did he punch them? Or did he throw his opponents? Or was it his legs? Did he kick them? Not even that much was clear. Jumbo did *something*. That was all they could tell.

"Elder!" Eltalihi, head of the House of Mercurian, tried to draw his sword to defend Elder Harumerial of the elves. He failed. He was sent flying before he could, with his head turned all the way around. His neck must have been broken.

Jumbo seized the iron king's throat with his right hand, Harumerial's with his left, and lifted them up high.

The dwarves who had been launched into the air fell around him like so many insignificant raindrops.

"Perhaps..."

What was that emotion seeping into the depths of Jumbo's deep voice? Pity?

Despite his actions being as merciless and unrelenting as the judgment of heaven?

"That may be the wiser choice. If you had surrendered to us, we'd have had no choice but to turn you over to High King Dif Gogun. It is certain you would meet a fate worse than death at his hands. I will shoulder the sin of killing you myself, then. Farewell."

Who did that orc think he was? There was no malice in him. Not a shred of hostility to be felt. He transcended logic, common sense, emotion, all of those things, seeming to exist in some place beyond them. In which case, there was no point asking how he could do this. Haruhiro could get fired up, make a lengthy speech criticizing him, and the orc wouldn't feel a thing.

Jumbo easily crushed the iron king and Elder Harumerial's throats.

He didn't release them when he was done. He held them in the air a while, probably long enough for them to die.

Then he bent his knees, crouched down, and softly laid their remains on the ground.

"Wh-what are you...doing?"

Kuzaku was trembling. Haruhiro couldn't understand why, but for some reason, the paladin was enraged.

What's there to get so angry about? Haruhiro wondered. *What good is getting mad at a guy like Jumbo? He's not like us. Nothing like us. Let's say there's an omnipotent, omniscient god out there somewhere. If he's all-knowing, and he's able to do anything, then why doesn't he help us?*

Haruhiro could complain all he wanted, but God probably didn't care what some powerless human thought. He wouldn't even bother to respond. As if to say, *Not helping you is the entire point. It's better this way. Not that you'd understand that, you little fool.*

Haruhiro had Takasagi's foot on his throat and a katana thrust through his right wrist. Takasagi would notice immediately if he went for the flame dagger with his left hand. That said, Takasagi wasn't even glancing at Haruhiro. He just lazily pulled the blade out of Haruhiro's right wrist, then thrust it through his left.

"Gaaagh!"

Haruhiro hated Takasagi far more than Jumbo. He could see what went on inside the guy's head. Or he felt like he could. The man was the same type as Haruhiro. Observing. Considering. Researching. Studying. Refining. With hard work and repetition, he'd ascended to the realm of the masters. But he could go no further than that. He'd bashed his head against a wall, and Jumbo the orc was beyond that wall, in the place he couldn't get to. He'd submitted to him, charmed by that transcendent prowess, and now worshiped the orc almost like a god.

Takasagi was fairly advanced, at least compared to Haruhiro and the party. But there was something decidedly normal about him still, hiding not quite out of view. Takasagi made good use of that inescapable mediocrity as he worked for Jumbo. Most people—no, almost all people—were mediocre, so in a group like Forgan there were going to be problems a superior man like Jumbo couldn't resolve. Takasagi was doing more than enough to help the orc. It probably satisfied him. And you know what? Living that way is perfectly valid. Maybe it's the only way that mediocre people *can* live.

Haruhiro understood that, which made him hate Takasagi all the more. Give him another decade, no, just five years, three even, and he'd be able to go beyond Takasagi. He could kill the man with his own two hands. Now, he wasn't completely confident of that. But he also wasn't convinced he couldn't. That was what made it so frustrating. Being unable to do anything like this. Haruhiro resented his own weakness.

"Whoa, you moron—" Ranta shouted at Kuzaku. Haruhiro probably wasn't one to talk, considering he was on the ground with a boot on his neck, but Ranta was sounding pretty weak.

"Damn you!" Kuzaku flung himself at Jumbo. Setora and Merry tried to stop him. But Kuzaku was too fast.

He was a good man. Better than anyone, that was what Kuzaku was. Just a really swell guy. He was a normal dude, with his heart in the right place. It made him lovable. He was the adorable youngest member of the party, and a trusted comrade, one they could truly rely on. It wasn't just that he was tall; he also had a high overall level of athletic ability. Haruhiro just wished he were a bit cleverer. That is to say, underhanded and calculating. If he could move that big body around with more cunning, he'd become something really incredible. But even without that, Kuzaku had incredible bursts of power. If he gave his all, there wasn't much that could stop him.

"Zwaaah!"

Kuzaku's large katana swung too fast for Haruhiro's eyes to follow. He could have cleaved through rock with that swing. It sliced its way into the thief's heart more impressively than any attack Haruhiro had ever seen. A swing Kuzaku couldn't have achieved without absolutely everything coming together perfectly. It was truly a once-in-a-lifetime slash.

Maybe it was even good enough to surprise Jumbo. That was the last thing they needed now. Why'd he have to show off such an amazing swing? Obviously Kuzaku was seriously pissed. He wouldn't back down, even in the face of Jumbo's transcendent nature. The orc was beyond them, in a place they could never reach, so anything he tried was going to be in vain. But Kuzaku hadn't thought about that. He'd gotten emotional, as he was wont to do. He couldn't let Jumbo get away with this. That was all he was thinking. A very normal, very human reaction.

Jumbo drew his katana.

Swinging as he drew, the orc didn't just deflect Kuzaku's blade, he broke it in half. If he could have gotten out of the way without breaking it, he would have. This was Jumbo, after all.

Then, on the return, he swung his katana down diagonally.

He cut Kuzaku in a straight line from his left shoulder to his right hip.

Kuzaku.

Ohhh, Kuzaku.

You're slipping.

Slipping along the line where he cut you.

You're going to fall apart.

He cut you in two, Kuzaku.

"You bastard!" Setora flew into a rage. Calm, collected Setora. She really did care about Kuzaku, huh? Though she always acted like he was a pain, she still adored him. But was that all there was to it? This was Setora, after all. Maybe she was drawing attention so Haruhiro could do something? But what? What should he do? What *could* he do? Maybe Setora had just snapped and lost it after all.

Setora charged at Jumbo, throwing her spear. The orc batted it away with his left hand. By that point, Setora had drawn her sword and closed in on him.

"Ngh! Ah!"

Sharp as her swings were, they couldn't even graze Jumbo. He danced around her with easy steps.

"This's tough to watch," Takasagi said with a laugh.

Why do I have to let this guy laugh at us? Haruhiro thought. The instant he did, Takasagi put his weight down on the thief's throat. He wasn't even free to breathe in his current state. Takasagi was reminding him of that.

"Damn it!" Ranta picked up his katana and was about to go help.

Takasagi wouldn't allow that. He jumped, sinking his foot hard into Haruhiro's throat as he did, and swung at Ranta.

Haruhiro was nearly knocked unconscious, so he didn't see what happened at that exact moment, but Ranta's face seemed to have a fresh wound on it.

"Ngah! Guh!"

What were Itsukushima and Yume doing? Was Haruhiro counting on them to do something? If so, he was probably barking up the wrong tree. Did Haruhiro even have the right to expect things from others when he'd been unable to do anything himself?

"Damn you!" Setora must have realized that she could swing that sword forever and it would do her no good. Wise as she was, there was no way she hadn't figured it out. And yet, she couldn't stop now. What else would she be able to do if she cast the sword aside? She couldn't stop until she'd burned herself out completely. Oh, now he saw it. Someone needed to force her to stop.

"Ahhh!" Merry fell to the ground, gazing up to the sky. "Help... Help... Help...!"

"Enough," Jumbo said, taking away Setora's sword. He almost made it look like she'd given it to him.

"Kh!"

It didn't stop Setora from continuing to attack. She grappled him from behind, wrapping both her arms around the orc's neck as she tried to choke him out. She even attempted to bite Jumbo's right ear. Where was this tenacity coming from? Why was Haruhiro giving up when Setora was still going that far?

"Stop." Jumbo tossed aside the sword he'd taken from Setora, and reached back to put his left hand over her face in order to hold her back. Then, a moment later, he threw her.

"Agh! Kuh!"

As Setora immediately bounced back to her feet, the great black eagle descended on her.

The bird seized Setora's head with its talons, flapping its wings to lift her off the ground a little. It then let go and immediately pinned her, pecking viciously.

"Uaghhhhhhhhhh!"

"Forgo!" Jumbo scolded the great black eagle, and it soon stopped feeding on Setora. Lifting off, it settled on Jumbo's shoulder again.

Yume nocked an arrow, training it on Jumbo's eagle. But her bow was shaking—no, swaying. She couldn't shoot properly like that.

"She accepted me," someone said.

Yume lowered her bow and looked off to the side.

At Merry.

Merry had been sitting. Not anymore. She was on her feet.

"It might not necessarily have been of her own free will, but since she was seeking aid, I had no choice but to answer her. I am here, but not by any design of my own."

It...wasn't Merry.

The way she spoke, the way she stood, everything about her was not Merry.

"Who...are you?" Haruhiro sat up. "What...are you?"

"I have no name. Only things people call me."

The thing that looked like Merry, but was not, turned her head and looked around. She raised her chin, looking at things with down-turned eyes. He knew that was a habit of the thing that wasn't Merry.

"Boss..." Takasagi bent his knees slightly, bracing himself. He seemed to sense something ominous.

"Mm." What about Jumbo? He was as calm and self-possessed as ever. Or he looked that way, at least.

The thing that wasn't Merry raised her right hand and looked down at Merry's palm.

"I simply became life at the end of a long process of trial and error."

She slowly clenched her hand into a fist.

"I was not alive. I was something else, and yet I happened to take on the form of life, and to become life. That is what I am. I have a wish. For us to live together, forever. It was all I wished for, and yet I was hated. Or perhaps feared. The people called me..."

The No-Life King.

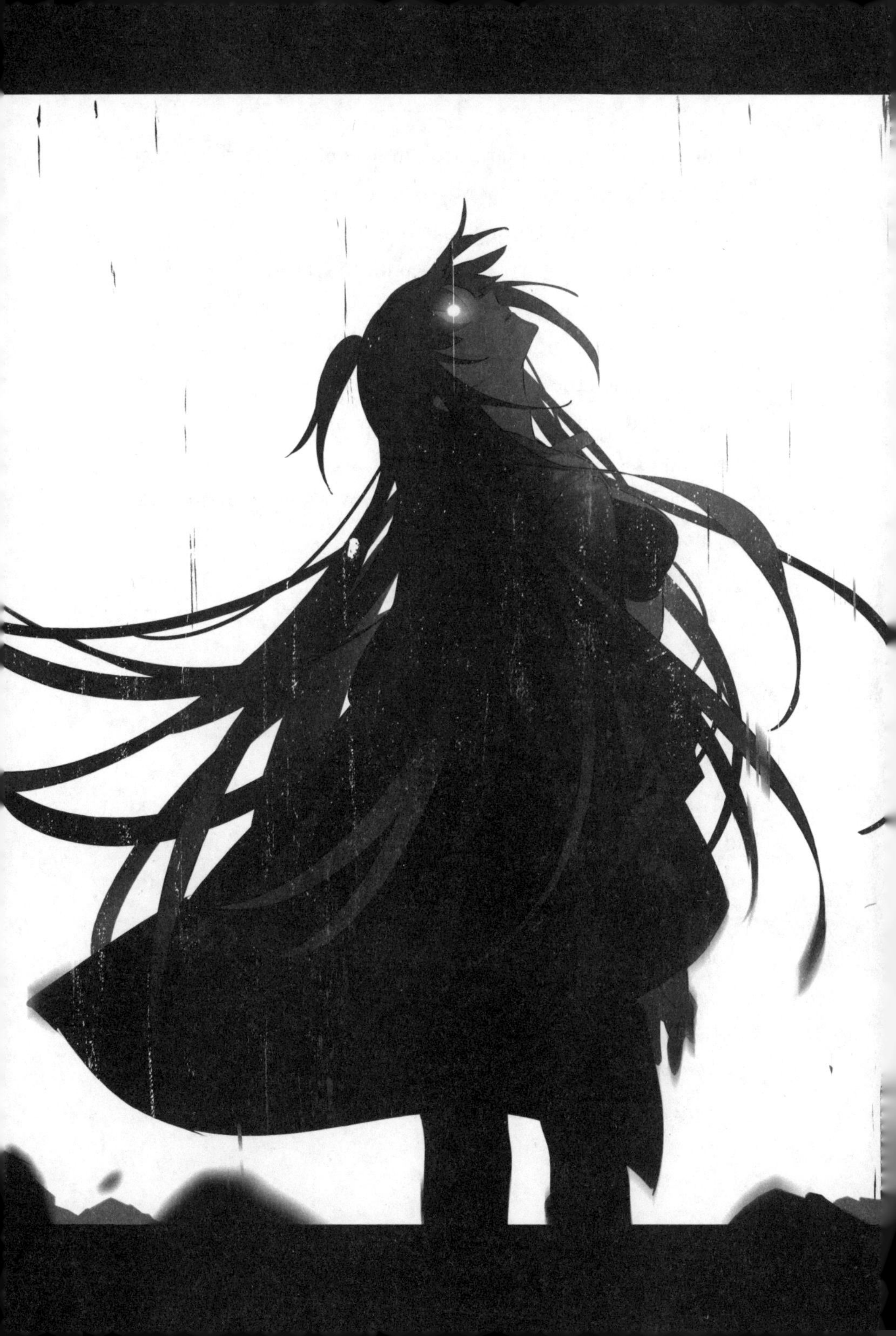

The name came to Haruhiro's mind before the thing that wasn't Merry could say it.

He'd suspected all along that this was who it might have been. Okay, no, he hadn't. But it was all too strange. Merry had died. Dead people don't come back to life. And yet, she had. No, perhaps she hadn't, not strictly speaking. Whatever this thing that people called the No-Life King was, it entered Merry's body after her vital functions had ceased. Then it remade her dead cells. It was borrowing her body, so her memories and personality remained. But it might be that Merry was gone, and only the No-Life King remained.

No. It's Merry.

Merry.

She came back to life.

Merry's still alive.

The No-Life King had said, *She accepted me.*

That he had responded to her cries for help.

True, Merry had been saying, *Help,* over and over. Haruhiro hadn't been able to do anything about it. At that point, Merry hadn't even been looking at him. She'd turned to the No-Life King inside her for salvation. And the No-Life King had responded. That was why he was here.

So, what about Merry?

Where did she go?

Did Merry hand her body over to the No-Life King?

If she did, then where is she?

"Even though I am life itself..."

HATE THE WORLD

The No-Life King hung his head as he spoke. He wasn't just looking down. His shoulders fell too, as if he were lamenting some great hurt and sadness.

"Humans said my existence was no life at all."

"They called me a monster."

"The humans were afraid. They didn't try to accept me."

"I wasn't the one who sought conflict. The humans tried to destroy me."

"If I have one fault, it is that I took Enad George as my vessel. The man who was king of the human nation of Arabakia. A fallen sovereign, betrayed by his friends and associates. That man found me when I had finally become life."

"He was on the verge of death then. I tried to save him. He, too, accepted me."

"I didn't want to simply exist as life."

"Enad did not want to die and have his memories and will vanish."

"Our interests were aligned."

"I became Enad, in a sense, and Enad became me in some ways too."

"Enad resented the people who had rebelled against him, trying to slay him through subterfuge. He didn't mean to kill them all, though. Enad was a king. He felt he should be welcomed as such in the nation he'd founded. Having learned the niceties of the human heart from Enad, I felt as though that might be expecting a little too much, but..."

What's it talking about?

It wasn't that Haruhiro didn't understand what the No-Life King was saying. He remembered hearing the legend of the founding of the Kingdom of Arabakia, or something resembling its history, from Hiyomu.

Humans had once believed in a paradise called Arabakia. One man called Theodore George set out and settled in a bountiful land where he founded a country. His descendant, Enad, was the first king of Arabakia. However, King Enad fled after being betrayed by his close associate, Ishidua Zaemoon. No one knew where he'd gone.

Enad then became the No-Life King. Was that what had happened? Or perhaps Enad was the first living being, the first human, that the entity they would later come to call the No-Life King infested. The No-Life King had just referred to the man as a vessel. Perhaps by using the toppled king as a vessel, it had assumed the form and shape of the No-Life King, or something like that.

Why was the No-Life King talking about all this now?

Why were they all listening to the No-Life King tell his story?

Because it was a story worth hearing? Haruhiro couldn't help but be interested. This was *the* No-Life King. His history was being revealed to them. And from his own mouth, at that. The mouth that belonged to Merry. On the outside, at least, he was Merry.

There was a strange tension in the air, an atmosphere that made it difficult to move.

No, this wasn't a matter of the air. It was the sound. There was *no* sound. No chirping of birds, buzzing of insects, or rustling of leaves. This silence was abnormal. Was that why the air felt so tense?

"I wasn't an enemy of humanity. Humanity decided I was their enemy."

"Enad wanted to be the king of humanity."

"I did not."

"You humans have a word that felt more appropriate to me..."

Haruhiro had thought the No-Life King was just eloquently telling his story.

When did that change?

Haruhiro only noticed it now.

The No-Life King had bent his right elbow, turning the back of his hand downward. And his right hand was lightly balled into a fist.

Was it flowing out of his right wrist?

That thin, threadlike strand falling from Merry's—the No-Life King's right wrist, was it a liquid?

Was it blood?

"I wanted to be their friend."

Suddenly, on Jumbo's shoulder, Forgo spread his wings. The great black eagle started letting out shrill, discordant shrieks.

The No-Life King's blood, the fluid that circulated inside Merry's body, wasn't what people would generally call blood at all. The bloodlike substance that had come out of Jessie and entered Merry's lifeless remains was something far more dreadful. It might even have been the No-Life King himself.

That was what the No-Life King was allowing to drip out of his body, albeit in small quantities.

What for?

What was the No-Life King trying to do?

"Gwah!"

Haruhiro hadn't expected to hear Kuzaku's voice. But it *was* Kuzaku.

Even though it couldn't be.

Kuzaku had been cut down by Jumbo. Bisected. He was dead. Haruhiro didn't want to accept it, so he'd tried to avert his eyes from the fact, but Kuzaku had died. Haruhiro had lost another comrade. One of his precious companions, someone who had been more to him than just a brother-in-arms.

"Gagh! Mwargh! Oaugh! Hah! Wahhhhh!"

Now Kuzaku was writhing in agony. How? Why? He shouldn't have been able to move. There was no way he could have. But the fact was, Kuzaku was groaning and moving. His head jerked up and down, and his right arm flailed. No, it wasn't just his head and right arm. His left arm and his legs too.

"No...way!" Had Ranta's legs given out? Haruhiro was shocked too.

"The No-Life King..." Takasagi murmured.

The No-Life King was the king of the undying, but so what? What did that matter? This was crazy, wasn't it? Kuzaku had been cut from his left shoulder to his right hip. Haruhiro couldn't be completely sure, but didn't that path slice through his heart? He must have died instantly. Cut in two. That was what Kuzaku's remains had been. He'd been split into two—the upper half, which included his right arm, and the lower half, which had his left. That was what should have happened. So why?

Why were they stuck back together?

"Warghhhh! Ahhhhhhhhhhhhhhhhhhhh!"

Kuzaku finally got up. He bent his knees, raising them off the ground, then, without putting his hands on the ground, he rose as if lifted by some unseen force.

"Ahhhhhhhhhhhhh! Huh?"

Kuzaku inspected his wound with both hands. It had left massive bloodstains, of course, and not only had the wound Jumbo'd given him not vanished, but it was still totally distinct. It was reddish black and writhing, bubbling, as the two sides connected.

"Ha ha!" Kuzaku started laughing. He shook his head, punched himself in the forehead, and tore at his own hair. He wrenched his neck back and forth, shoulders heaving.

"Ha ha hah! Wuh ha! Wa ha ha ha ha! Ha ha ha ha ha ha ha! Gyah ha ha ha ha ha ha ha! Uh-hyuh! Fwoh ha ha ha! Dobyah ha ha! Bwah ha! Gwah ha ha ha ha ha ha ha ha!"

It was like something had broken inside him. What kind of laugh was that? He was howling like an idiot.

"Kuzakkun!" Yume shouted.

"Aha aha aha aha! Weh heh aha oho! Bwaha! Doh ha ha ha ha! Gweeheh hoh oho ho!"

Kuzaku wasn't listening. Couldn't he hear her? He covered his face with both hands, throwing his head backward as he kept on cackling. What was so funny? Had he gone funny in the head? If so, how could he laugh about it? Haruhiro was completely distracted by Kuzaku.

319

At some point Setora had risen to her feet as well. More than that, she was walking around.

"S-Setora?" Haruhiro's voice trembled, cracking.

"Gee-hee! Eh hyah ha ha ha ha! Do-hee! Oo-hee ha ha ha! Goh ha! Zwee ah ha fwee hee hee!" Kuzaku was still laughing.

Setora was acting weird too. She was walking. Round and round and round, in an incredibly tight circle, maybe forty to fifty centimeters across, rapidly mumbling something under her breath as she went.

Forgo the great black eagle had made a meal of Setora's face. He was a large bird. It looked like the area from her right eye to her nose and upper lip, her skin, muscle, bone, and eyeball had taken extreme damage. It was a horrible thing to admit, but up until this point, Haruhiro hadn't been able to tell how badly she'd been wounded, or if she was even alive. It was possible that Forgo had dealt Setora a lethal blow. Maybe she'd died, just like Kuzaku.

Her face was a horrible mess, but the damaged parts were covered in a reddish-black substance. Haruhiro could only assume it was the exact same stuff that had stuck Kuzaku's wounds back together and was closing them up now.

"Noooo..." Yume collapsed. Itsukushima tried to support her, but they both ended up falling together.

"It's been a long time since I've done this," the No-Life King said, holding his right wrist with his left hand. "It will take time for them to adapt. I hope she will consider her wish granted with this. Unfortunately, it's the only means available to me."

"You..." Jumbo had his eagle Forgo take off, leveling his katana at the No-Life King. "What did you do?"

"I shared my blood with them." The No-Life King lowered his eyes.

"Ohah! Oh ho fwoh ha ha! Go-hee! Gwee hee hee fwee! Ga hee ga hee ga hee! Gwoh ha ha ha!"

Kuzaku was laughing. Setora was walking around in circles.

"Unlike Enad, I hold no resentment toward humans. I had no intention of ruling over them. I wanted to be their friend. But they feared and hated me. Out of hostility, they tried to destroy me. I was forced to fight." The No-Life King raised his face, or rather his chin, turning that usual downward gaze on Jumbo, Takasagi, Haruhiro, Ranta, Yume, and Itsukushima in sequence.

It wasn't Merry. But it was. It wasn't as if her voice had started echoing directly inside their heads, or her eyes were shining, or anything like that. It was still Merry, yet not. That was why, even at this late stage, Haruhiro was still thinking, *Is it really not Merry? Am I sure there hasn't been some mistake?*

Forgo shrieked noisily in the sky above. Haruhiro's breathing was painfully shallow and hurried. He didn't know how his lungs were managing to work so hard. His vision blurred. Something was off with his ears too. He kept hearing this low, heavy sound. Was it a sound? It could have been a vibration. That, or Haruhiro's senses had all gone haywire. If he'd gone insane, could anyone really blame him? The whole situation was nuts. It'd be crazier if he *didn't* go crazy.

But it wasn't just Haruhiro. Jumbo and Takasagi, Ranta, and Yume and Itsukushima seemed to sense something too. Everyone was looking around here and there.

"It's not only humans," the No-Life King said, furrowing his brow. "The world hates me too."

It was approaching. *Something* was. The thing Jumbo and Takasagi had sensed. Haruhiro sensed it too. He didn't know what it was, but he could feel it. He had no choice but to. Where was it coming from? Any particular direction? He couldn't be sure. Or rather, it was probably coming from all over. There was a buzzing. No, more of an NNNNNNNNNNNN... It was a heavy sound, crushingly so. So low that no creature could make it. The vibration came from the front, the right, the left, the back. The low, heavy sound, or vibration, was surrounding them all. The net was closing.

"I am being rejected by the world. The sekaishu will try to remove me."

That word. Sekaishu. Right. Sekaishu. From back then.

Black. He could see something black. Beyond the trees. Just black. Formless. A mass of black. It was coming. The sekaishu. Pressing toward them. They had to run. There was no fighting it. No resisting the sekaishu.

We've gotta run. To run and lose it. Let's run. Run away. But where to? The sekaishu is closing in from all directions.

"Wa ha! Aha aha aha! Eheh heh heh! Ga ha ho! Gu-hee! Gya ha ha ha ha ha!"

Besides, they couldn't run while Kuzaku was still laughing. Setora kept walking around and around in tight circles too.

"Boss, this is bad," Takasagi said. Jumbo sheathed his katana and took off running, with Takasagi following him.

Haruhiro almost shouted, *Wait! Where are you going? You're going to run away? Do you think you can escape?*

Don't leave us behind.

The thief was shocked. He'd never been so disappointed in himself. He was trying to cling to Jumbo and Takasagi. There was no way they'd have helped him. They obviously had no obligation to.

"Kuzaku, hey, come on!" Ranta was trying to pull Kuzaku by the arm. Kuzaku didn't shake free of the dread knight. He just got up close and laughed in Ranta's face.

"Uweh heh heh! Guh ha! Bo ho fwah! Ahyah hyah hyah hyah! Dohyeh hyeh heh!"

"This guy's a lost cause!"

"Setoran! Hey, Setoran!" Yume was clinging to Setora, who simply tried to keep walking, unconcerned.

"Yume!" Itsukushima tried to pull Yume off Setora.

Haruhiro couldn't do a thing. He should have been able to help Ranta or Yume. Why didn't he? Why was he just watching?

The black things, black masses, black waves—the sekaishu was getting closer.

The No-Life King had said, *The world hates me.*

It clearly had no love for Haruhiro either.

Yeah, well, I hate it too.

He felt that keenly.

I hate it.

I hate the world.

afterword

For various reasons, I had a bit more time to write this volume. Thanks to that, the story advanced a little more than originally planned.

The prelude to the final chapter is finally complete, and I'm going to try to run toward the finish line from here.

To my editor, Harada-san, to Eiri Shirai-san, to the designers at KOMEWORKS among others, to everyone involved in production and sales of this book, and finally to all of you people now holding it, I offer my heartfelt appreciation and all of my love. Now, I lay down my pen for today. I hope we will meet again.

—Ao Jyumonji

#1 | 937 Days Later

*W*HAT'S CHANGED *since then? A whole lot. So many things it's hard to count.*

What hasn't changed? The sun rises in the east, and sets in the west. The day-night cycle.

Haruhiro fed a branch into the campfire.

Oh, right. The color of these flames too. And the stars. The red moon.

"I'm grateful to you, Ranta."

"What're you saying out of nowhere? You're grossing me out, man." Ranta was sitting diagonally across from Haruhiro with his knees up, bending and snapping little branches to keep his hands busy.

Haruhiro tried to make some sort of expression with his face, but he couldn't seem to do it. "You know, when Ruon was born, it made me happy. Yume being a mother didn't feel all that far out there, surprisingly. But you as a father, man? It's still hard to believe." He had emotions. It wasn't like they were all gone. He just couldn't express them well.

"Oh, shut up." Ranta let out a nasal laugh. "We did the deed, and she got knocked up, that's all."

"I was just thinking, even with things the way they are, I can still feel happy."

"Yeah..."

"We've gotta protect Ruon until he gets bigger, huh? Yume ought to stay by his side until then, at least."

"Yeah, even I know that much."

"Don't you go and bite it on us, okay, man?"

"There's no way I'm gonna kick the bucket, leaving the woman I love and my son without me, and you know it."

"Yeah, I do."

"Haruhiro, I oughta say..."

"What?"

"Nah..." Ranta looked away, sniffling. "It's nothing."

The flames flickered. Beasts cried out into the night, far off in the distance. Were those even the voices of animals? They might have been something else. Haruhiro reached toward a pelt wrapped around an object. If need be, he'd use it. That is, if those voices or some other presence approached them.

"I'm gonna get it all back."

"Any idea how?" Ranta asked, dubious. He was always keeping an eye on Haruhiro, never sure when the thief might go off the rails and he'd need to be the one to stop him.

Wasn't it supposed to be the other way around?

If Haruhiro could have put on a strained smile, he would have. But right now, that was too hard for him. It seemed he'd forgotten how to smile at all.

"I'll find a way. Definitely. There's gotta be one. Relics must be the key."

Ranta started to open his mouth. But all he did was take a single breath. He didn't say anything.

I'll find a way.

Haruhiro repeatedly muttered, "I swear I'm going to find a way."

Grimgar of Fantasy and Ash

#2 | Fire, Stay with Me

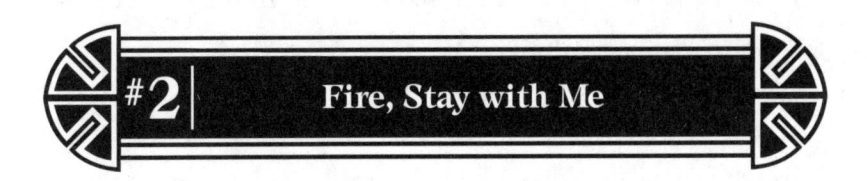

Haruhiro made a habit of picking up anything that he could use for starting a fire. Things like bark, or maybe a little dandelion fluff. When his clothes were getting too worn out to wear, he would cut them into thin strips and put them in his backpack. If he heated the scraps slowly to make char cloth, they were excellent tinder.

This was the forest, so there were dried twigs and branches lying around everywhere that provided a convenient source for kindling. Dead trees were easy to break, and their wood burned well. He could use those that had been felled by lightning strikes and the like too.

Haruhiro gathered his firewood and dug a shallow hole in the ground as an impromptu fire pit. He'd need to rebury it later, no doubt, and it wasn't so cold out that he would freeze if he wasn't by the fire all night, so he didn't have to take this part all that seriously.

He put his tinder at the bottom of what could only charitably be called a fire pit, and created a dome of dried branches over the pile. The branches, which were thicker, provided a framework. Then he placed pieces of firewood that he'd broken or cut into twenty-centimeter lengths on top.

He'd experimented with various ways of assembling fire pits in the past, but he tried not to be too obsessive about it. As long as it didn't collapse, that was all that really mattered. He laid the remaining kindling and the firewood he would use as fuel later around the outside of the fire pit.

Next, Haruhiro began starting the fire. He'd tried a number of different methods for this too, but he had settled on a quick method that didn't require flint or other tools. First he would cut a piece of soft wood, so that one side was flat, and carve a groove in that side. Then he would run a harder piece of wood up and down the groove. Other people might have different preferences, but Haruhiro found this suited him better than the method of making a hole in one piece of wood and spinning another around in it to create friction.

As the pieces of wood rubbed together, the wood fiber blackened from the heat. Eventually the wood fiber ignited and started to smoke. He piled on some tinder and blew into it. Once he started to see fire, he just had to push it into the bottom of the fire pit. In most cases, the fire would quickly spread to the kindling.

Today, the fire seemed weak. Haruhiro got down on all fours, then lowered his head further. With a little more air blown into the bottom of the fire pit, smoke began rising, and the crackling sounds started.

Haruhiro stopped blowing and sat in front of the fire pit.

It wasn't long before the red flames appeared. He stuck his hand out over them. Maybe this is obvious, but it felt hot.

It had gotten pretty dark out. Haruhiro took a breath, looking around the area.

Should he have lit a fire tonight? Was it safe? Or was it dangerous? He always hesitated. But if he was hesitant to do it, maybe he should have just not. He'd considered that, but he wanted a fire, even if that meant taking some risk. He couldn't deny the appeal.

Haruhiro hugged his knees.

For whatever reason, when he stared into the flickering flames, no extraneous thoughts clouded his mind. Extraneous thoughts... Were the things he thought about unnecessary, though? Not at all. He knew that. That was why he got lost in thought. But he didn't want to think. Thinking alone changed nothing. He couldn't get things back that way. Dwelling on it served no purpose. But pointless or not, he couldn't help but think.

A bird cried out in the night. The bugs chirred, each kind having its own unique voice.

The fire kept burning.

Haruhiro fed it a piece of firewood crossed over another.

There was just one good thing about the dark of night. The darkness made vision useless. He couldn't see anything in the dark. In order to detect threats, he perked up his ears instead, honing his senses to catch the slightest change. He could afford to stare at the fire.

Haruhiro kept staring intently into the flames. The night grew long, and his firewood ran out. He briefly fell asleep, still sitting, looking as if he had given up.

#3 Into Shelter

Haruhiro was alone that day.

He didn't mind being by himself. If anything, he found himself hoping for this kind of solitude a lot lately because it meant he didn't have to take responsibility. When he was alone, he only had to worry about himself. He could freely decide what he wanted to do. No matter what came of it, the only one to suffer the consequences would be him. Being like this was easy, and he liked it.

Obviously, that didn't apply in all cases. If Haruhiro messed up and died in a ditch somewhere, that would affect others somehow. But he didn't need to stay aware of those "others" at all times, even if he did think about them occasionally—and even if, ultimately, he would have no choice but to face them.

"It's gotten cold," he mumbled.

Raising the hood of his cloak a little with his fingers, he looked up to the sky. He was at a pretty high altitude. It had been drizzling on and off since last night. Not now, though. Still, it looked like it was ready to start pouring any moment. Heavy clouds covered almost the entire sky, leaving no breaks worth mentioning.

Haruhiro pulled out his dwarven pocket watch.

"Almost four o'clock, huh?"

He still had water. If he was sparing with his rations, he could eat three meals a day. The only other thing he needed to conserve out here in the wild was body heat. He was feeling chilly already, and exhausted. Soon it would be night, but he didn't think that he was going to die of exposure. He'd been through worse than this. But it was best not to get overconfident.

He had time before sunset. Haruhiro walked around the mountain, collecting little branches he could use as kindling.

Eventually, he found the stump of a tree that had died and fallen over. He touched it and found it was pretty sturdy and free of rot. It would probably work as a decent foundation.

"I guess here will do..."

Haruhiro laid out all his kindling, then began looking for materials he could use. What he needed was as long and sturdy of a stick as he could find. Once he had that, he'd need a lot more sticks, although those could be shorter. The more branches with leaves he could find, the better.

The key was to have a long stick to use as a ridgepole. If he didn't have one, Haruhiro would need to come up with a different idea than the one he was thinking of now.

Fortunately, there was a suitable stick lying around, and he was able to round up a decent number of short sticks without having to spend too much time on it. This was halfway up the mountain, so there were bushes all over the place. He could cut as many leafy branches off them as he liked.

While hunting for materials, he kept an eye out for droppings, fur, claw marks, and other traces that might have been left by animals, as well as any remains. If he came across the especially strong-smelling feces of a carnivore, there was a strong possibility it was still nearby. Obviously, there was always the risk that a dangerous beast that wasn't nearby now might come along later, but all he could do about that was remain alert.

Anyway, after scouting around, everything seemed to be fine. That didn't mean he could drop his guard, but if he was attacked while building the shelter, he was going to have to chalk it up to bad luck. He was confident enough in his safety measures to let himself feel that way.

With most everything he would need ready, Haruhiro stood one end of the ridgepole against his foundation, which had an indentation perfect for making sure the stick wouldn't slip out easily.

After that, he leaned the other sticks against the ridgepole from either side, forming upside-down V shapes with them. If the ridgepole was like the backbone, the shorter sticks were the ribs, like how a ship has a keel and ribs too.

With enough of the short sticks in place, he placed the rest so that they crossed the ribs diagonally to provide support. That would reinforce the skeleton of the roof. When he ran out of short sticks, he started laying the leafy branches over the top of the ribs, and then he followed them up with more and more of the dry fallen leaves he'd gathered.

By the time he couldn't see through to the other side of the roof anymore, it had gotten pretty dark out.

Haruhiro crawled into his finished shelter. There was no room to crouch in it, let alone stand. It was cramped, but that just made it warmer.

Haruhiro lay on his back in the shelter, taking a deep breath.

"Being alone isn't so bad...is it?"

Airship

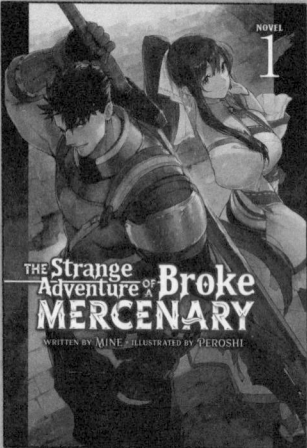

Discover your next great read at
www.airshipnovels.com

Let your imagination take flight with Seven Seas Entertainment's light novel imprint

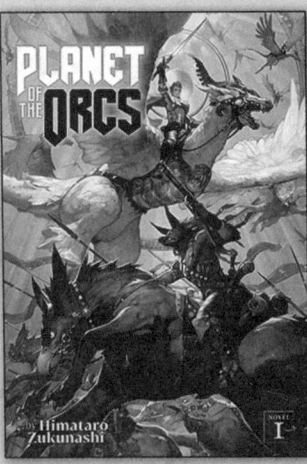

Print & digital editions available!

Visit and follow us on Twitter @gomanga and sign up for our newsletter for all Seven Seas has to offer

Airship

HEY ///////
▶ HAVE YOU HEARD OF
J-Novel Club?

It's the digital publishing company that brings you the latest novels from Japan!

Subscribe today at

▶▶▶ j-novel.club ◀◀◀

and read the latest volumes as they're translated, or become a premium member to get a *FREE* ebook every month!

Check Out The Latest Volume Of
Grimgar of Fantasy and Ash

Plus Our Other Hit Series Like:

- ▶ The Master of Ragnarok & Blesser of Eihenjar
- ▶ Invaders of the Rokujouma!?
- ▶ Arifureta: From Commonplace to World's Strongest
- ▶ Outbreak Company
- ▶ Amagi Brilliant Park
- ▶ Kokoro Connect
- ▶ Seirei Gensouki: Spirit Chronicles

- ▶ Full Metal Panic!
- ▶ Ascendance of a Bookworm
- ▶ In Another World With My Smartphone
- ▶ How a Realist Hero Rebuilt the Kingdom
- ▶ Crest of the Stars
- ▶ Lazy Dungeon Master
- ▶ Sorcerous Stabber Orphen
- ▶ An Archdemon's Dilemma: How to Love Your Elf Bride

...and many more!

In Another World With My Smartphone, Illustration © Eiji Usatsuka   Arifureta: From Commonplace to World's Strongest, Illustration © Takayaki